He realized he was naked.

His tone warmed with humor. "It appears somebody stole my clothes. Who do you think it could be?"

"I had no choice, Yale." She turned her head, avoiding his eyes. "You were bleeding so badly."

He caught her chin, forcing her to look at him. "I bet you're going to tell me you never looked, aren't you?"

She couldn't help laughing as she pushed his hand aside. "You're the most irreverent man I've ever known. Do you need anything?"

"Cara. Such a question. Especially when you're addressing a man with no clothes."

"Oh." She stood up, shaking down her skirts. "You're incorrigible, Yale."

"Also indecent. But exceedingly grateful to you for all you did." He looked up, searching her face. Despite his pain, the devil was in his eyes. "Careful, Cara. If you keep on treating me like this, I might learn to like it."

Badlands Legend

Ruth Langan

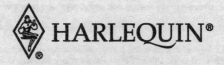

HARLEQUIN®

TORONTO • NEW YORK • LONDON
AMSTERDAM • PARIS • SYDNEY • HAMBURG
STOCKHOLM • ATHENS • TOKYO • MILAN • MADRID
PRAGUE • WARSAW • BUDAPEST • AUCKLAND

ISBN 0-373-29228-7

BADLANDS LEGEND

Copyright © 2002 by Ruth Ryan Langan

For families everywhere.

Especially mine.

Life's an adventure
Savor the journey

Prologue

Dakota Territory, 1867

Nine-year-old Yale Conover stood with the little party of mourners on a sun-baked hill, sweltering under a relentless haze of heat that held the land in its grip. Beside him his brother, Gabe, older by a year, stood tall and unflinching as half a dozen neighbors took turns tossing a handful of dirt on the wooden box that held the remains of their grandfather.

Deacon Conover, his father's father, had been a stern bear of a man who had taken Yale and his family in when they'd had nowhere else to go.

Whenever her children asked about their father, their mother, Dorry, told them proudly that after he'd finished soldiering in the Great War, Clay Conover had been sent on a secret assignment that had been authorized by President Lincoln himself before his untimely assassination.

Like his brother and sister, Yale yearned for the return of his father. But unlike Gabe, who wanted to welcome home a hero, or Kitty, who just wanted them to be a family once more, Yale's reasons were simpler. He was tired of taking orders from men he didn't respect. In fact, the only man who had ever earned Yale's respect was his pa. Besides, he figured Clay Conover would return a rich man, bearing a reward from a grateful nation. And why not? Wasn't he off risking life and limb? The way Yale figured it, those willing to take the risks ought to have the right to claim the gold.

Yale was so deep in thought he wasn't even aware that the service had ended until the neighbors began returning to their wagons and his mother called out, "You're all welcome to come back to our place for supper. I killed a couple of chickens. They're simmering in a pot right now."

Several of them paused until, seeing the scowl on her brother-in-law's face, were quick to offer their apologies and hasten back to their own ranches.

As Dorry was climbing into her wagon Junior Conover caught her roughly by the arm, stopping her in mid step. "What right have you got inviting them back to eat my food?"

She seemed genuinely surprised by his outburst. "Junior, these are your neighbors. They came all this way just to pay their last respects to your father. Some of them will be on the trail for hours before they get home. It's only right that we offer them our hospitality."

"Oh, you'd be good at that, wouldn't you? You know all about accepting hospitality."

At his uncle's outburst, Yale, who had just climbed into the back of the wagon, turned around in surprise, his hands clenched into fists, ready to do battle against anyone who would speak in such a tone to his ma.

Dorry's voice took on that quiet, respectful tone she'd learned to use around her husband's older brother whenever he was on one of his tirades. "What are you talking about, Junior?"

"I'm not Junior anymore." His voice seemed as hot as the sun. As hard as the baked earth. "I've always hated that name. With the old man gone, I'm Deacon now. Deacon Conover. And don't you forget it."

Dorry nodded. "Whatever you say."

"That's right." He glanced at the mound of dirt, then back at her. "It's whatever I say now. Not the old man. I told him he was a fool to take on four more mouths. But you fed him that lie about Clay, and he swallowed it whole."

"Lie? What are you…?" She glanced toward the back of the wagon and could see her three children watching and listening in horrified fascination.

"That pretty little sugarcoated story about Clay carrying on some secret mission for the President. You and the old man both knew it was a lie. Clay's never coming back for you." His voice lifted to a whine. "You could have had yourself a solid, dependable husband, Dorry. You knew I wanted you.

When we were kids, you were just about the prettiest girl around. With all that yellow hair and those big blue eyes."

Yale was ready to jump down from the wagon and start pummeling his uncle when Gabe clamped a hand over his wrist. "You don't stand a chance of beating Uncle Junior."

Yale's voice was little more than a strangled whisper. "Maybe not. But at least I could land a couple of solid blows."

Gabe held him back. "You might start it, but he'll end it. With a boot to the stomach or a knee in the groin."

They both knew that was their uncle's usual method of fighting. Of the two boys, Yale had borne the brunt of Junior Conover's quick-triggered temper. There was just something in Yale's nature that had him rebelling whenever he saw the unfairness of a situation.

Junior's tone hardened. "But you just had to go and give your heart to my reckless little brother, Dorry. And look what it got you. Three brats, and a husband who left you to run off with the most dangerous gang of outlaws in the land."

Yale heard his little sister's cry and saw the pained expression on Gabe's face. For himself, it wasn't pain he was feeling but a wild rush of excitement.

An outlaw? His pa was an outlaw?

Yale felt as if he'd just been struck by lightning, and a bolt of electricity had gone clear through his body. He was fairly twitching from the jolt to his system.

For the space of several moments, Dorry seemed frozen to the spot, unable to speak. Unable to move. Finally she drew in a long breath. "You'll be burdened with us no longer. We'll stay only long enough to fetch our things. Then we'll be through accepting your hospitality."

She climbed up to the wagon and flicked the reins. As they started across the hills, nobody spoke. Not the woman, the children, nor the man who rode his horse in stone-faced silence alongside them.

At the ranch Dorry moved from room to room, bundling up their meager belongings, supervising as Gabe and Yale secured them in the back of the wagon. She walked the garden, taking care to pick only half the rain-starved crop, leaving the other half for her brother-in-law. She did the same with the chickens, tossing half a dozen in a pen, along with a rooster. She tied a young cow behind the wagon, then ordered her children to climb aboard.

Junior stood in the doorway, grinning foolishly. "You want me to beg, don't you, Dorry? That's what this is about, isn't it?"

She said nothing as she picked up the reins.

His smile faded as he ran down the steps and started racing alongside. "All right. I'm sorry for what I said back there, Dorry. But the brats had to hear it some time. Besides, you know you can't really leave. Where will you go?"

She reined in the horse long enough to say, "I'm

heading for the Badlands. That's where Clay said he'd be. As for you, I never want to see you again." And then, because she'd been pushed to the limit, she added, "You'll never be Deacon Conover to me, Junior. You're not half the man your father was. Or your brother, Clay."

She urged the horse into a trot, leaving her brother-in-law standing in the dust, staring after her.

No one said a word. Yale could see the shocked look on Gabe's face, and the fear in the eyes of his little sister. But his own heart was pumping like a runaway stage. He felt like standing up and shouting.

Free.

He was finally free of his stern grandfather, who'd ruled with a belt to the backside for the slightest infraction. Free of his spineless uncle, who'd found fault with everything in their lives from sunup to sundown, and took out his anger and frustration on three helpless children.

It didn't matter to Yale that his father might be an outlaw instead of a hero. Anything, he reasoned, was better than the life they'd had up to now. Even a life on the run from the law. Especially since it meant that at least one Conover had found the courage to stand up against silly, useless rules.

The euphoria of freedom lasted a few days. After that, their little odyssey became a test of endurance. To spare their horse, the family walked as much as possible until, drained by heat and exhaustion, they would make camp during the hottest part of the day and begin walking again after sundown. While Kitty slept in the back of the wagon, Gabe and Yale would take turns leading the horse, with their mother walking beside them telling them tales of her childhood in Missouri or coaching them in spelling and sums.

"You owe it to me and your pa to make something of your lives, boys. You can't ever let life's trials beat you down."

Yale fell silent. He had no intention of ever being beaten by anyone or anything. It just wasn't in his nature. But the same couldn't be said for his ma. This journey had begun to sap her energy, until, within weeks, she was going on pure will.

Their family witnessed a variety of bewildering extremes. There seemed to be limitless expanses of space, but almost no people. They traversed sweeping treeless plains and steep, forested mountains, but spent hours searching in vain for water.

To Yale, their odyssey had become not a burden, but simply a new challenge. One he faced head-on with the same fearlessness he'd always displayed.

When Dorry Conover awoke one morning with a raging fever that gradually grew worse, he could already see what was coming, though his brother and sister were still in denial.

"You ride in the wagon with Kitty, Ma." Gabe helped her into the back and lay her down among the quilts, then took up the reins and began walking.

Yale, walking beside him, said softly, "What will we do when Ma dies?"

Gabe grabbed him by the throat, his eyes hot with fury. "She isn't going to die."

Yale shoved his hand away and lifted a fist, as always ready to stand and fight. "Who says? People die, Gabe. Gramps died, didn't he?"

"That was different. Gramps was old."

"Young people die, too. Remember Pa's friends who died in the war?"

"That was war. This is..." Gabe shook his head, struggling to find a word to describe the hell they were in.

"This is a different kind of war, Gabe." Yale lowered his voice. "It's just us against the Badlands. But it's war all the same." A war he had no intention of losing.

By the time they stopped for the night, Dorry was too weak to sit up. She clutched their hands and struggled to make herself understood.

"Your pa's a good man. An honorable man. Don't believe what your uncle said about him."

When Gabe agreed with her, Yale held his silence. In his heart, he'd already accepted the words tossed by his uncle. What other reason could his father have for staying away so long?

Dorry Conover's voice became little more than a whisper. "I'm not going to be with you on your journey. I can feel my strength ebbing. But I want you to know that my spirit will always be with you. Don't be afraid. You have your father's blood flowing through you. That Conover blood will make you strong enough to prevail over anything." She squeezed Gabriel's hand, and turned to look at her middle child, Yale, the rebel, and then her baby, Kitty, as though memorizing their faces. "You take care of each other, you hear me?"

"Yes'm." Gabriel nudged his brother and sister, and the two answered in kind.

Even as they were speaking, Dorry's eyes went sightless. In the whisper of a breath, she slipped away.

As they left the crude grave with its simple stone marker, and started out at first light, Yale swallowed back his grief.

Seeing tears on Kitty's lashes, he knelt down and urged her to climb up on his back. Then he ran ahead, trotting and snorting like a horse, until she forgot her fears and began giggling. It was a sound Yale had always loved. He would do anything to see his little sister's eyes bright, and her lips curved into a wide smile of delight.

By nighttime, as they made camp by a mud hole that had once been a raging river, he had a revelation. It came to him with blinding clarity. With no adults around, all the rules had suddenly been suspended.

While the others slept, he crept away, following the sound of a distant lowing. In the morning he returned to their small encampment, grinning wickedly.

"Where've you been?" Gabe's features were tight with anger.

"Getting us some supplies." Yale held up a jug and uncorked it, filling a tin cup with milk. He passed it to Kitty and watched with satisfaction as she drank it down in long gulps.

Gabe's jaw dropped. "Where'd you find milk out here?"

"There's a ranch about a mile from here."

"And the rancher gave you milk and supplies?"

"In a way." Yale's grin widened. "'Course, he doesn't know it yet. And I'd advise us to be long gone before he finds his prize calf slaughtered." He tossed a hunk of raw meat, as much as he'd been able to carry, in the back of the wagon and covered it with a blanket to hide the evidence.

"You stole his milk and butchered his calf?" Gabe looked horrified.

"That's right." Yale pushed him aside and lifted Kitty into the back of the wagon. "Now let's get. It'll be light soon."

They managed to cross a muddy creek and pass through a forest before making camp. But that night, for the first time in weeks, they went to bed with their stomachs full. And as Yale curled up beside his brother and sister, he pushed aside the little twinge of guilt over the meat and milk he'd stolen. Did he come by it naturally, through the blood of his father? Was that what his ma had meant when she used to call him her little rebel? Or was it just something inside him? Some demon that was fighting to be free?

Whatever the reason, he knew it was his skill that

had saved the day. And right or wrong, he would keep on doing whatever it took to keep his brother and sister not just alive, but strong and healthy.

Two weeks later, long after they'd gone through the last of their meat, they walked up over a rise and saw a small encampment of wagons and shacks. As they drew near they saw an old man tending a herd of cows. He looked up as their little party approached.

"'Afternoon, boys. Welcome to Misery."

The two brothers looked at each other.

Yale glanced around. "Misery?"

Seeing their surprise the old man laughed, showing a gaping hole where his teeth had once been. "That's the name of our little place. We figure we're all sharing in it together. My name's Aaron Smiler."

Gabe offered a handshake. "I'm Gabriel Conover. This is my brother Yale." He pointed to the back of the wagon. "And that's our little sister, Kitty."

At the sight of the little girl the old man touched a gnarled hand to his wide-brimmed hat in a courtly gesture. Then he turned back to Gabe, sensing that he was the spokesman for the family. "Where's your folks, son?"

"Our ma's buried along the trail. We're heading for the Badlands to join up with our pa." He looked at the old man hopefully. "You wouldn't happen to know him, would you? Clay Conover."

The old man shook his head. "Sorry, son. Never heard of him." He glanced at the weary little party before pointing toward a wood shack in the distance. "That's my place. Why don't you stop awhile and I'll make you some vittles."

At that the two younger ones perked up considerably.

Gabe held back. "We can't pay you, Mr. Smiler."

Yale gave him a sharp nudge with his elbow, hoping to silence him.

Aaron Smiler saw the range of emotions in these three. He could read simple honesty in the eyes of the oldest, and disappointment in the little girl's eyes. The middle brother was harder to read, but he sensed a simmering annoyance in Yale's eyes. This, he thought, was a boy impatient to become a man.

"Well, now," Aaron said simply. "Maybe you could lend a hand with some of the chores around here. I'm getting on in years, and I can't do all the things I used to."

Yale looked around at the hard land, wondering why anyone would want to settle in such a place. But Gabe was already agreeing, and nudging him to do the same.

Yale gave a reluctant nod of his head.

"All right then." The old man led the way. "Maybe, if you decide you like it here, you'll make Misery your home for awhile. Just until you're ready to resume your search for your pa, that is."

While Gabe and Kitty ran ahead, Yale took his time, looking over the old man and his land. He didn't much like the idea of living by Aaron

Smiler's rules, but for now it was a chance to stop and gather his strength. Then, as soon as he was old enough and strong enough, he would resume his search for his father. Then, he thought with a grin, he'd live his life as he pleased.

Chapter One

Dakota Territory, 1887

Yale Conover picked up his money and smiled at the gamblers who sat around the poker table, glowering at him. He'd been on a winning streak that appeared to have no end in sight. Some might call him lucky. But those who'd stayed around for the entire forty-eight-hour poker marathon knew it took more than luck to earn his reputation as one of the shrewdest gamblers in the Dakotas.

He looked the part of a charming rogue. Expensive black suit, soft white shirt, wide-brimmed black hat and boots polished to a high shine. While his opponents cast furtive glances at one another each time the cards were dealt, he merely smiled and drew on his cigar, looking as relaxed as a man after a good meal. And though he always ordered a glass of whiskey, he never drank it. It was just one of his props. Now he indulged himself, draining it in one long swallow.

"Thank you, gentlemen. It's been an...interesting and profitable experience."

He shoved away from the poker table and moved with catlike grace across the room. When he stepped through the swinging doors of the saloon into blinding morning sunlight, he scrubbed a hand over the rough stubble of beard and blinked. For a moment he was tossed back into another time. Another place.

He'd been sixteen, and amazed that he'd spent the entire night in a small-stakes poker game at the Red Dog Saloon in the little town of Misery, in the Dakota Territory. As always, the lack of sleep caused him no concern. He'd always been comfortable with the night.

He touched the money folded in his pocket before giving a lazy smile. It had been worth every minute, just to see the look on Buck Reedy's face when he'd set down his hand showing three queens, beating Buck's pair of aces. Yale's smile grew. He considered the ladies his lucky cards.

He crossed the dusty patch of road the residents of Misery called their main street and walked into Swensen's Dry Goods.

Inga Swensen looked up from the counter. "You're up and about early, Yale. Olaf and Lars are out back right now loading Aaron's supplies into the wagon."

Yale smiled, already planning how he would spend his bounty. After all, wasn't that what money was for? "I'll be adding a few things to Aaron's list, Mrs. Swensen."

Knowing his sister's sweet tooth he picked up a jar of honey. Then he added a pair of decent boots for Gabe, who'd been wearing the same pair for more than a year now. He paused to add a couple of cigars for Aaron. Thinking better of it, he took one more for himself. Sitting in the Red Dog with all the gamblers had given him an appetite for smoking. He knew Aaron and Gabe would disapprove. But he'd just save it for a time when he was alone with the herd.

When Inga Swensen tallied the purchases, he peeled off a couple of bills. As she was handing him his change she said, "If you'd like, you can ride back to Aaron's place with Lars. He'll be leaving within the hour."

Yale was about to agree when he caught sight of Cara McKinnon just walking in the door. She had the face of an angel, all smooth, creamy skin and big honey eyes, set off by a halo of ebony curls that just begged to be touched.

His heart gave one hard bounce before he managed to compose himself. "No thanks. I'm not ready to leave town just yet."

Inga walked away to wait on Cara's mother, and Yale followed the young girl to the back of the store, where she stopped to admire a display of fancy hair ornaments. She seemed mesmerized by a comb decorated with pale pink stones that glinted in the light.

"You like that, Cara?"

She whirled, then blushed when she caught sight of him. She seemed to always have that same reaction whenever she found herself close to Yale

Conover. He was taller than the other boys his age. Taller even than her own father. His body was already sculpted with muscle from his years spent working for Aaron Smiler and the other ranchers nearby. Every girl in Misery, from ten to twenty, thought he was just about the most handsome boy around. But though many were attracted, in truth most were a little afraid of him. There was an air of danger about Yale. An edgy sense that he would climb any mountain on a dare, leap any chasm, or break any rule that stood in the way of what he wanted.

And he'd made it plain for some time now that he wanted Cara. What frightened her even more was that she felt the same way. She wanted him. Desperately. Even though she wasn't at all certain just what to do about these strange feelings he caused.

To hide the color she knew was on her cheeks, she turned back, pretending to study the comb. "It's pretty. And my favorite color, too. Mrs. Swensen told my ma she just got these in a shipment from St. Louis. Can you imagine?"

"You ever been to St. Louis, Cara?"

"No." She shook her head, sending midnight curls dancing down her back.

Behind her, Yale couldn't help reaching out to feel. Her hair was as soft as a newborn calf's downy hide. He rubbed a strand between his thumb and finger.

At his touch, heat spiraled through Cara's veins and curled deliciously along her spine. She glanced over her shoulder. "I've never been anywhere but here in Misery. Have you been anywhere else, Yale?''

"Sure. I've even been across the Badlands."

"You have? When?"

He shrugged, uncomfortable talking about that time in his life. "When I was nine. That's when we came to stay with Aaron."

"My pa said you and your brother and sister are orphans."

His tone hardened. "We're not orphans." He hated that word. It made him feel that people would pity him. That was the last thing he wanted. Especially from Cara McKinnon. "We've got a pa."

"You do? Where is he?"

Yale lifted a shoulder. "We haven't found him yet. But we will." To change the subject he picked up the comb. "Why don't you see how it looks on you?"

She seemed shocked at the suggestion. "I couldn't do that."

"Why not?" Seeing an excuse to touch her again he settled the comb into a strand of her hair, then lifted her chin, allowing his fingers to linger on the soft flesh of her throat.

He stepped back, studying her intently.

Now her cheeks were blazing. To cover her embarrassment she turned and picked up a looking glass. What she saw startled her. Her cheeks were so pink, and her eyes so wide, she looked different somehow. Older. Prettier. And the jeweled comb tucked into her dark curls was just about the most beautiful thing she'd ever seen.

"Oh." The sigh escaped before she could stop herself. "I've never worn anything so elegant."

He stepped closer, bending so that she could see his face beside hers in the looking glass. "It isn't the comb, Cara." His breath was warm against her cheek, and his voice, already as deep as a man's, seemed to wrap itself around her heart. "It's you. You're so beautiful you take my breath away."

"Yale." She set down the mirror with a clatter, then reached up to remove the comb from her hair. When she turned, he was standing so close her body brushed his.

She started to step back, only to find the wooden shelf digging into her waist. She lifted her chin. "You shouldn't say such a thing."

"Why not? It's the truth."

She knew her face was flaming, and there was no place to hide. "But it's bold. Papa says you're too bold."

"Maybe I am." He was close enough to smell her. She smelled so sweet. Like a field of wildflowers. Her clothes smelled of sunshine. He'd seen that very gown flapping on the McKinnon clothesline just yesterday. He'd spotted a filmy chemise, as well, and had wondered at the time how Cara would look wearing only that. The thought had his blood heating, his heart speeding up.

He touched a hand to her arm. Just a touch, but he felt the way she jerked back before lowering her gaze.

"I want to kiss you, Cara."

Her head came up sharply. "No, Yale. Ma might see us."

His eyes narrowed. "Is that the only reason you're saying no?"

She seemed about to deny it, until she looked into those dark, laughing eyes. Without meaning to, her lips curved into a smile. "Yes."

"You mean, if we were alone, you'd let me kiss you?"

Before she could respond, a woman's voice shouted, "Cara. Your pa's here with the wagon. Let's go, girl."

"I'm…coming, Ma."

As she started away Yale reached out and caught her hand, holding her still.

His voice sounded urgent. "Tell me, Cara. Would you? If we were alone?"

She swallowed, then looked down at their linked fingers. His hand was so big. So workworn. And so strong. Yet he was holding her as carefully as if she were made of spun glass.

She gave just the slightest nod of her head before yanking her hand free and racing toward the front of the store.

When she was gone Yale stayed where he was, watching the flutter of her skirt as she followed her mother out the door.

Afterward it took several long minutes before his heart settled back to its natural rhythm. He knew there were some in this town who thought he was still a boy. But he knew in his heart he was already a man. With a man's powerful needs.

That very day he went to the hollow tree where he kept his stash and counted it out. Over five hundred dollars. And that was after settling Aaron's bill at Swensen's, and buying grain for next spring, and paying for the bull Aaron had been eyeing for the better part of a year.

Aaron often scolded him for being too generous. But that was just Yale's nature. He liked knowing he was paying his own way, so that he didn't have to feel like he was taking from Aaron without giving something back. Besides, he could see how much Aaron appreciated his gifts.

It was the same with his little sister. He loved seeing Kitty's eyes grow all warm and happy when he surprised her with something special.

Even straight-arrow Gabe hadn't been able to find fault when he'd presented him with a new parka and rifle last Christmas.

Though his family resented his gambling, they were willing to enjoy the fruits. For Yale, it wasn't the money. It was the thrill of winning. He couldn't explain it to the others. But he simply loved living on the edge.

Like my pa.

He frowned, and brushed aside the thought, wanting nothing to mar his happiness. Tonight he was going to show Parker McKinnon how much money he'd saved, before asking for his daughter's hand in marriage. Then he and Cara McKinnon would start a life together.

Together.

He thought that was just about the best word ever.

There wasn't anything he wouldn't do for Cara. He'd give up his wild ways. The gambling, the smoking, the occasional taste of whiskey. He'd settle down. Buy some land and build her a home. And together they would fill it with children. He'd be the best husband, the best father in the world. There would never be a night when he wouldn't be there with his family, looking out for them.

Oh, he might still drop by the Red Dog from time to time. Just to teach the ranchers who thought of themselves as gamblers a lesson in humility. He was grinning as he started toward the cabin he shared with Gabe and Kitty and Aaron Smiler.

He paused to study it with a critical eye. He intended to build one twice as big for Cara. One with a fine big cookstove. And a separate bedroom, so he and Cara could slip away after dinner and lie in each other's arms. The thought had him whistling a little tune as he slipped in the door and started washing up.

If Gabe and Kitty and old Aaron noticed his air of expectancy, they didn't let on. Over a supper of leathery beef and burned biscuits, they chatted about the day. Aaron was scolding Kitty about not keeping the cabin clean, and for refusing to learn to cook anything but beef and biscuits. She was reminding him that she'd spent as many hours in the field as he and Gabe, and she figured somebody else ought to help with the womanly chores, before staring pointedly at Yale.

He'd merely grinned, too happy to accept her invitation to spar. Though it was one of his favorite activities, tonight was different.

As soon as he could, he slipped away and helped himself to Aaron's plow horse, pulling himself onto the mare's bare back and digging his hands into her mane. He didn't need to ask permission. Aaron never went anywhere at night. Besides, he'd be back before he was missed. He smiled in the darkness. Oh yes. He'd be back. And he'd surprise his family with the big announcement of his pending marriage.

As he made his way to the McKinnon ranch, he thought about the money in his pocket. He'd have to use some of it to buy himself a decent saddle horse. It wouldn't be right for a family man to be seen riding an old swaybacked nag. And some proper clothes, he thought. After all, he and Cara would be expected to attend Sunday services, whenever the visiting preacher came to town.

He and Cara. His smile grew. From the time he'd been old enough to notice girls, it had always been pretty little Cara McKinnon. He couldn't imagine his life without her.

He slipped from the mare's back and stood a moment, staring at the flickering lantern light coming from the McKinnon cabin. Then he tucked the paper-clad present into his pocket and strode to the door.

As he knocked, he heard the sound of laughter suddenly cease. A moment later the door was thrown open and Parker McKinnon stood framed in the doorway.

He was a big man. Strong as a bull from his years

wrangling on his sprawling ranch. There were some who said he ruled his hired hands with an iron fist. But when it came to his wife and daughter, he was a very different man, clearly doting on them as he squired them into town from time to time like a proud peacock.

Yale stepped into the spill of light and extended his hand. "'Evening, Mr. McKinnon."

Parker McKinnon's eyes narrowed. "Something you want, Yale?"

"Yes, sir. I've come to see Cara."

The older man glanced over his shoulder and could see his daughter leap up and start toward the door. Instead of moving aside he remained where he was, keeping himself between her and this brash young man. "It's already past supper. I won't have her going out in the dark."

Yale gave one of his easy smiles. "I don't mind coming inside."

Parker McKinnon seemed about to refuse when his wife called, "Invite whoever it is in out of the night, Parker."

He stepped aside, allowing Yale to walk past him.

The room, with its fancy rug and fine, sturdy furniture became a blur when Yale caught sight of Cara. Her pleasure at seeing him was there in her eyes, wide with surprise, and in her lips, curved into the sweetest smile.

"You look..." He wished he had the words to describe what she meant to him. But all he could manage was, "...really pretty tonight, Cara."

She blushed and glanced over at her mother.

Remembering his manners, Yale reached up, yanking the wide-brimmed hat from his head as he smiled at her mother, seated across the room. "'Evening, ma'am."

Like her husband, Evelyn McKinnon's smile faded at the sight of the young man everyone in town considered bold and just a little bit dangerous. "Yale. What brings you here?"

"I came to speak to Mr. McKinnon." He turned to the older man and for the first time felt his courage slip a notch. He could almost feel the hostility coming in waves from Cara's father. "I came here to ask for your daughter's hand in marriage."

Cara clapped a hand to her mouth, but not before issuing a quick little squeal of delight. Then, seeing her father's dark look, she stared hard at the floor.

"What sort of nonsense is this?" Parker McKinnon's eyes were hard as flint. "What gives you the right to ask such a thing?"

"I know you think we're both too young. But I have feelings for your daughter, Mr. McKinnon. And have for years. And I have reason to believe that she feels the same way about me."

He saw the older man's head whip around, his mouth a hard, tight line of disapproval. "Have you been going around behind our backs, Cara?"

"Oh no, Pa." She looked at her father, then away. "But Yale's right. I...do have feelings for him."

His hand snaked out, grasping her arm, forcing her to look at him. "Just tell me if you've acted on those feelings."

"Pa!" Her cheeks grew as red as the coals on the hearth. "How could you even ask such a thing?"

"All right." Eyes narrow, he released her and turned to Yale. "Go home now, boy. And don't ever let me see you sniffing around here again."

"You don't understand. Maybe you think I'm just a boy. But I'm a man, Mr. McKinnon." Yale reached a hand to his pocket and withdrew a fistful of money. "I've been saving this to buy some land and build a cabin. I promise I'll take good care of Cara, if you'll give us your blessing."

"My blessing? My blessing? What the hell are you thinking, boy?" The words were tight. Clipped.

Yale glanced toward Evelyn McKinnon, who had risen from her chair to stand beside her husband. It occurred to him that these two had formed a wall of resistance, determined to end this unexpected intrusion into their orderly lives as quickly as possible.

Remembering the present, Yale reached into his pocket and handed it to Cara. "I bought this for you today at Swensen's. I know, by the way you were admiring it, how much you like it."

Before she could unwrap it, her father tore it from her hand and tossed it at Yale's feet. "And just how did you come by the money to buy my daughter a present? I'll tell you how. The same way you came by the rest of your money. By gambling. By spending all your time in the Red Dog with drunks and gamblers. I won't allow my daughter to accept a gift from the likes of you. Now get out. Before I'm forced to throw you off my land."

Anger burned in Yale's eyes, and in his throat.

He looked over at Cara and saw that all the color had drained from her face. Without thinking he touched a hand to hers. "Don't cry, Cara. I'll make this right, somehow."

For her father, that was the last straw. He caught Yale by the back of the shirt and spun him around.

Reflexively Yale's hands fisted, ready to fight back. His voice, when he spoke, was so cold he hardly recognized it. "Take your hands off me this minute, Parker McKinnon, or you'll live to regret it."

At the fierceness of his tone, Yale had the satisfaction of seeing the older man back up a step.

Yale turned to Cara. "I thought…I thought I could make your father see I'd be good to you. But he's like everybody else in this town. They see what they want. So I'm leaving. Not just this house, but this town. Are you coming with me, Cara?"

She glanced from Yale to her parents, who wore matching looks of absolute disbelief at his rashness.

With tears filling her eyes, she slowly shook her head. "I can't, Yale. I just…can't leave my father and mother."

His eyes were hot with fury as he spun on his heels and strode out the door.

As he pulled himself onto the back of his horse, he looked up to see Cara standing in the doorway, lantern light spilling over her in a yellow pool, the pretty jeweled comb clutched to her chest, the paper it had been wrapped in drifting around her feet.

With a furious oath her father tore it from her hands and tossed it out into the dirt. She was still weeping when her father reached around her and slammed the door.

It was an image that was burned into Yale's memory.

By the following morning he'd turned his back on his family, and on the town of Misery.

He'd never looked back.

He blinked, erasing the bitter memory. Even now, after a dozen years, it still had the power to churn his gut and twist a knife in his heart.

He folded the thousand dollars he'd won and stuffed it in his pocket before turning and walking back into the saloon. He'd thought he had his fill of this place. But he had a sudden need for another shot of whiskey. Maybe he'd just stick around and stir up a little more excitement before hitting the trail.

He wasn't in the mood for his own company right now.

Chapter Two

Yale slowed his mount as he crested a hill. Down below was a string of mustangs in a corral. He'd been pushing his horse to the limit, ever since he'd had to hightail it out of Elmerville after beating the sheriff out of a high-stakes jackpot. The saloon keeper had warned Yale about the sheriff. As corrupt as they come. Figured his title as a lawman gave him the right to lose and still keep his money by threatening gamblers with jail. When he'd tried that line on Yale, he'd met his match. The entire saloon had been stunned by the fire in Yale Conover's eyes.

"I don't take orders from spineless scum who break the rules, then hide behind a tin badge." In the blink of an eye Yale had wrapped a muscled arm around the sheriff's throat, while pressing a six-gun to his temple. "To my way of thinking that makes you worse than any outlaw. You're flaunting the very law you claim to uphold."

The men in the saloon had gone eerily quiet. It

wasn't just the way this gambler used his gun. It was the fire in his eyes. And the deadly softness of his voice that spoke of suppressed rage.

He'd made his point, and had been allowed to ride out of town. But he knew, by the icy fingers along his spine, that a posse wasn't far behind.

He needed a fresh horse if he intended to keep one step ahead of Elmerville's corrupt lawman.

He slid to the ground and quickly removed the saddle and bridle, turning his horse loose. From a position on the ridge he watched as his horse trotted toward the corral, in search of food and water.

Minutes later a grizzled old man, hearing the sound of hoofbeats, stepped out of a crude cabin and looked the horse over before opening a gate. Yale stayed where he was, watching intently as the old man poured water into a trough before returning to his shack.

Yale had fully intended to help himself to a fresh horse and be on his way. But the sight of the old man triggered something in him. Something so deep, so primal, he couldn't walk away. This man in this deserted cabin, on the edge of the Badlands, could possibly know about his father. Could, in fact, be his father. Though he knew the odds against it, he couldn't leave until he found out one way or the other.

Tossing the saddle over his shoulder he made his way down the hill and crept toward the shack. Once there he peered through the cracks of the log wall, hoping for a glimpse of the old man's face.

Just as he crouched in the grass, he felt the press of a gun's barrel against the back of his head, and a raspy voice called, "You so much as breathe hard you'll be dead, stranger."

Yale froze.

"Toss your gun aside real slow."

He did as he was told, then lifted his hands and turned to find the old man aiming a rifle at his chest. "Thought you'd help yourself to my mustangs, did you?"

Yale nodded. "Just one of them."

"I figured, when I saw that horse all lathered and dust-covered, somebody around here needed a fresh mount." The old man's eyes narrowed. "Why didn't you just offer to buy one of my horses? Got no money?"

"I've got enough." Yale gave one of his lazy grins. "But it's just not my nature to pay for what I can get for nothing. Besides, it was a fair exchange. My horse for one of yours."

"If you believed it was fair, you'd have come here like a man and offered, instead of planning to steal from me."

Yale nodded. "You're right, old man. I guess I've been on the wrong side of the law so long, I've forgotten how to play by the rules." He studied the figure before him, trying to find something that even remotely stirred a memory. "What's your name?"

"What's it to you?"

Yale gave a negligent shrug. "Just wondered if we'd met before."

"If we had, I'd remember." The old man spat a stream of yellow tobacco juice. "The law says I have the right to shoot a horse thief."

Yale chuckled. "You don't waste any time, do you, old man?" He lifted his hands, palms up. "All right then. Fire away."

The old man took aim, watching Yale's face. Seeing no fear he slowly lowered the rifle. "You're a cocky one. A man ought to have a healthy fear of dying."

Yale shook his head. "Not me, old man. I don't care if I live or die, as long as I'm free to make my own rules along the way."

"I know what you mean. I've lived the same way all my life." The old man stuck out his hand. "My name is Otis Conley. What's yours?"

"Yale. Yale Conover." He waited a beat, to see if the name triggered a response. Seeing none, he sighed. "I was told my father came to the Badlands about twenty years ago. His name was Clay Conover. You ever hear of him?"

The old man thought a minute before saying, "Sorry. Can't say I have. You want to bargain for a horse? Or you still thinking of stealing one?"

Again that slow, lazy smile as Yale reached into his pocket. He peeled off a couple of bills and said, "I'll want the best of the lot."

Otis Conley's eyes lit as his fingers closed around the money. "You can have your pick. That black stallion is the fastest. But he's also the meanest. You don't want to get behind him or he'll knock you clear back to Oklahoma Territory.''

''Thanks. I'll keep that in mind.''

Yale looked over the herd, then lassoed the black and tied him to the gate while he saddled him. Minutes later he rode off, lifting his hat in a salute as he did.

As he disappeared into a dense woods, he found himself wondering about the conflicting emotions churning inside. He certainly hadn't wanted that grizzled old man to be his father. Had he?

Why then this emptiness each time another encounter ended without a resolution?

For twenty years now he'd been looking into the eyes of every man of a certain age, wondering if this one might turn out to be Clay Conover.

He muttered a rich, ripe oath and urged the stallion into a gallop. What the hell did he need with an old man? He'd been taking care of himself for years now. And doing just fine, thank you. Finding a father now would just be a complication in his life. And that was something he could do without.

Footloose and free. That was the way he liked it. No woman to tie him down. Nobody checking up to see when he got home, when he left, or where he was headed.

He brushed aside the dull edge of memory and urged his horse faster. It didn't matter where he was headed. Just so he never had to look back.

The day had been long, the trail rough. Thanks to that crooked lawman, Yale had left Elmerville in such a hurry, there'd been no time to make provisions for a journey. His canteen was nearly empty. There was no food in his saddlebags. And he hadn't caught sight of any game along the way. On top of that, there was the relentless sun, causing the sweat to run in rivers down his back and under the brim of his hat. Not even a whisper of a breeze stirred the air as dust clogged his lungs and burned his eyes.

At the first sound of gunshots he reined in his mount. Slipping from the saddle he tethered the stallion and crept around a mountain of boulders to stare at the scene below him.

A man, obviously wounded, lay slumped behind the cover of a rock. Up ahead were more than a dozen horsemen, fanning out to surround him. Whenever one got too close the wounded man would fire off a shot. But it was obvious that before long he would be overcome by the sheer number of his adversaries.

Thinking quickly Yale pulled himself into the saddle and, keeping to the cover of rocks, made a wide circle until he was behind the group of horsemen. Then, knotting the reins around the pommel, he gave a nudge of his knees, urging the stallion into a run. With his rifle in one hand and his pistol in the other, he charged in with both guns blazing.

Caught by surprise, the horsemen scattered. Though several returned his gunfire, they were too startled to stick around to see just how many men were after them.

Within minutes they'd disappeared over a hill, with only the sound of their horses' hooves retreating in the distance.

In the stillness that followed Yale cupped a hand to his mouth and shouted, "You can put away your guns. They've gone."

The man behind the rock made no reply.

He shouted louder, "I'm tossing aside my weapons. I come in friendship."

Again there was only silence.

Though he shoved the rifle into the boot of his saddle, and returned his pistol to his holster, he kept his hand there just in case he had to draw fast.

When his horse rounded the boulder, he realized why the wounded man hadn't responded. He lay still as death in an ever-widening pool of blood.

Yale was out of the saddle and feeling for a pulse. Finding one, he worked as quickly as possible to stem the flow of blood. While he did, he felt the slow, feeble heartbeat, and heard the almost inaudible moans of the wounded man.

It took more than an hour to remove the bullet from the man's shoulder and dress the wound. After wrapping him in a blanket, Yale started a fire, then spent the next hour searching for food and water. As darkness settled over the land, he sat by the hot coals and rested his back against his saddle while he ate the remains of the rabbit he'd killed. In a blackened pot nestled in the coals steam rose from the broth that was simmering.

From the stranger's saddlebag Yale had rescued

a bottle of whiskey. He helped himself to a healthy swig, then corked it, figuring the wounded man would need some when he woke up and had to deal with the pain.

He studied the sleeping man, wondering who he was. There had been nothing in his saddlebags to give a clue. But the very fact that he was traveling so light made Yale think he was a drifter.

Since the stranger was sleeping in his only blanket, he had no choice but to curl up close to the fire for warmth. His stomach full from the rabbit meat, his blood warm from the whiskey, and his mind at peace that he'd done what he could, he fell into a deep sleep.

It was the sound of the man's moans that woke him. For a minute Yale lay still, struggling to get his bearings. Then, by the light of the moon, he made his way to where the stranger was thrashing around, trying to untangle himself from the confines of the blanket.

"This what you're looking for?" Yale held the man's pistol in his hand.

"Yeah." The voice was weak, raspy. "Feel naked without it."

Yale nodded, understanding. "I just didn't want you shooting me first, and asking questions later."

The man smiled before hissing in a breath of pain. "Can't say I blame you." He nodded toward his saddlebags, lying nearby. "I could use some whiskey."

Yale uncorked the bottle and held it to the man's lips.

When he'd had his fill, the man lay still a moment, studying him intently. "Why'd you get involved in my fight?"

Yale shrugged. Grinned. "I didn't like the odds. Figured I'd at least give you a fighting chance."

"I'm obliged." The man nodded toward the bottle and Yale helped him drink more before corking the bottle and setting it aside.

The stranger lay back, taking in shallow breaths until the pain subsided. "My name's Justin Greenleaf."

"Yale Conover."

"What makes you think I was worth saving, Yale Conover?"

Yale gave him a slow, easy grin. "Didn't figure it was any of my business. Like I said, I just wanted to even the odds."

"You got anywhere you have to be, Yale?"

He shook his head. "Just so it isn't Elmerville. There's a lawman there I'd rather not run into for a while. I figure he's just a few miles behind me by now."

Justin Greenleaf seemed to think about that a moment before saying, "I'd know a thing or two about lawmen. My name's on Wanted posters from here to Oklahoma Territory. The last thing I want to run into is the law. I'm on my way to join some friends in the Badlands. Want to come along?"

Yale considered. "What kind of friends live in the Badlands?"

"Friends like you and me who want to avoid the law. Interested in joining us?"

Yale took his time crossing to the fire where he poured broth into a cup before returning to hold it to Justin's lips. While the man drank, he thought about the posse that would probably catch up to him by morning. If he left now, he could stay one step ahead of them. Of course, he'd be leaving this stranger at their mercy. And since he'd already had a taste of the sheriff's brand of justice, he'd be condemning Justin Greenleaf to jail. But if he took him along, Justin could direct him to a hideout in the Badlands, where no posse would ever dare to follow.

But there was an even more compelling reason to ride along with this stranger. The very thought of the Badlands had Yale's heart racing. His father. Clay Conover had disappeared in that very place, more than twenty years ago, never to return.

Maybe one of Justin's friends would be able to fill in the missing piece of his life. Though it was a long shot, if there was even the slightest chance that he could learn about his father, he had to risk it.

His lips curved into a smile. He'd never been able to resist a gamble. "I think I might be interested. How soon can you ride?"

They were in the saddle before dawn. And by the time the sun was high in the sky, they had long ago crossed into the forbidding landscape considered so

dangerous, that the Sioux called it *mako sica,* bad
land, and nervous French trappers dubbed it *les
mauvaises terres a traverser,* bad lands to travel
across. There were few travelers brave or foolish
enough to risk survival in this place of granite
mountains, dizzying pinnacles, and huge, yawning
caverns. But it was notorious for offering shelter to
gangs of reckless men who had chosen to live outside the law.

Despite his wounds, Justin Greenleaf was able to
lead the way across high ridges and barren mesas,
until they came to a narrow gorge carved between
massive rock formations. A man holding a rifle suddenly appeared on the very top of the ridge.

Justin gave a whistle and the man returned the
signal. Minutes later several more men came riding
toward them, rifles at the ready.

"Who've you got there, Justin?" one of the men
shouted.

Justin lifted a hand signaling Yale to halt. Urging
his horse ahead he called, "He's a friend. Name's
Yale Conover. Saved my life."

The men spoke in low tones, and Justin responded.

One of the men separated from the others and
started toward Yale. "Justin says you can be trusted.
What do you say?"

Yale kept both hands where the man could see
them. "I guess you'll have to decide that for yourself."

"You could be the law."

Yale gave a negligent shrug of his shoulders. "I could be. But I don't think many lawmen would be foolish enough to come in here alone. What good would it do them?"

The man nodded. "No good at all. Only a fool would try it." He drew his horse closer, staring into Yale's eyes. "And you don't look like a fool to me." He wheeled his mount, shouting over his shoulder, "Follow me."

Minutes later they drew up to a campsite where more than a dozen men were seated around a fire, eating the remains of a roasted deer.

While Jason Greenleaf told the others about Yale's courage during the gunfight, the men listened with rapt attention. When he was finished, one man stepped forward. At once the others fell silent.

The man's face was heavily bearded, his clothes filthy and bloodstained. But it was his eyes that held Yale's. Eyes that seemed nearly opaque, as though absorbing the light. They looked, to Yale, to be as pale as a ghost's.

"You want to join up with us, pretty boy?"

Yale shrugged. "That depends."

"On what?" The man wasn't smiling. Nor were the others now.

"I'm a gambler, not a thief. I don't take orders." Yale glanced around, seeing that he had the attention of everyone. "And I live by my own rules."

Those strange eyes were fixed on him with fierce concentration. For nearly a full minute, no one moved. No one spoke. Finally the man nodded.

"That's how I live my life, too. But I want you to know I don't trust you. Not yet, anyhow. But then, I don't trust anybody. Especially men in fancy suits with soft hands and pretty-boy faces. My name's Fenner. Will Fenner."

He turned away without a handshake.

Yale realized that he'd just stumbled into a den of rattlesnakes. The infamous Fenner gang was known and feared by every lawman and every law-abiding citizen in Dakota Territory.

Chapter Three

"Where you been?" Will Fenner scowled when he caught sight of Yale dressed as always in his neat dark suit and white shirt, without a trace of trail dust.

Yale dismounted and strode into the circle of firelight. Up close Fenner and his men seemed even more dirty and ragged than when he'd last seen them.

It had been more than a month since Justin had introduced Yale to the gang of outlaws. Now, more than a hundred miles from the Badlands that usually offered them refuge, the men appeared even more desperate than usual, causing Yale to question why he'd ever allowed himself to become entangled with such men. For, though he had no scruples about participating in an occasional theft of a horse or cow when food was scarce, he was far more interested in the next hand of poker than in stealing. In fact, the others had grown accustomed to leaving him behind in every small town where he managed to find a willing card partner. He lived, he'd explained, for the thrill of the game. He was simply far more suited to gambling than stealing. And though he was a man who scorned most of the laws made by mere men, he never actually considered himself an outlaw. He preferred to think of himself as a law unto himself.

His biggest regret was that he'd joined these men hoping one of them might know something about his father. It had been one of his rare gambles that hadn't paid off.

"It took me a while longer than I'd expected." He pulled a roll of bills from his pocket and began counting them out to the eager, outstretched hands. It was his most endearing quality, and the reason Will Fenner tolerated him. Even though this newcomer rarely participated in the crimes they committed, he had a generous heart, always sharing whatever he won. Fenner knew he'd be a fool to send Yale Conover packing. Especially since he seemed to be the only one making money these days.

Yale looked around. "Why the sad faces? Another robbery gone sour?"

Justin Greenleaf nodded. "We had it all planned. The time the train would be passing through Twisted Fork. The number of passengers aboard. Figured we'd all be sleeping on satin sheets tonight with fancy women. But we hadn't counted on Federal troops riding along."

"Soldiers?" Yale cocked a brow.

"Yeah. Thanks to them, we lost Tim and old Frank."

Yale's eyes narrowed. "Dead?"

Fenner's scowl deepened. "And Jed here badly wounded." He pointed to the man who lay nearby, shivering under a bloodstained blanket. "Probably won't make it to morning." He studied the worried faces of his loyal followers. "What's worse, we figure those soldiers are little more than a day's ride behind us, if that. They'd have caught up with us by now if they hadn't had to stick around to deal with the passengers."

"Couldn't the conductor handle that?" Yale stuffed the rest of his money back into his pocket.

"Could have. If he was still alive." Fenner's lips peeled back in a smile. "I caught him with my first shot, the engineer with my second. That's how we managed to take control of the train."

Yale felt his heart sink. It wasn't just a train robbery now. It was murder.

Fenner's voice lowered with urgency. "We need a plan. Something that will offer us a place to hide and enough food until we can shake that posse and make our way back to the Badlands, where we'll be safe."

"I might know a place." A burly man whose face bore the scars of a dozen saloon fights and was known only as Rafe, sipped coffee thick as mud. "While we were waiting for the train, I caught sight of a ranch north of here. Thought it strange that I never saw any wranglers tending the herd. Caught a glimpse of a woman once, though."

"Pretty?" Justin asked.

The others laughed, knowing Justin spent every waking minute thinking about women. That is, when he wasn't thinking about ways to steal enough money to impress women.

Rafe shrugged. "Wasn't close enough to see. But she and a couple of kids are all I ever spotted near the house. If you ask me, she's probably a widow, or her man ran off and left her. Anyway, she and the kids seem to be running the place by themselves. Ought to be easy marks."

Seeing that he had the interest of the others he set aside his coffee. "If she's alone, nobody'd be wise to us being there. We could hole up until the soldiers give up on us. If they should come poking around her place looking for us, we could find a way to make her tell only what we wanted her to say." He snorted out a laugh. "And we could have some fun with her before we help ourselves to her cattle and head on back to our hideout."

Yale felt his stomach muscles tighten. This just kept getting worse. A conductor and engineer dead. And now they were talking about violating a helpless woman.

He kept his voice deliberately calm. "What about the kids? You said she had children."

Will Fenner swore. "I won't have any squalling brats around. As soon as they've served our purpose, we'll get rid of 'em."

Yale felt a buzzing in his brain, and suddenly the voice speaking wasn't Will Fenner's, but that of his uncle Junior, talking in that same contemptuous tone at his grandfather's gravesite.

His hands fisted at his sides. He vaguely heard Fenner's voice droning on.

"As for the woman, hell, keep her around as long as you please. She can't do much to stop us." He gave a chilling smile to the others. "Might as well sample her charms at the same time we're helping ourselves to her home and herd."

The outlaws were still howling with laughter when Yale stood, stretched, then walked slowly to his bedroll.

Fenner scowled. "Where're you going?"

Yale was wearing his gambler's face now. It was a look he'd perfected over the years. Whatever feelings might be seething inside were now carefully hidden behind the mask, "I'll grab some sleep and take the midnight watch."

"Good." Fenner nodded. "Slick's up on the bluff now, keeping an eye out for the posse. He'll be glad for the break come midnight."

Yale pulled his hat over his face to shield the firelight from his eyes. But sleep was the farthest thing from his mind as the others began to drift toward their bedrolls. His mind was racing as he plotted how to slip away under cover of night and warn the widow to take her children to town while she still had time.

Then he'd have to make himself scarce as well. If there was one thing the Fenner gang didn't take lightly it was disloyalty.

Not that he minded. He'd been ready to move on almost from the moment he'd met this band of cut-throats. But he'd held on, hoping one of them would get drunk enough and talkative enough to recall some information about his long-absent father.

When would he stop this foolishness? He'd spent a lifetime chasing after smoke and shadows. Now he'd have to pay the price.

Because of his association with this gang, he'd be wanted by half the lawmen in the territory. But what was even worse was that after tonight, he'd be wanted desperately by the Fenner gang. The only trouble was, their justice would be swifter and deadlier than anything a judge would impose.

When he left here tonight, he would be a marked man. And if he didn't play his cards exactly right, he'd be a dead one.

"Hey, Slick." Yale slid from the saddle and tethered his horse, taking care to move sluggishly, as though he'd just dragged himself from sleep. "I've got the midnight watch."

"Luck of the draw." The stick-thin cowboy got to his feet, using his rifle for a crutch. "Glad my time's up. These old bones are getting too stiff for this." He limped toward his horse and pulled himself into the saddle, thrusting his weapon into the boot before leaning down to say softly, "Better stay alert. Those soldiers were mad as a nest of hornets. They'll come in with guns blazing."

"Yeah. That's the way I figure it, too." Yale

stood watching as the old man nudged his horse into a trot, eager for his bedroll.

Minutes later the sound of the horse's hooves faded, leaving only the silence of the night.

Yale stood on the high ridge for half an hour more, just to be certain that Slick's return to camp hadn't awakened any of the others. When he was assured that nobody was stirring, he caught his horse's reins and picked his way down the steep trail on the far side of the high ridge of rock. When he reached the valley below he pulled himself into the saddle and headed north, determined to find the widow's ranch before he was missed.

He used the time in the saddle to go over his plans. He would rouse the woman and her children and send them off to the nearest town, with orders to stay there. Then he'd head in the opposite direction, putting as much distance between himself and the Fenner gang as he could.

Even though Fenner would be hot for revenge, he'd have to put his feelings aside until the problem of the soldiers was solved. His immediate solution would be to hole up at the widow's ranch and stay out of sight until he was certain the posse had given up. That could take weeks. By the time he and his men were free to follow Yale's tracks, it would be too late. Yale intended to be halfway to San Francisco. He'd given this a lot of thought. He was tired of the dusty little towns and the smoke-filled saloons. They no longer offered any challenge. There was nothing to keep him here in Dakota Territory.

What he craved now were the pleasure palaces that could only be found in the big cities. And San Francisco had the best. He'd been there several years ago, and had stayed until the wanderlust had taken hold of him, forcing him back in the saddle. Back to the Badlands.

No more.

This time, Yale thought with a smile, he'd put himself up in the biggest and best pleasure palace of all, and sit in on high-stakes poker games until he walked away a millionaire or a pauper.

As he crested a ridge he thought he saw the flicker of lantern light in the distance. Just as quickly it was gone. He urged his horse into a run. There was no time to waste. He needed to be long gone by morning.

Yale heard the lowing of the cattle first, alerting him that a ranch was nearby. The herd seemed small; not much bigger than the one he'd once tended for Aaron Smiler.

The thought of the old man who'd opened his home to Yale and his brother and sister brought a quick, unexpected flash of pain. He hadn't seen any of them in more than a year. How was that possible? Where had the time gone? He'd dropped by unannounced one day, after a successful poker game in a nearby town, his saddlebags filled with presents, which had brought murmurs of appreciation from all of them. Aaron had been unable to hide his pleasure at the box of fine cigars. Kitty, now grown and un-

expectedly beautiful, despite the buckskins she wore
to tend her herd of mustangs, had laughed delight-
edly at the store-bought gown. Even Gabe's usual
scowl had turned to a smile when he'd unwrapped
the Winchester rifle. To a lawman like his brother,
there couldn't have been a finer gift.

Gabe, a lawman.

Yale shook his head, considering. They were so
different, it was hard to believe they were brothers.
Gabe, the dour, serious loner, determined to follow
the straight and narrow, no matter what it cost. Yale
had no doubt his brother had become a lawman just
to make up for all the laws he figured his younger
sibling was bound to break.

He remembered the day his brother, no more than
sixteen, had returned to the ranch wearing that shiny
new badge. He'd been bursting with pride, until he
learned that his first arrest would have to be his own
brother. Lucy Fairfax had accused Yale of stealing
her prized filly, and selling it to a snake oil salesman
passing through Misery on his way to Montana.
Yale had protested his innocence, but Gabe felt
honor-bound to arrest him until he could get to the
truth. In the end Gabe had ridden over two hundred
miles before returning to turn his brother loose and
arrest Buck Reedy for the crime. But it was too late
to undo the damage. Most people in Misery didn't
care who stole the filly. They knew only that Yale
Conover had spent time in jail, and no doubt had
done plenty of things to deserve it.

Was that when he'd stopped trying to please others and had begun caring only about himself?

He shook his head at the thoughts that had suddenly begun crowding his mind. There hadn't been any one defining moment. In fact, he'd been breaking the rules since he was born. Hadn't his ma always called him her little rebel?

It was in his blood. There was no stopping it.

Like my pa.

Up ahead he could just make out the roofline of the barn, and then the small ranch house, all in darkness.

He'd been debating the best way to handle this. But now that he was here he realized that the urgency of the situation left little time for formalities. With a frown of impatience he slid from the saddle and strode to the front door, where he rapped loudly before leaning a hip against it. He'd expected the door to be secured. But he was surprised by the ease with which he was able to force it inward.

"Hello." Even while he shouted a greeting, he was striding across the room.

The fire on the hearth had burned to glowing embers. But even that faint light was enough to reveal a ladder leading to a loft. On the far side of the room was an open doorway.

He stepped into the small bedroom and glanced around. A second fireplace gleamed with hot coals, revealing a chair, a small table on which rested a pitcher and basin, and beside it, a crude bed. The figure in the bed sat up, staring in dazed surprise.

"Who…? What…?" A woman's voice gave a gasp of surprise. "Oh, sweet heaven."

Before she could cry out he was beside her, clapping a hand over her mouth. "I'm not here to rob you or hurt you. I'm here to warn you. A gang of outlaws is heading here to take over your ranch. You and your children have to leave here right now. This minute." The mattress sagged as he pressed her back against the pillows, determined to drive home his point. "I'm going to remove my hand now. When I do, I'll take a step back. You understand?"

She gave a slight nod of her head.

He lifted his hand and moved quickly to reassure her that he meant what he said. When he did, he felt the press of a rifle against his back and a small voice that quavered with nerves.

"Don't move, mister, or I'll have to shoot."

"Oh, thank heavens, Cody." The woman tossed aside the blankets and started to step around Yale.

As she did he caught her by the shoulder and dragged her close, wrapping an arm around her throat. In the same instant he turned, so that the rifle that had been pressed to his back was now pointed at her stomach.

"Just put away your weapon, son." Yale deliberately kept his voice calm when he saw how young the boy was. No more than seven or eight. And shaking like a leaf. He was apt to pull the trigger without even meaning to. "You wouldn't want someone to get hurt, would you?"

"N…No sir. But you have to let my mama go."

"I will, son. Just as soon as you lay down that rifle."

"No, Cody." The woman's voice was soft, breathy, and it occurred to Yale that she seemed much younger than the image of the widow he'd been carrying in his mind. "If you do what this outlaw tells you, we'll be helpless."

"I'm no outlaw, ma'am. I'm here to help you and your children." To prove it, he released her.

As soon as she was free she hurried to her son's side and took the rifle from his trembling hands.

"Light the lantern, Cody," the woman said.

"Yes'm." The boy hurried to light a candle from the hot coals, before holding it to the wick of the lantern.

As he did, a little boy of perhaps five or six scurried down the ladder and rushed over to stand silently beside his mother.

Minutes later the little cabin was filled with light. As the older boy carried it close, the woman gave a cry. In that same instant Yale recognized the spill of midnight curls. The warm, honey eyes.

"Cara McKinnon." Her name came out in a burst of surprise as Yale found himself staring into a face from his past.

A face that had teased and taunted him every night for more than a dozen years.

Chapter Four

They stared at each other in stunned silence, while the two little boys looked from one to the other in puzzlement.

"Mama?" One boy lifted the lantern higher studying his mother's pale face.

"I'm all right now, Cody." She lowered the rifle and continued staring at the Yale as if he were a ghost. In a way, she thought, he was. A ghost from her past. Looking so much better than he had in her memory.

Then he'd been a handsome, reckless boy in cast-off clothes and dung-spattered boots. Now that boy was gone. In his place was a man who looked every inch the successful gambler he was reputed to be, in his fine clothes and shiny boots. His eyes still glinted with equal parts danger and humor, though his face had more sharp angles, with that square jaw and lean, hollow cheeks. He was, if possible, even more handsome than anything she could have imagined.

She had to mentally shake herself before she

could speak. "This man is Yale Conover. We grew up on neighboring ranches back in Misery. My name is Cara Evans now, Yale, and these are my sons, Cody and Seth."

He studied them intently, trying to see Cara in her children.

The older boy looked just like his mother. Coal-black hair and dark, serious eyes. Eyes that were assessing him with interest, and more than a little dislike.

The younger one had dark hair as well, but with glints of gold dancing in the lantern light. Like his mother, his eyes were amber pools ringed with a darker shade of honey. There seemed too much sadness in them. A sadness that tugged at Yale's heart.

Cara's voice brought his attention back to her. "What is this about, Yale? Why are you here?"

"A band of outlaws is planning on taking over your ranch and using it as a hideout." He marveled that he could still speak. The sight of her had his tongue tied and his brain muddled. "They've figured out that there's no man here. Are they right?"

Her tone was flat. "My husband is dead."

When she didn't move he grew agitated. "I'm sorry for your loss. But don't you understand? You and your children are in grave danger."

She took a step back. "How do you happen to know about this?"

"Because I..." He hesitated, knowing whatever he said now would only add to her mistrust. "It doesn't matter how I know. There's no time to waste. They'll be here by morning. You have to leave now and get to the nearest town.''

''That's not possible. Crescent Butte is more than fifty miles from here. All I have is an old plow horse and a small wagon. We'd be lucky to make ten miles a day.''

Frustrated, he turned away. ''Ten miles is a whole lot better than being here when the Fenner gang arrives.''

''The…Fenner gang?'' She blanched. ''I've heard of them. Of what they've done to their helpless…'' She glanced at her children, her attention suddenly sharpened. ''Cody. Seth. Get yourselves dressed and ready to travel.''

''What should we take, Mama?'' the older boy asked.

''Nothing more than is absolutely necessary.'' Yale answered for Cara. ''There's no time.''

Cara absently agreed with him. And though she seemed distracted, she quickly gathered a few things. A bearskin. A warm shawl. Some cooking utensils, which she piled into Yale's waiting arms.

She gave him a look of cool appraisal. ''We'll need the wagon. It's out in the barn.''

Yale was pleased to see that she wasn't going to weep and wail and bemoan the fact that they were in peril.

He turned away. ''I'll take care of it. You and the children can meet me out there when you're dressed.''

She nodded and watched as he let himself out the door and sprinted off the porch.

A short time later, when he'd finished hitching the plow horse to the wagon, Yale walked back to the house calling, "We're wasting time. You should be ready by now. We have to get moving."

He shoved on the door, but it didn't budge. Caught by surprise, he nudged it with his hip, but it remained closed. Annoyed, he rapped a fist on the door. "Cara. What's going on in there? What are you up to?"

Her voice sounded muffled through the closed door. "I want you to leave Yale. Get on your horse and go."

"Go? What are you saying? What's this all about?"

"It's about you. I only sent you to the barn to buy some time."

"Are you crazy? Why?"

She stepped in front of the window. Cradled in her arms was the rifle. She'd changed into a faded gown of dull gray. Her sons stood several paces behind her, the younger one looking absolutely terrified, the older boy looking as angry and determined as his mother.

Cara's voice was clearer now, her eyes narrowed in concentration. "I figure there's only one way you could have known what the Fenner gang was planning. They would have had to trust you enough to tell you."

"Cara, listen to me. You're wasting valuable

time.'' He slammed a fist against the door. ''Open this now. Or I swear I'll break it down.''

She shook her head. ''The boys and I moved the table against it. You'll never get through.'' She took aim with her rifle. ''Leave now, Yale. But before you do, tell me the truth. Are the rumors true? Are you riding with the Fenner gang now?''

He gave a hiss of frustration. ''It's true that they took me in as one of them. I'm not proud of it. But none of that matters now. When I heard what they planned here, I came as quickly as I could to warn you, even though I had no idea it was you, Cara.''

''Then I thank you for that, Yale. But you have to go now.''

''What about you and the children?''

She backed away from the window. ''We'll take our chances here. We have nowhere else to go.''

''Your parents…?''

''They're both dead.''

He made a sound of disgust. ''You can't stay here. You don't stand a chance against a dozen or more guns.''

She was shaking her head and struggling not to weep. ''Go away, Yale. I need to think.''

As she turned away she heard the sound of shattering glass. She whirled and saw Yale, blood streaming from his hand, stripping away the shards of glass before climbing through the window.

She lifted the rifle and took careful aim. ''You stop right there or I swear I'll shoot.''

''Then you'd better do it fast.'' He didn't even

pause. Instead he was across the room in quick strides. One hand snaked out, snagging the rifle from her hands.

With a cry her older son sprang at Yale, his little fists flailing out harmlessly until Cara caught him in her arms and forced him behind her, where the younger one had taken refuge.

She turned to face Yale, lifting her chin in defiance. "Go ahead then. Do what you want with me. But at least spare my children."

"What I'd like to do…" The bitter oath died on his lips when he caught sight of little Seth's face, crumpled and tear-stained, peeking out from behind his mother's skirt.

He remembered the fear he and his brother and sister had faced when their serene lives had suddenly fallen apart in childhood.

Without realizing it his tone softened, despite the frustration that seethed inside. "I came here to warn you of danger. If you want to hate me for being part of a gang, do it later. Right now you can't afford to waste any more time. Let's move aside this table and get to the wagon."

As he set aside the rifle and started toward the door he heard a distant sound like thunder.

"I'm warning you, Yale. My children and I…" The words died in her throat when he lifted a hand and called for silence.

Crossing to the broken window he listened intently while peering into the darkness. He turned. "They're coming."

"Who's…?" Her eyes widened. "I thought you said they wouldn't be here until morning."

"They must have found out I'd deserted and figured out that I was headed here." His tone hardened. "How many guns do you have in the house?"

"Just the rifle."

"Do you know how to fire it, or were you bluffing?"

She stood a little taller. "I can shoot well enough to defend myself. If I'd wanted to shoot you, you'd be dead now."

He managed a quick smile. "Then I'm glad you spared my life. Get all the ammunition you have. Then find a place to hide the children." He looked around. "Is there a root cellar?"

She nodded.

"That would be the safest place for them. And for you," he added as she started away.

Cara hesitated, then turned. "This is my fight, Yale. I have no intention of hiding."

"Suit yourself." He was already busy moving the rest of her furniture out of the way and taking up a position beside the broken window.

This hadn't been part of the plan. But then, he thought, none of his life had ever gone as he'd planned. Why should this be any different?

He felt a hand on his arm and looked up to find Cara standing beside him, holding up a pouch of bullets.

Her voice was as soft as he'd always remembered.

"This isn't your fight, Yale. You don't have to stay."

In the moonlight his gaze held hers. "I'm not leaving. Not this time."

"Why?"

For a moment he had no answer to that. Though he'd initially intended only to warn this family of their peril, and then make good his own escape, everything had now changed. The moment he'd seen Cara, he'd known that he couldn't walk away. Not again.

He shot her that wonderful lazy grin that had the ability to warm her heart like no other. "Maybe because I've always liked playing the long shots."

For the space of several seconds she stayed where she was, seeing the boy he'd been and the man he'd become. Then, hearing the hoofbeats growing closer, she gathered her sons into her arms and murmured words of love and caution before lifting a trap door in the floor.

"I'm not going, Ma." Cody stood, feet planted, ready to resist. "I'm not leaving you alone with this man."

"Shh. Cody." Cara brushed a kiss over his face. "I know you want to stay with me. But think about Seth. I don't want him in any danger. I know if you're with him, you won't let anything happen to him."

"But what about you, Ma?"

At his brother's outburst, little Seth started whimpering.

Seeing it, Yale walked over and knelt down until the little boy's eyes were even with his. "You don't have to be afraid, son."

Cody stepped between Yale and his little brother. "Seth doesn't talk. He hasn't since…"

He stopped. Glanced at his mother, who said softly, "Seth hasn't spoken a word since his father died."

"I see." Yale looked beyond Cody to Seth. "Have you ever played hide-and-seek, son?"

The little boy nodded solemnly.

Yale smiled. "Think of this as a game. It's your job to hide down there and stay hidden, no matter what you hear. Think you can do that?"

Seth glanced at his brother.

Cody spoke for him. "He won't go unless I go with him."

Yale turned to the sullen little boy. "How about it, Cody? Want to help your brother play?"

Cody glanced from the man to his mother, before giving a slight nod of his head. "I guess I can."

"Good boy." Yale squeezed the boy's shoulder, then tousled Seth's hair.

As Cody took his little brother's hand and began descending the crude ladder, Cara called, "You can't light a candle. And you're not to come up here, no matter what you hear. Do you understand?"

The little boy nodded.

"When it's safe, I'll summon you." Cara tossed down blankets and pillows. "Stay close. But remember. If the voice calling you isn't mine, you musn't answer. It could be a trick to find you.''

She waited until they were huddled together on the dirt floor of the root cellar. Then, regretting the fact that they would be left in the dark, she lowered the door slowly, before covering it with a rug.

When she looked up she saw Yale watching her in silence.

''Thank you,'' she said softly.

''For what?''

''For making them think this is a game.'' Though there were tears shimmering in her eyes, she resolutely picked up the rifle, waiting for what was to come.

Yale braced himself. From the thunder of hoof-beats, the gang was riding hard and fast. He knew them well enough now to expect that they'd come in with guns blazing, hoping to strike terror into the hearts of their opponents.

He turned to the woman beside him and whispered, ''Hold your fire as long as possible. That way they might be fooled into thinking we've already fled. Once you do open fire, make every bullet count.''

Cara nodded and peered into the darkness. The trees outside danced and swayed in the night breeze, sending shadows flitting across the open spaces. Every little movement deepened her fear. But though her heart was thundering, and her palms damp with sweat, she stood quietly, watching and waiting.

Suddenly the silence was shattered by a volley of gunfire that seemed to split the heavens and echo through the darkness. Cara stood up, intending to return the gunfire. Yale launched himself at Cara, knocking her to the floor, where he covered her body with his.

He could feel the way she trembled as bullets sprayed the walls of the cabin, shattering the tiny bedroom window, splintering wood, ricocheting off the stones of the fireplace.

His face was buried in her hair, his body pressed firmly to hers. He knew he was too heavy, but there was nothing he could do to ease her discomfort. He lay perfectly still, alert to any sound that might signal that the outlaws were about to storm the cabin.

At long last there was a lull in the gunfire, and Yale eased himself up and crawled toward the window.

Yale recognized Rafe's voice just beyond the porch.

"You think he got the widow and her brats clean away?"

"Could be." Will Fenner's words were clipped. "Or he could be on the other side of that door, waiting for us."

Yale saw several horsemen slip from the saddle and start toward the cabin. Without a word he motioned to Cara, who crawled across the room to kneel beside him.

"I'll fire high, you fire low," he whispered. "On the count of three."

Seconds later, the silence was shattered by more gunfire. This time it was the outlaws who were surprised. Two of the three men gave out cries as they slumped forward. The third man managed to crawl to safety, but it was plain that he'd been wounded.

Will Fenner's voice was high-pitched with fury. "Yale Conover, you just cost me two of my best men. Now you and the female are going to pay. Mark my word, Conover. You're already a dead man."

Gauging the distance, Yale took careful aim and fired. The bullet whistled past Fenner's head, causing him to drop to his knees with a savage oath.

At his shouted command, the rest of the band fell back until he joined them for a whispered conference.

Yale peered into the darkness, and saw the band of men break into two groups.

He turned to Cara. "They'll attack from both sides now. I'll need you to fire first out this window, then through that one. Think you can do that?"

She nodded. "Where are you going?"

He pointed to the loft. "I need to get to the roof."

"There's a tiny window. I'm not sure it's big enough to get through."

He winked. "If it's big enough for a cat, I'll get through it. You just keep on firing until you're out of bullets."

She waited until he'd climbed the ladder to the

loft. Then she turned and took careful aim, waiting until the first man appeared at the broken window. The sound of his cries as he fell had her shuddering. Then, shaking off the dread, she turned and fired across the room just as a second man started inside through the rear window. She blocked out the sound of his cry as she turned this way and that, firing again. And again. And again.

She had no idea how long she'd been shooting. Nor how many men she'd faced. She knew only that her children were listening for the sound of her voice. She couldn't fail them. She was all they had.

It was the only thought that kept her going as the night air was filled with the sound of thunder.

Up on the roof Yale crouched behind the chimney and took advantage of the fact that he could fire in any direction. He managed to drop three men before he realized his rifle was out of bullets. In one smooth motion he reached for his pistol and resumed shooting.

The gang, taking fire from above as well as inside the cabin, had nowhere to hide.

Suddenly Yale heard a shouted command and watched as the men fell back. From his position he could see that there were only six men left standing. He had no idea how many of the others were dead and how many wounded. But at least for now, the odds were a whole lot better than they'd been an hour ago, when the siege had begun.

Slipping through the narrow window, he climbed

down from the loft to check on Cara. She was still kneeling in the middle of the floor, waiting for the gunfire to resume.

Instead, there was nothing but an eerie, unnatural silence.

She looked up as Yale walked toward her. "Do you think they've given up?"

He could see the light of hope in her eyes, and hated that he had to be the one to extinguish it.

He shook his head. "They're just regrouping. They weren't expecting us to put up such a vigorous fight. Now they have to figure out another way to beat us."

"But there are less of them now. Don't they know we'll just keep beating them back?"

"Cara." He touched a hand to her arm. Just a touch, but he felt the heat sizzle through his veins.

Instead of warming him, it chilled him to the bone to know that the old feelings were still there between them. It would have been easier somehow if he could have felt nothing. For he knew, without a doubt, that whatever tiny spark they might have coaxed into flame would be extinguished before it even had a chance to ignite. Their time together was about to end. Fenner would see to that.

Cara pointed to the darkened outline of men pulling themselves into their saddles. "Look, Yale. They're leaving." Before he could respond she threw her arms around his neck. "We've won. Look. They're leaving."

She gave him a hard hug that sent his heart spiraling out of control before lodging in his throat. And though he didn't intend it, his arms came around her, molding her to the length of him.

"Thank you for staying, Yale. I'll never forget this."

She saw the smoldering look in his eyes and quickly pushed herself free of his arms. She was just turning away when she heard the soft thud on the roof. With a puzzled glance she looked up and saw a strange red glow.

"What is...?" She clapped a hand to her mouth when she realized what it was. "Oh, sweet heaven. Fire." Her voice was little more than a strangled whisper.

Yale swore, even though he'd anticipated as much. "They can't get us with their bullets, so they're going to burn us out."

She turned to him, her eyes reflecting the flames that were already licking along the roof. "If you knew, why didn't you join them? Why did you stay and fight on the losing side?"

He shrugged before giving her that roguish, heart-stopping smile. "Hell, a man can't always choose when he's going to die. But sometimes, if he's lucky, he can choose where and how. If I have to die tonight, I can't think of a better place to do it than right here, with you."

And because he figured their time together was about to end, he dragged her close and covered her mouth with his. A jolt of lightning would have been less startling, as heat sizzled and snapped between them.

Cara felt the floor beneath her feet sway and tilt and was forced to hold on to his waist to keep from falling. As she did, she felt an explosion of stars behind her closed eyes.

It wasn't so much a kiss as an assault on her senses. She could feel her blood heating, her bones melting, as he drew out the kiss until her mind seemed to go blank. She couldn't think. All she could do was feel. The warmth of the hands holding her. The hard muscled body pressed to hers. The taste of him. So fierce. So potently male.

When he finally lifted his head and held her a little away, her breath was coming in short bursts. She could see twin points of flame reflected in his eyes. Then he smiled. That wonderful, over-the-edge smile that had always done such strange things to her heart.

"Too bad it took us so long to do that. But it was worth waiting for, Cara."

He deliberately turned away and picked up his rifle to keep from touching her again. But the need for her was still vibrating through him. And the taste of her was still on his lips.

Chapter Five

For the space of several seconds both Yale and Cara seemed mesmerized by the glow of flames licking along the roof.

"We'll have to give up." Her voice was filled with despair. "I have to think of my children. I can't let them pay this price. I'll summon them."

Yale held up a hand to stop her. "Fenner and his men are expecting that reaction. They're waiting just beyond the door. I don't mind for myself. They'll just kill me. But what they have in mind for you and the children is much worse."

He saw her shudder and wished he had the time to comfort her. But time was a luxury neither of them could afford now.

Suddenly he looked around as a thought struck. "Do you have a bucket of water?"

She pointed to a bucket and basin beside the wooden table.

He started across the room. "I'll get it while you fetch all the linens you have."

"All right, Yale. But why? What good will it do?"

He shook his head. "There's no time. Get them now."

Minutes later she found him lifting the rug that covered the trap door. He waited until she climbed down the ladder, then he followed, carrying the bucket and an armload of linens.

Even the darkness of the root cellar was illuminated by the eerie red glow. As Cara dropped to her knees, the boys, who had been cowering in a corner of the cellar, hurried to her side. Immediately Seth began crying softly against his mother's shoulder.

"What's that sound, Ma?" Cody asked.

"The outlaws have set fire to our cabin."

"Are we going to burn?" he asked.

Cara turned to Yale, who gave the children a wink. "Now we wouldn't want to do that, would we?"

When the boys shook their heads he knelt down beside them and said, "How would you like to wear masks?"

"Like outlaws do?" Cody asked.

"That's right, Cody. Just like outlaws." Yale soaked strips of linen in the water and handed them to Cara. "We'll tie these around our lower faces to help us breathe. When the fire gets closer and hotter, we'll soak the rest of these and use them to cover ourselves."

He watched as Cara secured them around the children's noses and mouths before doing the same for herself.

While she did that, Yale began a thorough inspection of their hiding place. It wouldn't take long for the fire to burn through the dry logs that served as support beams beneath the cabin. When that happened, the entire structure would begin to cave in on itself, trapping them beneath a mound of flaming rubble.

On the far side of the cellar he found the earth gradually sloping upward. Following it, he reached up to find a crude wooden door above his head.

He turned. "Where does this lead?"

Cara glanced over. "It opens near the garden. We positioned it here so that I'd be able to haul my crops in at harvest time, for easy storage."

Yale felt the first slim ray of hope.

"There's a chance we might be able to make good our escape without being spotted. Unless I miss my guess, Fenner and his men are standing watch on the far side of the cabin."

Unless, of course, one of the men had already found this entrance to the root cellar. If so, he and Cara would find themselves facing rifles when the door was pried open. Still, it was a chance he had to take.

Above their heads they could hear the crash of timbers and the deafening roar as the flames fed on rugs and curtains and raced through the tiny cabin. Yale knew if they stayed here much longer, they would have no chance to survive.

"Cara." He beckoned her close. "How is this outer door secured?"

"We use a wooden brace."

He nodded, feeling hope grow. The same fire that could snuff out their lives would burn through the wood that kept them locked in this fiery tomb.

Quickly he told her his plan. "We may find ourselves staring into Fenner's guns. But I don't see that we have any other choice."

She nodded, then drew her arms around her sons. "I'll risk whatever I have to for the chance to save their lives."

As the flames burned closer, Yale tied a wet rag around his face, then leaned a shoulder into the overhead door. It didn't budge, even though the heat of the fire could be felt clear through the wood.

He stepped away and poured water over himself, then took several deep breaths before trying again and again, until he felt the door start to give. Despite the precautions, his clothes were smoldering. He took no notice as he continued his assault on the door.

Finally, sensing that the door was about to give, he turned to Cara. "When I get the door open, you and the boys need to run as fast as you can toward the cover of woods. Don't look back or wait for me. Is that clear?"

She seemed about to argue until she saw the look of fierce determination in his eyes. She swallowed back her protest. "I'll do whatever you ask, Yale."

"Good." He touched a hand to her shoulder. Just

a touch. Then he took a deep breath and pushed against the door with all his might.

The burning door slipped free, sending a shower of fiery sparks and debris over them. Seeing Cara hesitate, Yale drew his pistol from its holster, prepared to defend them against attack. Instead of armed men, he faced a fireball that reached as high as the treetops. He holstered his gun and lifted Seth into his arms, then caught Cody by the hand, dragging him through a wall of flame. When Cara faltered he lowered Seth to the ground and placed his hand firmly in that of his brother.

"Run," he said fiercely. "Now."

Gathering Cara into his arms he carried her through a wall of flames and into the cover of the woods that ringed the ranch.

When they found themselves in the coolness of the forest, they dropped into the grass, coughing and retching, their eyes and lungs burning from the smoke.

"Did they see us?" Cara asked when she could manage to speak.

"If we'd been spotted, they'd have come at us with guns blazing. But just to be sure…"

Yale caught her hand and helped her to her feet, then put the exhausted Cody up on his shoulders and lifted Seth into his arms, leading them deeper into the woods until they came to a stream. There they knelt on the banks and drank, before splashing water on their soot-blackened flesh.

At the sound of thrashing in a nearby thicket they

froze. Seeing the look of terror in Cara's eyes Yale lay a hand on her arm. "Hide yourself and the boys. If you hear gunshots, run as deep into the woods as you can. Whatever you do, don't ever stop. And don't look back."

Before she could say a word he was gone, heading toward the sound. She led the way through thick underbrush. There, hearts pounding, she and her sons watched and waited for what seemed an eternity.

The woods were so dark they could barely make out the shadow of a man and horse. When they heard Yale calling softly to them, they stepped out of their hiding place to find him leading the plow horse, still hitched to the little cart.

Cara gave a delighted laugh. "It's old Sadie. How did she find us?"

Despite Yale's soothing tone, the animal's eyes were wide with terror, its nostrils flared. "Looks like she must have bolted after being spooked by the fire. She ran until the cart became hopelessly entangled in brush." As he spoke, he continued running his hand along the horse's neck until the quivering began to ease up. He pointed to the cart. "It appears that most of the supplies are still there. I suggest you and the children climb inside. We have only a few hours left before dawn. If we hope to get away, it has to be now, under cover of darkness."

Cara lifted her sons into the back of the cart. Then she suddenly looked up. "Where will we go, Yale?"

"Which direction is Crescent Butte?"

"North of here."

He glanced up at the sky, barely visible beneath the canopy of trees, studying the path of the stars. "That's where Fenner will expect us to go. What's south of here?"

She shook her head. "Nothing. Just wilderness."

He took up the reins, eager to escape. "Then that's where we're headed. Let's just hope we find a place to hide by the time daylight comes."

Suddenly the enormity of what she was about to do seemed to come crashing down upon her. Cara leaned a hand against the wheel of the wagon and slumped forward, pressing her other hand to the nerves fluttering in her stomach. She lowered her head to hide the sudden rush of tears. Her voice was choked. "What about our cabin? The barn? Our cattle?"

"Don't think about that now, Cara." Yale knew he had to move quickly. Right now, it was absolutely essential that he get them as far away from here as possible. He couldn't afford to allow emotions to get in the way of doing whatever was necessary to survive.

He took her arm and helped her up onto the hard seat of the wagon. Then he climbed up beside her and flicked the reins.

As the horse started forward Cara turned for one last glimpse of the flames destroying her home. Then, turning back, she folded her hands in her lap and took a deep, steadying breath.

Yale thought about his mother, and the stoic way

she had faced leaving his grandfather's farm, despite her hasty preparations. Her death along the trail had thrust her children into a life unlike anything she'd ever imagined.

This was different, he told himself as he urged the horse into a faster pace. Unlike his mother, Cara wasn't alone on her odyssey.

He was a man now, not a helpless boy. What's more, he knew how to survive in the wilderness. If anyone had to die along the trail, he vowed, it wouldn't be this woman and her children. On that, he intended to stake his life.

Cara clung to the hard wooden seat as they moved through the darkness into the unknown. So much had happened in such a short time, she was still trying to sort it all out in her mind.

It didn't seem possible that she was calmly sitting beside Yale Conover while they escaped the clutches of a gang of outlaws. She glanced over her shoulder, relieved to see that both children were sound asleep. If only she could do the same. But her mind was whirling in a dozen different directions, feeling again the shock when she'd found a man in her cabin, ordering her and her children to flee. When she'd discovered that the man was Yale, her shock had turned to wonder, and then to fear, when she'd figured out his relationship to the Fenner gang.

He was one of them.

She had to keep reminding herself of that. It would be so easy to think of him as the boy she'd once loved. The wild, restless young man who had turned his back on his family, on his town, and had asked her to do the same.

She had never forgiven her father for what he had done that night. She'd wept buckets of tears, until there were none left. Still, if she had followed her heart, where would she be now? What would her life have been like, tied to an outlaw?

He glanced over. "You should climb in the back with your children and try to get some sleep."

She shook her head. "I'd never be able to close my eyes."

He shrugged. "Suit yourself. But sooner or later it's going to catch up with you."

"I know. I'll sleep later." She studied the big hands holding the reins. Soft hands. A gambler's hands. He had long ago left the respectable life of a rancher to ply his skill in saloons with drifters and women of the night. She'd heard the rumors about him. Rumors that had grown until he had become a legend in the Dakota Territory. Yale Conover was the envy of most men, who saw his life of ease and excitement as the exact opposite of their own lives of unending, thankless chores, failure and despair. The women who spoke of him did so in whispers. And though they claimed to disdain his lifestyle, they were clearly fascinated by the man, who seemed larger than life.

She lifted her gaze to study his rugged profile. "What do you think will happen now?"

"I'm not much good at predicting the future. But

at least for the time being we're still alive." He grinned. "Considering the odds against that, I'd say we're already winners."

"Do you think the Fenner gang will follow? Or will they give up now that we've managed to slip away?"

His smile grew. "You're asking for another prediction? I'm not sure I have it in me."

She shook her head, sending dark curls tumbling around her face. "How can you smile after all this?"

"That's easy." He surprised her by closing a hand over hers and squeezing gently. "Haven't you heard? I'm a born gambler. I've always loved beating the odds."

Despite her fears she felt the warmth of him seeping into her and marveled that even this simple touch had the ability to bolster her courage.

"You're not afraid, Yale?"

"Are you?"

"I'm terrified."

"Come here." He brought his arm around her, tucking her close against him. "You just close your eyes awhile, and let me do the worrying for both of us."

"I can't."

"Yes, you can." His hand moved across her shoulder, and along the top of her arm, gently massaging the knots of tension. "Go ahead. Give it a try."

Though she was reluctant, she did as he asked, closing her eyes, and forcing herself to relax.

There was something so comforting about the warmth of his body, the surprising strength of the arm that encircled her. Resting here against him it was difficult to remember that he was an outlaw. Instead she found herself slipping back to that time in her youth when she'd been so blindly in love with him, she hadn't been able to think of anything else.

She'd be tending to her chores, when she would spot him on the hill overlooking her father's ranch. And suddenly the chores were forgotten. All she could think of was watching him. He had a way of walking. As though he knew exactly where he was going, yet had all the time in the world to get there. Her father had called him cocky, arrogant. To Cara, Yale Conover had been merely confident. A man forced to live in a boy's body, a boy's world. A man who always played by his own rules. A man who made no secret of the fact that he wanted her. And she'd wanted him. Wanted to be with him. Only him.

The yearning in her heart had been so overwhelming, it frightened her. She'd never wanted anyone or anything the way she'd wanted Yale. And yet she'd been too young, too afraid, to defy her father. Added to that was a fear of Yale. A fear of the things that drove him to be so different from all the other boys she knew.

Maybe what she'd feared the most was that she wouldn't be able to measure up in his eyes. He was willing to take any risk, choose any road, without regard to where it led. A true gambler. She'd always wanted to know exactly where she was going and what she would find at the end of the road. She hated surprises. And was afraid of the unknown.

And so she'd married Wyatt Evans, a man hand-picked by her father. His ambition had pleased her mother. His plainspoken ways had pleased her father. And their approval had overcome whatever reservations she'd had about marrying a man twice her age.

If there had been no excitement in their marriage, at least there had been no estrangement from her parents. She could take comfort in that. And now they were all gone. Her father and mother. Wyatt. But she and her children were safe for now. And though it seemed a bitter irony, she owed their safety to that wild, restless boy from her past.

What strange twist of fate had brought him back into her life? And for what reason?

There seemed more questions than answers. More shadows than clear images. But this much she knew. Though the danger was far from over, she felt a measure of safety knowing she didn't have to face whatever was to come alone.

Weary beyond belief, she slept in Yale's arms.

Chapter Six

It was the sudden stillness that woke Cara. She opened her eyes to see dawn light streaking the sky, and was shocked to realize that she'd been asleep in Yale's arms for several hours.

Yale lowered the reins. "Sorry I had to wake you. But it's getting light. And we need a place to hide, in case Will Fenner's on our trail."

She glanced around and saw that they were in a desolate, rock-strewn area of wilderness. "Where can we hide around here?"

"I may have spotted a place." He scrambled down. "I'll be right back."

He strode behind a tumble of boulders and disappeared. When he didn't return after long minutes Cara began to worry. But suddenly he stepped out from behind a boulder, wearing a smile.

"There's a cave just beyond here. It's big enough to hold the horse and cart. I took the time to look around." His grin widened. "Just to be sure we wouldn't have to share it with a bear or mountain lion.''

He caught the reins and began leading the horse. Minutes later they were inside a cave. Though the entrance was barely big enough to admit a horse and cart, once inside it was roomier than her cabin.

Yale had taken the time to light a torch and set it into a niche in the wall of rock. The flickering light illuminated even the far corners of the cave.

Yale reached up and lifted her down. As he did, his hands brushed the underside of her breasts.

Cara felt her cheeks grow warm as he set her on her feet and walked away. Even now it was impossible to forget the kiss they'd shared. It shamed her to realize that such a simple thing had left her shattered and defenseless.

Working quickly Yale gathered branches and brush, using them to cover their tracks. Then piling them in a haphazard fashion, he was pleased to note that they actually concealed the entrance to the cave.

In the back of the cart Cody sat up rubbing his eyes. ''Where are we, Ma?''

''We're in a cave.''

''Why?'' he asked as little Seth sat up beside him.

Cara lifted the younger boy in her arms, holding him close. ''We have to hide from the bad men who burned our cabin.''

Seth looked around with wide, frightened eyes.

Cody gave voice to his brother's fear. ''Are they following us?''

Yale walked over to give them both a wink. ''I

think we got clean away. But we don't want to take any chances. So your ma and I thought we'd play a game. Would you two like to play?''

Seth looked at his brother, and it was clear that he took his cue from him.

Cody studied Yale with serious, solemn eyes. ''Maybe. What do we have to do?''

Yale touched a finger to his lips. ''We have to be really quiet. We can whisper, but softly enough so our voices won't carry beyond this cave. And we're going to search to see if there's another way in and out of here. The first one to find another entrance gets this.'' He reached into his pocket and pulled out a gleaming gold piece.

The boy's eyes widened with excitement, before Cody backed up with a look of wariness. ''Where'd you get that? Did you rob a bank?''

''Cody.'' Cara put her hands on her hips. ''I expect you to respect your elders....''

''It's all right.'' Yale knelt down, so that his eyes were even with the boy's. ''That's a fair question, Cody. You have a right to wonder about me. But the fact is, I've never robbed a bank. I earn my money by gambling.''

''My pa said all good men earned their living by ranching.''

''Some do. I chose a different way.''

The little boy studied him. ''Do you sit in saloons with fancy ladies and drink whiskey?''

Such wise old eyes, Yale thought. He nodded.

"Sometimes. But the fancy ladies and whiskey don't appeal to me. It's the games of chance that I crave."

"Why?"

Yale shrugged. "I don't know. I've just always wanted to take risks. Whether in cards, on a horse race, or just to bet my money on one man wrestling another to the ground. Now, would you like to earn this gold coin? All you have to do is find another way out of this cave."

"Come on, Seth." Cody caught his little brother's hand and led him away.

When they were gone Cara turned to Yale with a look of surprise. "You didn't mind his questions?"

"He has a right to ask."

"But you didn't evade or make excuses."

"Why should I? He deserves the truth."

She studied him with new respect. "You're really good with children."

He tugged on a lock of her hair. "Maybe that's because I'm still a kid myself. Didn't your father once warn you that I'd never grow up?"

She watched as he walked away to join the children in their search, then pressed a hand to her stomach. The same nerves were fluttering there now, and she knew that this time it wasn't from fear, but from something far different. She marveled that even now, after all these years, Yale Conover had the ability to affect her this way with the simplest touch.

"We found it. We found another way out of the cave."

Cody and Seth came dancing into the firelight.

Cara touched a finger to her lips, reminding Cody to lower his voice.

"Come on, Ma. Mr. Conover." Cody was twitching with excitement as he led them deep into the cave. "Look." Cody proudly pointed to a spot high above them where sunlight filtered through a small hole in the rock.

"Good work." Yale pulled himself up, hand over hand, along the rock wall until he'd reached the spot. Rummaging around, he suddenly disappeared from sight, only to re-appear minutes later. He climbed down until he was standing beside them. "There's a shelf of rock up there, which leads to another wider opening. I think it's big enough to fit through." He knelt down between the two children, holding out the gold coin. "Now which of you found it?"

The two boys eyed the coin with naked hunger.

Suddenly Seth pointed to his brother.

Cody shook his head. "Not really. It was Seth who spotted the sunlight first. I just figured where there was sunlight there had to be a hole in the rock."

"Well now. This is quite a puzzle. Who should get the reward? Seth thinks it should go to you, Cody. And you're trying to give it to him." Yale looked from one to the other, then smiled. "I know." He reached into his pocket and withdrew a second gold piece. "You've both earned the prize."

The children couldn't seem to believe their eyes. This was more money than they'd ever seen.

Cody looked up at his mother. "Is it all right to take it, Ma?"

She seemed about to refuse when she suddenly smiled. "Go ahead. I don't think Mr. Conover would offer it unless he wanted you to have it."

Yale held up a hand. "I'll give it on one condition."

Cody drew back with a look of suspicion.

Yale winked. "You have to call me Yale. Think you can do that?"

Cody bit his lips and glanced at his mother. "I guess I can call you Yale."

"See? That didn't hurt, did it?" Yale handed them the coins and the children danced away to study the gold more closely by the light of the torch.

As they turned away Yale started climbing toward the beam of sunlight overhead.

Cara felt a clutch of fear. "Where are you going?"

He glanced over his shoulder. "I'm going to take a look around. See if there's any sign of Fenner. And while I'm at it, I'll see if I can catch us something to eat."

She almost told him to be careful before stopping herself. Yale Conover had spent too many years on his own. He certainly didn't need her telling him what to do.

When she saw him slip over the rock face and disappear from view, she couldn't stop the tremors that snaked along her spine at the knowledge that she and her children were all alone. She'd been alone with her children now for more than a year, since Wyatt died, and though it had been a struggle, she'd survived. But this was different. Now she had left behind all that was familiar for a frightening cave in the wilderness. If Yale didn't come back, she had no idea what she would do.

If she dared to leave, she might run headlong into the Fenner gang. If she didn't leave, she wondered just how long she and her children could survive, without heat or food or water.

She whispered a little prayer that she would never have to find out the answers to those questions.

Cara and her sons slept briefly, bundled together in the bearskin. She found herself grateful that she'd originally given it to Yale to pack, even though it had all been a trick to get him out of her cabin. Now she realized what a lifesaver these meager supplies might prove to be. They weren't much. Besides the bearskin there was a warm shawl and a few cooking pots. But at least she would be able to keep her children warm and, hopefully, fed.

Though she tried to keep busy, she found herself spending much of her time watching the slim beam of daylight fade into evening. With each passing hour she felt her fear grow. And with fear came a rush of doubts.

What if Yale had decided that a woman and two small children were too much responsibility? After all, he'd spent the past years looking out only for himself. And from the looks of him, doing a fine job of it.

She couldn't seem to shake the image of him when she'd first caught sight of him in her room. The perfectly tailored suit. The shiny boots. That proud, almost arrogant look of self-assurance. Even her father, with all his success, had never looked so grand. It wasn't just the clothes, she realized. There was something about Yale that set him apart from every other man. Even in a room filled with handsome, successful men, he would stand out from all the rest.

She twisted her hands together, wondering how much longer she should wait. Was she being a fool for trusting him? She glanced at the fading light. She would wait until dark, then she and the children would start out in the opposite direction toward Crescent Butte.

Shivering, she turned away and decided to risk a fire. "Come, boys." Remembering the way Yale seemed to turn everything into a game she said, "Let's see who can find the most firewood."

With eager cries the children scurried around, hunting up sticks in the far corners of the cave. When they'd gathered enough wood, they took turns with the flint until they'd managed to coax a tiny flame. Soon the warmth chased away the chill, lifting their spirits considerably.

Suddenly Cody leapt to his feet and pointed. "Look, Ma."

The shadow of a man appeared on the inner rock shelf, dragging something through the narrow opening. When it cleared the hole he leaned down and they could see that it was Yale. He tossed his heavy burden to the floor below before leaping down to follow it, then dropped to his knees beside the bloody carcass of a fawn.

"Where have you been?" Cara hated the accusing note to her tone, but it couldn't be helped. She was so relieved to see him she wanted to throw herself into his arms. Instead she held back and watched as the children danced around him in excitement.

"It took a lot longer than I'd expected to lure something into my trap." He looked from her to the boys. "I was afraid to fire a shot for fear of revealing our location. So I had to set a trap and wait."

Working quickly he began skinning the young deer before gutting it. While he worked he said, "I'm glad to see you were able to start a fire."

"I was afraid the smoke might give us away. But the children were so cold."

"Don't worry about the smoke. By the time it works its way up there..." he pointed with his bloody knife "...it's swept away by the strong winds."

He threaded chunks of meat onto a stick and set them over the fire to roast. Then he finished the rest of the carcass and tied it over a long pole, allowing it to cook more slowly over the fire. The organs were tossed into a blackened kettle into which he added water from his canteen. He passed a second canteen of water around to the others. They drank greedily.

"We should have enough food cooked by morning to last us along the trail."

Cara looked up sharply. "We're not staying here?"

He shook his head. "I don't think that's wise. We'll have to keep moving if we want to stay one step ahead of Fenner and his men."

"Did you see them?"

"No. But I saw dust in the distance. The sort of dust you'd expect from half a dozen horses."

"That could be anybody."

He nodded. "It could." His eyes met hers across the fire. "But I trust my instincts. And they tell me Fenner's not the sort to let us walk away. It's become personal now. I crossed him. He's going to want to see me pay."

He turned to the children, keeping his tone light. "Want to help me with this hide?"

"What'll you do with it?" Cody asked.

"I'll stretch it out across a rock and let it dry completely. Then I'll cure it and tan it until it's so soft, you'll both want to wear it instead of those clothes you're wearing."

Seth giggled.

Yale turned to Cody as he began draping the hide over a rock, smoothing out all the wrinkles as he worked. "What's so funny about that?"

"Nobody but Indians wear deer hides," the boy said emphatically.

"That's not true. I happen to have a little sister who prefers wearing buckskins to dresses."

At Yale's words the two boys turned to their mother with matching looks of surprise.

Cara laughed. "I know Yale's sister. Her name is Kitty. And I've never known her to wear a dress."

Seth giggled.

"Does she look funny?" Cody's voice held a trace of skepticism.

Cara paused to consider. "As a matter of fact, she looks so natural in her buckskins, I'm not sure I'd recognize her in a dress."

She could see that her two children were having trouble picturing a female in buckskins. "She lives on a ranch outside of Misery."

"Isn't that where we used to live with Gram and Grandpa before they died?" the boy asked.

Cara nodded, surprised by the sudden lump in her throat. When she realized that Yale was watching her she turned away and busied herself at the fire.

Sensing her sadness Yale knelt on the opposite side of the fire and began telling the children about his sister. "Kitty is just about the best horse handler I've ever known. She tames mustangs and breaks them to saddle, then sells them to neighboring ranchers."

"But she's a girl." Cody was already shaking his head in denial.

"That she is. And a pretty one, too."

"If she's pretty, why doesn't she just get married

and let her husband tame the mustangs?" Cody's voice held a note of skepticism.

"Not all pretty women are married."

"They aren't?"

Yale shook his head. "Look at your ma."

Cody's eyes widened. "You think she's pretty?"

Yale wasn't aware that his voice lowered for emphasis. "Just about the prettiest lady I've ever seen."

Cody glanced at his mother, trying to see her through the eyes of this stranger.

Cara blamed the fire for the heat that burned her cheeks. She cleared her throat. "I think this food is ready to eat."

They sat around the bearskin, leaning their backs against rocks warmed by the fire. Cara slipped the chunks of roasted meat off the stick, allowing them to cool before passing them around. Then she poured the broth from the kettle into tin cups and passed that around as well.

"How did you catch the fawn?" Cody asked.

"Dug a pit and covered it with branches, then sat behind a rock and waited." Yale smiled. "I was beginning to think we'd have to go to sleep hungry, when all of a sudden this deer and her two fawns stepped into the clearing. At first it looked as though they wouldn't go near the pit, and I was tempted to shoot. But I decided to give it another few minutes, and that patience paid off. The next thing I knew, the fawn had walked right into my trap. Of course, the minute the first one fell, the other two ran off and disappeared into the woods.''

Cara shook her head. ''I wouldn't have expected you to have that much patience.''

Yale leaned back, replete, content. He shot her a lazy smile. ''I guess I've changed some from the boy you knew.''

She felt the heat rise to her cheeks as she thought about the kiss they'd shared. That hadn't been a boy kissing her. He'd been a man. All man. Even now, just thinking about it had her heart behaving in the strangest way.

She glanced over and saw that Seth had nodded off. Grateful for the chance to be busy she picked up the bearskin and shook it, before setting it near the fire. Then she crossed to where the boy was sleeping.

Before she could lift him Yale was beside her, touching her arm. ''There's no need. I'll do that.''

He bent and scooped up the little boy, carrying him easily to the bearskin.

Cara felt her heart take a quick jolt at the sight of him, so big and strong, carrying her little son with such care.

He knelt and deposited Seth on the fur, watching while Cara covered him.

Then she turned and beckoned her other son. ''Come on, Cody.''

''I'm not tired,'' he protested.

Though the boy's eyes were heavy, he was reluctant to leave his mother alone with this man. He'd seen something pass between them that made him uneasy.

"Suit yourself. But at least you can lie here and be warm."

The boy gave a grudging nod and crawled into the fur beside his brother. And though he made a valiant effort to stay awake, his body betrayed him. He was asleep within minutes.

Chapter Seven

Yale leaned a hip against a rock and watched as Cara moved around the fire, adding wood to the hot coals, turning the spit on which the rest of the meat was roasting.

There was such simple grace in every movement. The way she bent forward to adjust the cooking pole, the way she shook down her skirts when she stepped back from the fire.

He'd had plenty of occasions to observe exotic women in gentlemen's clubs, to see close-up some of the most beautiful females employed in big-city saloons. Many of them had been gowned in silks and satins, smelling of the finest perfumes, and coached in the ways of pleasing a man. And yet none of them had ever touched his heart the way this one simple woman did.

He'd never expected to see her again. He'd carried the image of her in his heart all these years. The shy, sweet beauty, too timid to defy her parents, too afraid to risk what he'd offered. But the pretty girl she'd been couldn't hold a candle to the graceful woman she'd become. In many ways she was still shy and sweet. He'd tasted her sweetness in that kiss. A kiss that he couldn't get out of his mind. It teased and tantalized him, making him ache for more.

But there were new strengths in her as well. He'd seen the way she'd faced up to a dozen rifles when her children were threatened. The way she'd braved a wall of flame in order to save them from a fiery grave. And he'd seen the pain in her eyes at the thought of leaving behind all that was familiar for the unknown. But she'd done so, without complaint, when it became necessary.

Needing to do something, he took a cigar from his pocket and lifted a flaming stick from the fire, holding it to the tip. He exhaled a cloud of rich, fragrant smoke before tossing the stick onto the fire.

"I'm sorry about your parents, Cara. How did they die?"

She lifted her head. Tucked a stray curl behind her ear. "My father had a stroke and lingered for more than a year. Not long after he passed on, my ma took sick. It wasn't easy with Cody and Seth both needing me, but I did the best I could to care for her. She held on for a few months longer. Then…our fortune took a turn for the worse, and Wyatt and I were forced to leave Misery. We took what furniture we could haul in a wagon, and took up ranching on a little piece of land that Wyatt owned a hundred miles distant."

She looked away, and Yale realized she was thinking about the fact that everything from her childhood was now gone for good. What little she'd been able to salvage would have been destroyed by the fire back at the cabin.

"And your husband?" The word nearly stuck in his throat. But he needed to know. Was hungry for every detail of her life.

"He was thrown from his horse. When his mare came home without him the children and I went out searching. It took us two days before we found him. We probably never would have, if it hadn't been for the buzzards circling a rock ledge halfway down the side of a cliff. He was still alive, but by the time I managed to haul him up with the aid of ropes tied to our plow horse, it was too late. He died in my arms. With the children around him. I guess it was the shock of his death that robbed Seth of his voice. He hasn't spoken one word since."

"I'm sorry, Cara."

She swallowed. "Ma used to say life is hard in the Dakotas. I've often wondered if it gets easier in other places."

Yale shook his head. "I've been other places. I don't think it makes any difference. Life is the same no matter where you go."

She brightened. "Tell me about the places you've been, Yale."

He drew on his cigar, thinking. "Most of the territories. Wyoming. Montana. Up into Canada. I went as far west as California one year."

"California." She spoke the word on a sigh. "Did you see San Francisco?"

He nodded.

Without thinking she stepped closer and touched a hand to his. "Is it as beautiful as they say?"

He looked down at the small hand touching his and wondered if she felt the same rush of heat that he was experiencing.

"I guess you could say it's beautiful. At least the color of its money is."

"Then it's true that the people are all rich."

He shook his head. "There are some who are very rich. And they're more than willing to part with their money." He gave her that quick, dangerous smile. "As a gambler, I appreciated their generosity. But there are a lot more who are destitute. They've come from other lands, hoping to find a city paved with gold. Believe me, I'd rather be poor in the Dakotas than poor in a city filled with men desperate enough to slit your throat for a penny."

At his words she gasped and brought a hand to her own throat. "Did you see such men?"

"A time or two. But mostly I saw the saloons and pleasure palaces. In San Francisco, no matter the time of day or night, a determined gambler can always find a game of chance and a few generous souls willing to part with their money."

"It's true then? That's all you do for a living? Gamble?"

He nodded, wondering why that little note of censure in her tone should rankle.

"Why did you leave California, if you found it so satisfying?"

He stared at the glowing tip of his cigar. "Wanderlust, I suppose. I've never been able to stay in one place very long. I haven't decided if that's a blessing or a curse."

She ducked her head. "I envy you the ability to pick up and go whenever you please."

"You shouldn't. Don't ever envy me, Cara." He touched a hand to hers. The merest touch. But he saw her head come up sharply. Saw the wary look that came and went in those wide honey eyes.

He thought about ignoring the quick sexual jolt to his system. This wasn't the time or place. But then, that had never mattered to him before. Besides, it was too late. The need was too strong.

He tossed the cigar into the fire. In one smooth motion his hands were at her shoulders, drawing her firmly, inexorably toward him. His mouth was already seeking hers. When his lips covered hers he heard her little moan of pleasure.

And was lost.

How had he lived so long without this? How had he faced each new day without this woman in his arms? How was it possible to draw a breath, without first tasting this sweetness?

As he took the kiss deeper Cara couldn't seem to stop her heart from hitching, or her hands from moving up his chest. His tongue flicked over hers, sending little darts of pleasure straight through her core. It occurred to her that he knew a great deal about how to kiss a woman. And though she'd been a wife, she knew little about pleasing a man.

She hated the way her body was reacting. Blood heating until it flowed like lava through her veins. Bones growing so soft and pliant, she wasn't certain how much longer she could stand before she would simply slide to the floor. And her poor heart. Pounding in her chest as though it would surely explode.

He changed the angle of the kiss. Took it deeper. As he brought his hands up her sides his thumbs skimmed the tips of her breasts, sending the most amazing sensations skittering along her spine.

He thrilled to the way she shivered. As he drew her closer he could actually feel the tiny tremors that rocked her.

With an effort he lifted his head, though what he really wanted to do was simply kiss her until they were both beyond reason.

His voice, when he finally spoke, was gruffer than he'd intended. "You'd better get some sleep now."

"I…yes." Confusion darkened her eyes as she turned away.

He stopped her with a hand to her shoulder. Even that small touch brought a trembling response.

He struggled to soften his tone. "I'll wake you and the children in a couple of hours. We'll travel while it's still dark."

She didn't turn to look at him, afraid he would read the desire that still shimmered in her eyes. "What if Fenner anticipates that?"

"It's a risk we'll have to take."

She nodded. "As you said, you're very good at taking risks. But I have my sons to think about."

He said nothing as she crossed to where her children were sleeping and lay down beside them. He watched as she wrapped herself in her shawl and rolled to her side, keeping her face hidden from view.

He decided to climb up to the opening and keep an eye out for campfires in the distance. It would give him a chance to breathe cool night air. And maybe give his heart a rest, as well.

His hands, he noted, were shaking. And the sweet taste of her was still on his lips.

"Cara."

Yale's voice was little more than a whisper, but she was awake instantly. She sat up, uncomfortably aware of how her body brushed his as she drew the shawl around her shoulders.

Instead of moving aside he remained where he was, absorbing the warmth of her body. She looked pleasantly disheveled, her hair spilling around her face in a tangle of curls, her eyes still heavy-lidded from sleep.

"It's time to leave." He stood and offered his hand.

As he helped her to her feet she felt the strength in him. And the heat. It seemed to be always there, simmering between them.

"I'll wake the children."

As she turned away she noticed that the fire had

been allowed to burn down to embers. The deer meat, fully cooked, had already been cut up into small bundles, and wrapped in the deerskin before being loaded into the cart.

As soon as the boys were up she folded the bearskin and spread it in the back of the cart.

After spreading dirt over the hot coals to extinguish any fire that might remain, Yale moved aside the brush and tree branches that had covered the mouth of the cave.

He helped Cody and Seth into the back of the cart, then assisted Cara up to the seat before climbing up beside her and flicking the reins.

Outside the cave, the sky was black as midnight. Giant boulders loomed around them, dwarfing the little cart and its occupants. The children were soon asleep, lulled by the sound of the horse's hooves, and the slow, jarring movement of the cart as it rolled across the barren landscape.

Cara's voice was a hushed whisper in the night. "Do you think the Fenner gang will stay on our trail? Or do you think they'll give up on us and head off in another direction?"

Yale toyed with the idea of sugarcoating his reply, to give her some peace of mind. But in the end he merely said, "Their intention had been to use your ranch as a hideout until the soldiers who are chasing them gave up the search. Now, with that plan ruined, they have to keep moving, or risk being caught. And since they're in a mood to teach me a lesson, I figure they'll keep on my trail for as long as it takes."

"Why are soldiers after them?"

"They stopped a train, and killed the conductor and engineer."

She turned to study his profile. "Were you with them?"

"No. I was busy doing what I do best. Beating some cowboys out of their wages in a nearby saloon. When I heard what had happened, I knew I had to part company with Will Fenner and his men."

"How did you come to join them in the first place?"

He told her about the shoot-out, and his introduction to the gang. "I thought one of them might know something about my father."

"You've never found him?"

He shook his head.

Cara lay a hand on his arm. "I'm sorry, Yale. It must be hard, never knowing what happened to him."

He thought he could shrug off her sympathy the way he always had in the past. But he felt an odd tightness in his throat. "It's pure foolishness. I can't imagine it would do me much good now to find some broken-down old man. After all these years, the only thing we'd ever share is the same last name."

"But you can't help searching, Yale." She kept her hand on his arm. Squeezed. "It's the not knowing that drives you."

"Yeah." He turned his head. Moonlight glittered in his eyes, turning them to icy chips of blue. "I've always hated not knowing whether he's alive or dead. Whether he'd abandoned us, or made a real effort to make it back. It shouldn't matter, but it does.''

''I can understand that.'' She lifted her head and studied the blaze of starlight. ''My father made a lot of mistakes in his life. Some of them…hurtful. But now that I have children of my own, I realize that he did what he thought was right, because he loved me and wanted to protect me.'' She forced herself to look at Yale. To keep her hand on his arm, though the mere touch of him had heat dancing along her spine. ''I've always had the satisfaction of knowing that my father, for all his faults, loved me. I can't imagine what it would be like to always wonder where he was, and what sort of man he was, and whether or not I mattered in his life.''

''That's the worst of it.'' He closed a hand over hers. ''Though I've never put it into words.''

As they rolled across a high plateau, a coyote sang its mournful song to the moon. A night bird called to its mate and the answering notes were high and sweet. Insects hummed and chirped, adding to the rhythm of the horse's hooves and the sounds of the cart's wheels on the hard-packed earth.

Yale felt something he'd rarely experienced in his life. Oh, he'd known often that keen edge of excitement during a high-stakes poker game. And the satisfaction of winning the jackpot. But this was a very different feeling. With Cara here beside him, he felt a rare sense of peace. As though every road he'd taken had been leading him toward this time, this place.

And though the stakes were much higher this time around, he had no choice but to play the hand that had been dealt him. For he truly believed that the woman beside him and her children were now his responsibility.

He was prepared to risk whatever it took, even his life, to save theirs.

Chapter Eight

As the first silver streaks of dawn began to light the sky, they spotted the remains of a barn in the distance.

Cara looked up hopefully. "Maybe we could stay the day in there?"

Yale shook his head. "Too obvious. That's the first place Fenner would look."

He could see the weariness etched in her face and hated that he had to be the one to snatch hope from her grasp.

He touched a hand lightly to her shoulder. "I promise you, we'll find a safe haven."

They had to. With every passing minute, the sky would grow lighter and they would become an easier target.

Yale's gaze scanned the horizon, searching for something, anything that might offer them refuge. But all he could see was earth and rock and sky. And in the distance, the brooding Black Hills.

He flicked the reins, urging the horse into a trot.

If he didn't find anything else, they could always take shelter in the forest. It would mean another day without sleep for him, for he would have to keep an eye out for Fenner and his gang, and move Cara and her family deeper into the woods if danger drew near.

The children, wakened by the quickening pace, sat up and stared around at the unfamiliar country-side.

Cody rubbed his eyes. "Where are we, Ma?"

"We're just coming into the Black Hills." She pointed up ahead to the dark and somber mountain peaks looming on the horizon.

"Are there any ranches around here?" the boy asked.

Yale glanced over his shoulder. "No ranchers, son. But a few miners are still here. And Sioux, though most have been driven off their land by the men searching for gold."

The little boy's eyes widened. "Did you ever think about coming here and digging for gold?"

Yale chuckled. "I like gold as much as the next man. But I prefer mine clean and neatly piled at a gaming table. The thought of digging for it just never appealed to me."

He maneuvered the horse and cart between narrow boulders and started down a ravine when he suddenly brought the horse to a halt.

"What's wrong?" Cara looked at him in alarm.

"Nothing's wrong. I just want to take a look at something." He leapt to the ground and walked some distance before disappearing. When he returned a short time later he was wearing a broad smile.

"I just found the perfect place to spend the day." He caught the reins and began leading the horse toward what looked like nothing more than a small depression in the ground. But as they entered, they discovered they were inside an abandoned mine.

Yale had taken the time to light a torch, which he'd stuck between two braces in the wall. Now, as they moved deeper into the mine shaft, they could see glimmers of daylight here and there, punctuated by patches of darkness.

He stopped the horse and reached up to help the children from the back of the cart. Then he moved to the other side and helped Cara down.

"There was probably a shack directly above us at one time." He pointed to a crude ladder that lay resting against one wall. "The miner could enter his mine shaft from a trap door inside the cabin. That's why we almost missed seeing the outer entrance. He must have dug it in such a way that no one would be tempted to sneak in here and steal from him. I think with the aid of a few small rocks and some tree branches, I'll be able to make it as invisible as it once was."

While Cara and the children unloaded their meager belongings, Yale worked quickly to conceal the outer entrance to the mine. After rolling a couple of boulders into place and tossing dried twigs and branches around them, he examined his handiwork.

When he was satisfied that no one could spot it, he made a thorough study of the surrounding area and found that only bits of the miner's cabin remained. Fire and weather had reduced it to rubble. Nature had already begun concealing what remained, with shrubs and tufts of grass working their way through the sod floor, where bones attested to the fact that the prospector who had dug this mine had been dead a good many years.

He returned to the mine shaft, taking the torch with him, and found Cara preparing breakfast, while the two children stared around at the gloom.

"Want to take a look at where you'll be spending the rest of the day?"

Though Seth looked curious, Cody held back. "No. It's dark in there."

"Don't be afraid." Yale lifted a torch high enough to pierce the gloom.

The older boy couldn't resist the challenge. "I'm not afraid."

"Come on, then." Yale kept the torch high, illuminating the darkness, and led the way, with the two children following. Every so often he would wedge the torch into a niche in the wall and light another one, moving deeper into the mine with each one.

"Is the gold just lying here?" Cody asked. "Or is it under the ground?"

Yale grinned. "If gold could be found lying around, this place would be swarming with prospectors, instead of being abandoned. The gold lies deep in the ground. Some of these mines go down hundreds of feet.''

Cody's eyes lit with sudden excitement. "Do you think the miner might have missed a few nuggets?"

"Are you thinking you'd like to dig and see what you find?"

He nodded. "Could we?"

Yale shrugged. "I don't see why not." He pointed to a rusted shovel resting against a timber. "Maybe the two of you could take turns seeing what you can dig up."

While Yale anchored the torch, the older boy picked up the shovel and began to dig. By the time Yale walked away the two children were eagerly sifting the loosened dirt between their fingers, examining every stone and rock with barely concealed excitement.

When he returned to unhitch the horse, Cara looked around anxiously. "Where are Cody and Seth?"

"Digging for gold." When he saw her arched brow he winked. "I figured it might help them pass the time."

She couldn't help smiling. "I can't think of a better way for them to spend the day. In fact, I was just wondering how I could take their minds off the fact that they'd be spending so many hours in a mine shaft."

"It can't be easy for them." Yale poured water from a canteen into a bucket for the horse. "They've been through a lot in a short time. But they're bright enough to think of ways to fill up the hours.''

Cara sighed as she began cutting venison into bite sizes. ''You can't imagine what a comfort they've been to me in the past year.''

''Is that how long it's been since Wyatt died?''

She nodded.

''Why didn't you return to Misery?''

''There was nothing left for me there. With my parents gone, I have no family left. The ranch was gone.'' She looked away, avoiding his eyes. Her voice lowered to a whisper. ''I told myself I was staying because Wyatt's ranch was my home now. But the truth is, the town of Misery always made me think of you. And that always made me sad.''

Her honest admission caught him by surprise. ''Well, now. I wouldn't want you to be sad.'' He ignored the sudden hitch of his heart and turned away.

Seeing him heading toward the mine entrance she started after him. ''Now where are you going?''

''Just out and about. I need to scout the area.'' Seeing the little frown between her brows he touched a finger to the spot. ''Don't worry, Cara. I'll be back before you've even had time to miss me.''

She caught his arm. ''Promise?''

His eyes narrowed. And though he hadn't meant to, he found himself dragging her close for a hard, quick kiss. ''You have my word on it.''

There it was again. The heat, the flash, the fire

that always seemed to assail him the moment he kissed her. The hard, quick bounce of his heart in his chest, and the thrill he felt as his hands moved over her.

No other woman had ever affected him like this. One touch of Cara and his mind was wiped clear of all thought. Need pulsed through him. The need to taste all of her. The desire to touch her everywhere. The thought of taking her here, now, was like a living, breathing pressure building inside him.

It would be so easy. He could tell, by her response, that she was as affected by this kiss as he was. That had him taking it deeper, until he could hear her breath shudder. Could feel her pulse throbbing with the same intensity as his.

It took all his willpower to release her and walk away.

Yale crouched behind some rocks and peered into the distance. Far off he could see a faint cloud of dust. At the sight of it, his eyes narrowed in frustration.

The feeling in his gut told him it wasn't a stage, or a couple of prospectors. It was Will Fenner and his men, following his trail. He'd been so careful, sticking to high, rocky ground. Still, even if they hadn't found the distinctive wheel marks of Cara's cart, there were other signs a good tracker could follow. The fresh droppings of the plow horse, for instance.

If he'd been traveling alone he would have taken

the time to conceal such signs. But he'd had to concentrate all his energy on keeping up the spirits of Cara and her children while staying one step ahead of his enemy.

His enemy.

He'd known that Will Fenner was a man who would never forgive or forget an act of disloyalty. In Fenner's eyes he had committed the ultimate betrayal.

Not that he'd had any choice. Though it had been years since he'd allowed himself to think about his childhood, the pain was still there. It had been buried deep, but the scars were still tender when probed. The thought of his uncle Junior's fists had his own tightening. The thought of his mother's death along the trail had a muscle working in his jaw. The minute he'd heard Fenner plotting against a helpless widow and children, the decision had been made for him.

It was a decision he would never regret.

Feeling weary beyond belief, he made his way back to the mine entrance, taking care to cover his tracks before slipping past the boulders and brush.

"Did you see anything?"

He nodded. "Dust from a number of horses. Headed this way. They should be here in the next couple of hours." He glanced at the bearskin. "I think I'd better grab a few minutes of sleep. I want to be fresh when they get here."

Cara watched as he dropped down on the fur and tipped his hat over his face. Within minutes he was fast asleep. She watched him for some time, aware that her heartbeat had begun to speed up the minute he'd drawn close.

She picked up a bundle of meat and made her way deep into the mine shaft, following the sound of her children's laughter.

"Look, Ma." Seeing her, Cody held up a rusty nugget. "Think it could be gold?"

She examined it by the light of the torch, then handed it back to him. "I wouldn't know a gold nugget from a stone. But I think you ought to keep it in your pocket, just in case."

"You do?" Her older son's eyes were wide with excitement as he closed his hand around the pebble. "Can I take it to Yale? I bet he'll know if it's gold."

"You can show it to him later. Right now he's catching some sleep. And I think it would be wise if we keep our voices low so we don't disturb him."

Cody nodded and tucked the nugget into his pocket. When he looked at his mother, his tone was cautious. "Yale thinks you're pretty."

She could feel the heat rush to her cheeks.

"Did Pa think you were pretty, too?"

She met his assessing gaze. "I should hope so."

"Did he ever say so?"

She shrugged. "I...guess he did."

"Did you ever kiss Yale?"

Cara was grateful that she could speak the truth without evading. "No, Cody. Your pa was the first man I ever kissed."

"Do you think, if you'd kissed Yale first, you might have married him instead of Pa?"

She took a deep breath. "I'm afraid that's one thing we'll never know. I'm not sorry I married your pa."

As her words sank in, she could see the relief in her son's eyes.

She opened the bundle to reveal bite-sized chunks of venison. "Now, how about some food before you go back to mining?"

The two boys were grinning happily as they set aside the shovel and sat down to eat. A few minutes later they returned to their work, taking turns with the shovel, before sifting through the dirt.

Cara watched them for nearly an hour before she turned away and returned to where she'd left Yale sleeping. She was surprised to find him up and drinking from a canteen.

"That wasn't nearly enough time to sleep, Yale. If you'd like I'll go to the entrance of the mine and keep watch while you get a little more rest."

He shook his head. "No need to worry about me. There've been plenty of times when I've gone without sleep for days, if the other players were willing."

"You'd take such punishment for a game of cards?"

He grinned. "You call it a game. I consider it my livelihood. And when the stakes are high enough, I'm willing to forego a little sleep."

Before she could reply he touched a finger to his lips and lifted his head, listening intently.

"What is it, Yale? What do you…?"

He lifted a hand and whispered, "Bring the boys here. Tell them not to make a sound."

Minutes later she returned with Cody and Seth following.

Yale held up a gold coin and whispered, "Want to play a game? The winner will get this."

"What do we have to do?" Cody asked, eager to play.

"First you have to sit over there on the bearskin, while I extinguish all our torches. Then you both have to stay absolutely still. The one who can remain that way the longest will win."

Cody waited until Seth had hurried off to the fur before saying, "You might be able to fool my little brother, but you don't fool me. Are the bad men back?"

Yale nodded. "They are. And I need you to help me, Cody. If Seth should cry out, or make any sound at all, it might give away our hiding place. Do you understand?"

The boy nodded before turning away.

As he hurried around extinguishing their torches Yale called softly, "You'll hear some sounds. You may even hear voices. But no matter what you hear, you can't move or speak. Do you understand, Seth?"

The little boy nodded.

"Good." He handed a rifle to Cara, touching a hand to her arm as he did.

There was no time for words. He managed a quick grin before picking up his rifle and heading toward the outer entrance to the mine.

Minutes later they heard the unmistakable sound of horses' hooves thundering directly toward them.

While Yale peered through the brush that covered the entrance, he could see Will Fenner and his men pass within mere inches. Suddenly one of the horsemen urged his mount up the steep incline until he was passing directly overhead.

The children's eyes were wide with fear. Little Seth actually opened his mouth to cry out. But Cody clamped a hand over his brother's mouth and reminded him about the glittering gold coin awaiting them when this ordeal was over.

The two children watched as shadows danced overhead.

Soon there were more horses scrambling up and over, while the men talked among themselves.

"Looks like a miner's shack."

"What's left of it," came Will Fenner's voice.

The sound of it had Cara shivering. Seeing her reaction, Yale moved as silently as a cat until he was beside her. Without a word he took her hand in his, linking their fingers.

The minute he touched her she willed herself to stay calm and focused, for the sake of her children. But her finger tightened on the trigger of her rifle.

"Think Conover came this way?"

"I'm sure of it," Fenner shouted.

"Then why can't we find any trace of him? Not so much as a footprint."

"I don't know," Fenner snarled. "But I can smell him. He's somewhere nearby. Let's fan out and see if we can pick up his trail."

Minutes later the hoofbeats faded as the men began circling around, hunting for anything that might lead them to their enemy.

Yale and Cara and the children remained perfectly still, watching the shadows that drifted across the upper timbers, at times obliterating the sunlight, at other times permitting it to reappear.

When the voices faded and the hoofbeats could no longer be heard, they all gave long, drawn-out sighs of relief.

Yale's voice held a trace of a smile. "I seem to be traveling in some mighty fine company." He dug into his pocket and removed two coins. "Once again it seems we have two winners."

As the boys accepted their reward, Cody dug out his nugget and held it up alongside the coin. "I found this back there in the mine. Do you think it could be real gold?"

Yale held it up to the tiny rays of sunlight that filtered through the rocks and timbers above, turning it this way and that as he scratched at the rusty surface. "Hard to say, Cody. It could be real. Or it could be fool's gold. I guess you'd better keep it until we can have an assayer take a look at it."

"You mean it? You think it's worth keeping?"

Yale nodded.

The boy turned to his mother. "Can we go back to our digging now?"

She shook her head. "It's too dark back there, and it wouldn't be wise to light a torch just yet. But if you'd like, you can dig here, where there's a little light." As the children started off to fetch the shovel she added, "Remember. You can speak only in whispers. Will you do that?"

The two boys looked solemn as they danced away.

Cara turned to Yale. "Who would have ever believed that they would care more about digging in the dirt than about fretting over a gang of outlaws who are chasing after us?"

"It's the beauty of being young." He smiled, and then, because he wanted to gather her close and just hold her, he turned away and called over his shoulder, "I think I'll stand guard at the entrance. Just in case they decide to circle back."

Cara watched him walk away, then sank down on the bearskin and rested her face in her hands.

Though she'd forced herself to remain perfectly still for the sake of her children, she'd been absolutely terrified that one of the Fenner gang would discover their hiding place.

What had made it tolerable had been the touch of Yale's hand on hers. He hadn't moved. Hadn't flinched. But she'd seen something in his eyes. Something so fierce, so determined, she had no doubt he'd have found a way to save them.

She was beginning to see that he hadn't changed all that much from the absolutely fearless boy she'd once known.

Watching him, being with him, made her almost believe they could survive this.

She closed her eyes, willing herself to let go of the terrible tension that held her in its grip. For so long now she'd been forced to be strong for the sake of her children. She'd almost forgotten what it felt like to share the burden with another.

She took a deep breath and decided that, for a little while at least, she would let Yale be strong for both of them. With a hand over her eyes she lay back, emptying her mind until her heartbeat steadied.

Chapter Nine

Throughout the late afternoon and evening they could hear the horsemen backtracking, as they searched for some sign of their elusive prey. Several times the sound of horses' hooves overhead had their little party dropping to the floor of the mine, where they huddled until the sounds receded.

As daylight faded, the mine shaft was becoming increasingly darker and colder.

Cara was grateful for the deer meat, which she passed around while they sat together on the bearskin. She saw Seth shiver and settled her youngest son on her lap, wrapping her shawl around him. "Is that better?"

The little boy nodded and rested his head on his mother's shoulder.

Cody turned to Yale. "Will we be able to build a fire?"

"Not tonight, son. I wish we could, but I have a feeling Fenner and his men are going to circle around all night, hoping we'll let down our guard. I figure, if we can see their shadows down here, they'd be able to see the light of our fire up above.''

The little boy thought a minute. ''If they're your friends, why don't you leave us and join them?''

''Cody!'' Cara couldn't hide her shock. ''How can you ask such a thing after all Yale has done for us?''

''It's all right, Cara.'' Yale stared at the little boy. ''Is that what you would do to a friend? Leave him when things got too dangerous, and join forces with his enemy?''

Cody looked down at his hands, then up at the man seated across from him. ''No, sir. Not if he was my friend. Is that what you are? Our friend?''

Yale nodded. ''I'd like to think so.''

''If those men find our hiding place, are you going to die with us?''

''If I have to. But I give you my word, Cody, I'll do everything in my power to see that doesn't happen. You and Seth and your mother have a whole lot of living ahead of you. And I mean to see that you get to enjoy it.''

''What about you? When this is over, will you go back to being a gambler?''

Yale was aware that Cara had turned to look at him. But he kept his gaze fixed on the boy. ''That's what I am. It's all I know how to do.''

''That's not true.'' Cara couldn't help herself from coming to his defense. The words seemed to slip out of her mouth before she could stop them. Then, too embarrassed to look at her children, she said, "You know how to trap a deer and skin it and cook it. And you know all about finding safe hiding places. And best of all you know how to make everything seem like fun."

Yale leaned over and brushed his lips over her cheek. Just the slightest touch, yet they both drew back quickly.

"Thanks for reminding me of that, Cara. I guess I needed to know that I could do something besides win at cards."

Cody stepped between Yale and his mother. "When this is over, and the outlaws are gone, can we go home?"

"Oh, Cody." Cara closed her eyes against the pain and rocked her son gently. "Let's not think about tomorrow. Let's just get through tonight."

Seth tugged at his mother's hand.

Cara looked down at him. "What is it, honey?"

Cody spoke for him. "He wants you to tell us a story."

"All right." Cara settled her two sons in the bearskin, then drew the edges around them. When they were warm and snug, she sat beside them, leaning her back against the rough wall of the mine. "Which story would you like to hear? The one about Noah and the great flood? Or Jonah and the whale?"

Cody answered while his younger brother stifled a yawn. "Tell Seth's favorite. The one about the son who leaves his family and squanders all his talents."

"Oh. The Prodigal Son." She crossed her feet at the ankles and folded her hands in her lap as she began to tell the old, familiar tale of the son who demanded his share of his inheritance, only to travel to foreign lands where it was eventually used up, until he found himself alone and destitute.

As she spoke Yale took up a position near the entrance to the mine, keeping his gaze fastened on the gathering darkness. But as the minutes passed, he could feel himself being drawn into the tale. Cara's voice, as soft as when she'd been a girl, washed over him, touching a chord deep inside. He'd always loved the sound of her voice. The slight breathiness. The rhythm. The cadence. As he got caught up in the story, he realized it was one from his own childhood. He could recall his mother reciting that same tale.

Always, his brother Gabe had cheered for the good son, who had remained on his father's land, caring for the herds. Their little sister Kitty had often declared that she would forgive a brother anything, as long as the family could be reunited. For himself, Yale had always had a special fondness for the Prodigal. He understood the wanderlust that would drive a man to travel to distant lands. Perhaps he'd gone in search of something he couldn't find at home. Adventure. Excitement. Freedom. Respect. Or perhaps he'd simply wandered the world to escape the pain of rejection.

He heard Cara's words as she neatly ended the story.

''The father called together his friends and family and asked them to rejoice with him because what had been lost to him was now found. The son who had been dead to him was now alive, and had returned to the family who loved him.''

Cody's voice sounded muffled and sleepy. ''Seth wants to know if they lived happily ever after.''

''Yes, honey.'' Cara leaned down to press a kiss to her son's cheek.

''Will we, Ma?''

Cara brushed the hair from his eyes. ''Yes, Cody. We will.''

The boy rolled to his side, a hint of annoyance in his tone. ''If I was his father I would have made him pay his brother all the money he'd lost before I'd take him back.''

''I hope when you're old enough to be a father you change your mind, Cody.'' Cara tucked the bearskin around her son's shoulders to hold back the chill. ''The wonderful thing about family is that we're allowed to make mistakes and still be loved.''

''Did you still love Pa after he lost Grandpa's ranch in a poker game?''

At the boy's words Yale went perfectly still. It dawned on him that Cara had held back some vital parts of her life story.

He glanced across the distance and could see, in the shadows, the way Cara gave careful consideration before saying softly, ''Yes. I still loved him.''

''But I heard you tell him he'd squandered your inheritance.''

''I…was angry. But afterward, I forgave him.''

''Like the father in the story you just told us?''

"Yes. Like the father." Cara sat beside her children for long minutes, until their breathing grew soft and rhythmic. Then she got to her feet and shook down her skirts.

When she glanced toward Yale he was still peering into the darkness, the rifle in his hand. He gave no outward sign that he'd overheard. But there was no way he could have missed what Cody had said.

Squaring her shoulders she walked up beside him. "I owe you an explanation."

"You don't owe me anything, Cara."

"Yes I do." She took in a breath. "Now that Wyatt is gone, I'm trying to keep a certain image of him alive for his children."

Yale's eyes, though still fixed on the distance, narrowed slightly. "So a little thing like the fact that he lost your father's ranch in a poker game is now to be forgotten?"

She shrugged. "Something like that. Yale..." She touched a hand to his arm and felt him stiffen.

His tone was harsh. "Are you wondering if I was the gambler who won your father's ranch, Cara? Do you think I'm the one who stole your inheritance at a poker table?"

"Of course not. I know who beat Wyatt out of my ranch. It was Buck Reedy."

Yale made a sound that might have been a laugh or grunt of anger. "Good old Buck. Still palming cards and dazzling the locals with his talent." He turned to meet her eyes. "Does your son know this?

Or does he think I'm the one who beat his father at poker?''

She lifted a hand to her mouth. ''Oh, Yale. I never thought of that.''

''Didn't you?'' His eyes blazed. ''To a boy that young, one gambler is the same as another. No wonder he resents me so deeply. He'll never know for certain if I'm the man who stole his mother's inheritance, and played his father for a fool.''

''Then I'll tell him the truth. But I...need some time. I've tried so hard not to say anything unkind about Wyatt to Cody. He needs...'' She took a breath. ''A boy needs to think highly of his father. Especially a father who is no longer here to defend his own reputation.''

''Yeah.'' Yale turned away from her, his eyes scanning the horizon. ''I guess that's what my mother was thinking when she told us our father was off on a secret mission for the President. Somehow that was a lot easier to swallow than learning he was an outlaw.''

''But Wyatt wasn't an outlaw. He was simply a good man who...discovered a weakness in himself.'' Cara lowered her head. ''Oh, I don't know anymore. I'm so confused. I thought I was right to protect his good name. I told myself I was doing it for his children. But maybe I was really doing it for myself. So I wouldn't feel like such a fool.''

Yale shot her a quick look. ''Why should you feel like a fool over something your husband did?''

''Don't you see the irony in all this, Yale?'' Her

voice lowered with emotion. "I allowed myself to be married off to a man I didn't love because my parents thought he was fine and upstanding and respectable, only to discover that he was weak and selfish and incapable of taking care of his family. And all this time I've had to live with the knowledge that I'd given up a good, honest decent man, a man I loved, because he was a wild, reckless gambler whose very boldness frightened me."

His eyes were hot and fierce as he gripped her upper arms almost painfully. "Say that again."

"That you frightened me? You did. You still do, Yale."

"No." He dragged her close, his eyes never leaving hers. "That you loved me."

"I did. I've...never stopped."

For the space of several seconds he merely stared at her, trying to take it all in. Then slowly, so slowly she felt her heart begin to stutter and her throat go dry, he lowered his mouth to hers.

This wasn't at all like the hard, quick kiss they'd shared before. This time he poured himself into it. Like a man starved for the taste of her.

Feeling the way she held back, he tasted and nibbled, allowing her to slide slowly into the kiss.

"Yale." She brought her hands to his chest. "We shouldn't."

"It's too late." He smiled, and she could feel her heart tumble wildly. "I just have to kiss you, Cara."

He returned to her lips. But this time she could

feel the passion. Could taste the need, as he took the kiss deeper, until her head was swimming.

He caught her fists and opened them, lifting her palms to press a kiss to each. Then he looked into her eyes. "Kiss me back, Cara. Quick. Before I die of hunger."

"Oh, Yale." She gave a laugh, then wrapped her arms around his neck and stood on tiptoe to cover his lips with hers. She heard his quick intake of breath a second before his arms banded around her, molding her to the length of him.

She wasn't prepared for the heat. For the sudden flash of light behind her closed eyes, or the slide of liquid fire deep inside. Hadn't expected this quick slice of panic that had her by the throat, or the hot, hungry need.

Her laughter died, replaced by a low moan that seemed, to her ears, more animal than human.

"I want you, Cara. I've never stopped wanting you." With his eyes steady on hers he backed her up until she was pressed against the wall of the mine.

She could feel the imprint of his body on hers. Was aware of his arousal. And of her body's urgent response.

This time she was taken fully into the kiss. A kiss that was all fire and flash and need. His tongue found hers, mated, while his hands moved over her, igniting tiny sparks along her spine.

He ran hot wet kisses down the smooth column of her throat, sending chills racing through her. But even as she thought to resist, her body betrayed her. She arched her neck, giving him easier access, then moaned, low and deep in her throat, when he buried his mouth in the sensitive hollow of her neck.

"Cara. Cara." His mouth moved lower, taking her breast, and despite the barrier of her gown and chemise she felt her nipple harden.

She jerked back, her eyes dark and wild, her breath burning her throat.

"Yale. We can't. The children..."

She looked over to where Cody and Seth lay sleeping.

He kept a hand on either side of her head, holding her when she thought to slip away. Then his smile came. That wild, roguish smile that always sent her heart tumbling. "You once objected to kissing me because your mother might see us. Now it's your children." He leaned close, until his lips whispered over hers. "One of these days it's going to be just you and me, Cara. And when that day comes, oh, the things we're going to do."

He saw the flush that stained her cheeks and couldn't resist brushing his mouth lightly over each bright spot. "I've had a lot of years to think about you, Cara. A lot of years to fantasize about all the things we would have, could have, should have done."

He kissed the tip of her nose, then rested his forehead against hers. "Now I'm more resolved than ever to get us safely out of this mess. Think of all the things we have to look forward to."

Though it took all his willpower, he stepped back. "Go to sleep now, Cara."

"What about you?"

"I'll keep watch."

She touched a hand to his cheek. Just a touch, but she saw his eyes darken, and realized that he was very near the breaking point.

She quickly withdrew her hand and walked away.

As she covered herself with the shawl and curled up beside her children, she looked across the distance that separated them and could see him, standing where she'd left him, watching her with a quiet intensity that had the heat returning.

She touched a hand to her poor heart. It was still racing out of control. She clutched her hands together to stop the shaking.

In all the years that she'd been a wife, she'd never known such feelings. Had never believed any man could awaken such an overwhelming desire in her.

It shamed her to admit that she wanted him every bit as desperately as he wanted her. And had it not been for the presence of her children, she would right now be lying in Yale's arms, begging him to take her.

Chapter Ten

Cara was awakened from a sound sleep by the thundering of horses' hooves directly overhead. She sat up, struggling to see through the layers of darkness that seemed to swirl about the mine shaft. But in the inky blackness, it was impossible to see anything.

Then she caught the sound of voices above.

"I'm tired of this, Will. When are we going to call it quits and make camp for the night?"

"When we find that stinking gambler. He's around here. I can feel it."

Horses clattered over rock, sending debris drifting down from the rotten timbers that supported the roof of the mine.

In his sleep little Seth gave a cry of distress.

Instantly Cara reached out in the darkness and laid a hand over her son's mouth. With her lips pressed to Seth's ear she whispered, "Hush, now. Don't make a sound."

She felt a big hand on her shoulder and realized

that despite the darkness Yale had hurried over to kneel beside her. For a moment she rested her cheek against his hand.

In the silence that followed, a voice up above called out, "What was that?"

"What?" shouted another.

"I heard something. Like a kid's cry."

"Or a bird," someone said.

"I tell you it was a kid."

"I didn't hear anything."

"Come on, Will," shouted a rough voice. "I'm sick and tired of going over the same trail a dozen times. In this darkness we couldn't find Conover if we tripped over him. I say we make camp, and start fresh in the morning."

Several voices chimed in agreement, and Will Fenner could be heard muttering an oath before saying, "All right. We'll make camp here. But only until dawn. Then I want that gambler. I'm not leaving here without him."

Gradually the sound of men and horses faded. But from the way their voices occasionally drifted on the breeze, they'd chosen a campsite close by.

Cara moved her hand away from her son's mouth. Then, feeling tears on Seth's cheeks, she lifted the little boy into her arms and began to rock him.

Against his temple she whispered, "I know you're frightened, Seth. Just hold on."

"But the outlaws are right outside, Ma," Cody whispered.

"I know."

Yale's muted voice chimed in. "What they don't know is that we're down here. Now all we have to do is stay hidden. Sooner or later they're bound to give up."

"Do you think so?" Cody kept a hand on his little brother's arm as he lifted his head and sniffed back his tears.

"Yes, I do."

"So do I," Cara said softly as she drew her shawl around Seth before continuing to rock him. "Now you two close your eyes and go back to sleep. Hopefully by morning the bad men will be gone. And we can leave this place."

She felt Yale's hand squeeze her shoulder and brush her hair before he moved away. And found the touch of him oddly comforting.

Thin morning light filtered through the overhead timbers and layers of rock, piercing the darkness of the mine shaft. Cara awoke to find herself covered by Yale's black coat. Seth had been returned to the bearskin, where he slept peacefully beside Cody.

Cara sat up and glanced toward the entrance, where Yale was kneeling, rifle in hand. She crossed to him and handed him his coat. "You must be freezing."

He shook his head. "You keep it." He drew it around her and felt her shiver.

"Have you slept at all, Yale?"

"I'll sleep later." He turned his attention to the entrance, peering into the distance. "Right now Fen-

ner's men are starting to stir. I need to stay alert."
He nodded toward the sleeping children. "I think
you ought to wake Cody and Seth and take them as
deep into the mine shaft as you can. Take the meat
and a canteen of water, and the hides for warmth."

"What about you? What are you planning?"

"As soon as it's safe, I intend to leave here and
circle around Fenner and his men. I need to lure
them away from here. Otherwise, sooner or later
they're bound to stumble onto us." He pointed to
the rotted timbers. "Besides, I'm afraid too many
horses passing overhead might send that entire mine
crashing in on itself. If that happens, we could be
trapped in here."

He saw the fear she couldn't hide and touched a
hand to her cheek. "We've come this far, Cara.
Don't give up on me now."

She shook her head. "I'm not giving up. But I
don't want you to risk yourself."

"It'll only be for a little while. Until I can draw
Fenner and his men away. Then I'll come back and
we can get out of this tomb."

The minute the word was out of his mouth he
regretted it. But hearing a commotion outside, he
was forced to turn away.

Over his shoulder he whispered, "They're breaking camp. Take the children. As soon as I can, I'm
going to slip away. Promise me that no matter what,
you'll stay hidden in here."

She needed to touch him. If only for a moment.

Laying a hand on his sleeve she whispered, "All right. I promise. Please hurry back, Yale."

He closed a hand over hers. "You know I will."

Yale watched until the men broke camp and pulled themselves into the saddle. He strained to hear the orders Fenner was issuing.

"We'll break into two groups. One heads east, the other west. Follow every track, no matter how faint. When you spot his trail, signal by firing twice in succession. Understand? I want that gambler. And I want him before noon today."

Hearing this, Cara felt a chill pass through her. There was such venom in Fenner's voice. She turned for one last glimpse of Yale, but he was already completely absorbed in the actions of the outlaws. With a sigh she turned away and picked up the supplies before waking the children and leading them deep into the darkness.

As soon as the horsemen were out of sight Yale slipped between the boulders, taking care to see that the brush was replaced, leaving no sign that an opening in the ground existed.

He watched the twin clouds of dust, then set out on foot toward a distant mountain peak.

In the heat of afternoon Yale removed his shirt, tying it by the sleeves around his waist. Then he climbed hand over hand until he'd reached the shelf of overhanging rock atop the mountain. From there he could see in all directions. Far below he could make out the line of horsemen circling back on their trail. Farther on he could see the others, making a slow arc around the mine.

On the far side of the mountain he could see a trail carved deep into the earth, made by the hundreds of miners who had converged on the Black Hills years earlier, when gold had been discovered. These hills had given up their gold, at the cost of so many lives. Miners had clashed with the Sioux, who considered this ground sacred. Many of the Sioux still kept watch over their land, though most had been driven from it. The miners, too, had left, except for the few stragglers who simply couldn't give up the dream of untold riches.

Suddenly he caught sight of the one thing he'd been hoping for. Coming along that trail was a lone man in a horse-drawn wagon. The man was traveling fast enough that it would take Fenner and his men until dark to catch him, since they would first have to navigate the wall of mountain that stood between him and them.

He was so busy watching the man in the wagon, he never even heard the sound of someone coming up behind him. When he heard a man's voice ordering him to unfasten his gunbelt, and felt the press of a gun's muzzle against his back, he froze.

"Well, well. Won't Will Fenner be happy with me when he sees what I just found."

With his hand on his gunbelt Yale turned to see the skinny outlaw known as Slick grinning like a fool. "Why aren't you with the others, Slick?"

"I told Will I'd ride on ahead, in case you'd made

a break for it in the night. Looks like I was right.''
He glanced around. "Where'd you hide the woman
and her kids?''

Yale gave a disgusted shake of his head. "I
should have known you'd be the one to figure me
out, Slick. I guess that's how you earned that
name."

"That's right." The old man spat a wad of tobacco juice. "Now where's the woman and her
brats?''

Yale nodded with his head. "Behind those
rocks."

"Hooee! I bet old Fenner will have an extra chug
of whiskey for me tonight after this."

"Is that all you want? Extra whiskey? What about
a share of the gold?''

The old man's eyes narrowed. "What gold you
talking about?''

"The gold the widow had hidden in her barn.
Didn't Fenner share it with the rest of you?''

"Will didn't mention any gold." Anger flared,
quick and hot. "Why'd he keep that from us?''

Yale shrugged, and managed a quick frown.
"You know what gold does to some men. Makes
them greedy.''

"Yeah. Never figured Fenner to cheat his own
gang though." Slick motioned with his pistol.
"Take me to the woman. I want to know more about
this gold." As Yale turned away the old man called,
"But first you'd better drop that gunbelt, gambling man."

"Right. The gunbelt." Yale reached a hand to it, then spun around. In that split second it took to fire his weapon, he realized his miscalculation. At almost the same instant that he fired, Slick did the same.

He felt the force of the bullet knock him backward. Felt the white hot pain that had his pistol slipping from nerveless fingers to drop on the ground moments before his knees buckled and he found himself sitting with his back to a rock, staring wordlessly at the blood that flowed down his chest and pooled in the dirt.

Far below, the first cluster of men heard the two gunshots and turned away from the mine to head toward the mountain. Minutes later the second column of men turned and did the same.

Far above on the mountain there was only an unbroken stretch of silence.

"What was that, Ma?" Cody tugged on his mother's sleeve. "It sounded like gunshots."

"I heard them, Cody." Cara clutched her arms around herself as each gunshot echoed off the mountain peaks and seemed to reverberate through her body, causing a series of tremors along her spine.

"Do you think they spotted Yale?" The boy's voice was a frightened whisper.

"No. Of course not. He said he'd be careful." But her words lacked conviction even to her own ears.

She and the children had been deep in the mine

shaft since early in the morning. Without the comfort of a fire for warmth and light, the cold and darkness seemed to close around her, chilling her to her very soul.

Seth started to cry.

At once Cody said, "He's afraid, Ma."

"Here, now." Cara reached down and gathered the little boy into her arms, wrapping the heavy shawl around him. "I think it's time for another story."

She reached out into the darkness until she felt her older son's hand. With an arm around his shoulder she drew him close. "Why don't I tell you about Jonah and the whale. Now there was a desperate situation. I'll bet it was even darker in the belly of that whale than it is in here. And think how lucky we are. We have one another. Poor Jonah was all alone."

While the children clung to her in the darkness, she told them, in whispered tones, the familiar story. And though it was her intention to help them find strength from the tale, she feared her own faith was faltering.

The sounds they'd heard had been unmistakably gunshots. Two of them. Had Yale been merely using the signal to lead Fenner and his band on a merry chase? Or was he even now lying dead or wounded somewhere? What if he needed her, and she was too timid to go after him?

Yale had ordered her to stay with the children. Of

course, he had also given her his word that he would return.

She prayed he was strong enough to keep that promise. And that she wouldn't be playing a fool's game if she kept hers.

Chapter Eleven

Cara and the children lay huddled together, wrapped in the bearskin for warmth. She had no way of knowing how long they had been hiding deep in the mine shaft. In the pitch blackness, day and night seemed to blur together, leaving her brain as sluggish as her body.

She knew that she'd dozed several times, as had Cody and Seth. When they weren't sleeping, they kept up their strength by nibbling on pieces of deer meat. To hold their fears at bay she told them stories. As many as she could recall. But as the hours dragged on she had to work harder to keep up their spirits. And her own.

Where was Yale? What if he had been captured? Or worse, killed. The thought of him lying somewhere in this wilderness caused such a pain around her heart, she found herself pressing a hand to her chest and taking quick, shallow breaths.

For the sake of the children she managed to hold back the panic for what seemed an eternity. Suddenly she knew she couldn't take another minute in this place. Yale had called it a tomb. That's what it felt like to her. A black, bottomless pit, closing in on her. Trapping her within its icy walls of timber and rock and earth when she tried to break away. She could almost feel it closing in around her, collapsing into itself and sealing them in forever.

With a cry of terror she jerked up. The children, lying on either side of her, stirred.

"What is it, Ma?" Cody asked in whispered tones.

"We're leaving here." She scrambled to her feet. "I want the two of you to take hold of my skirts so we don't get separated in the dark."

The boys stood up and did as they were told, clinging tightly to her skirts. Cara folded the hide over her arm and, using one hand to feel along the dirt wall of the mine, began making her way toward the entrance.

When at last they came to the spot where the gap in the timbers afforded a little light, Cara breathed a sigh of relief. Even though the daylight had faded to early evening, it wasn't yet dark.

"Cody." She tossed the fur in the back of the cart, then reached a hand to the horse, tethered nearby. "We're going to need old Sadie to help us roll aside those boulders at the entrance."

The boy's eyes widened. "We're going out there, where the bad men are?"

"That's right."

"But what about Yale?" he asked.

"We have to search for him."

"You think he's been shot, Ma?" Cody hadn't moved.

"I don't know what to think. But I do believe he should have been back here by now. So it's time we went looking for him." She led the mare to the entrance, then tied the harness around the first boulder. While Cody and Seth gently coaxed the horse forward, Cara strained behind the rock until it had rolled far enough to allow them to pass through. Then she did the same with the next boulder, and the next; rubbing her hands raw, leaning every bit of her strength into the effort until the entrance was cleared.

"Good work, boys." Cara wiped her bloody hands on her skirt, ignoring the pain of her torn flesh. "Now let's get Sadie hitched to this cart."

Mother and sons worked quickly, easing the leather over the mare's head, hitching the cart to the harness. When they were through, Cody helped his little brother into the back while Cara climbed up to the seat and flicked the reins.

"How do you know where to go, Ma?" Cody asked.

"I don't. But we have to begin somewhere. We'll use those mountains as our compass."

Minutes later they started out, keeping the peaks of the brooding Black Hills always before them.

Yale put one foot in front of the other and forced himself to keep walking. He'd managed to climb down from the mountain peak, though he didn't know how. At first he'd feared that his wounded body would refuse to move. The sight of all that blood had him wondering how he could possibly still be alive.

And then there was Slick. He couldn't allow the outlaw to fire off another shot. Even in his befuddled state, Yale knew that two shots had already been fired. If there were no more, Fenner and his men would think it was the signal they'd been waiting for.

He'd drawn his knife, intending to fight to the death. But when he'd pounced on the old outlaw, Yale realized that Slick was already dead. His single shot had found its mark. Though for the life of him he could barely recall firing his gun.

He'd experienced one quick moment of triumph, knowing he'd been given a second chance. Fenner and his men would already be riding to the other side of this mountain range, just in time to follow the wrong man in the wrong cart. By the time they discovered their mistake, he and Cara and the children could be gone.

If he lived long enough to get back to them.

He'd tied his shirt around his chest, hoping to stem the flow of blood. Gingerly touching a hand to the spot he realized the shirt was soaked with his blood. And still the wound continued to bleed. Unless he made it back soon, it would be too late. He'd surely bleed to death. And if he did, what would happen to Cara and the children?

The thought of them was what kept him going. One more step, he told himself. Just one more. And though his mind had gone numb, and his body was one aching mass of pain, he forced himself to keep putting one foot in front of the other, walking toward the mine in the distance.

"What's that, Ma?" Cody pointed. "Up ahead."

Cara lifted a hand to shade the setting sun from her eyes and could see something along the trail. It appeared to be a man leaning against a rock, but it was impossible to tell, since the figure was nearly doubled over.

Handing the reins to her son, Cara took aim with her rifle. Her hands were trembling as they drew near. Whoever this was, he didn't even react to the approach of a horse and cart. He seemed not to even hear them until they were nearly on top of him.

And then she saw his head come up. Saw his hand go to the pistol at his hip.

"Yale." She set aside the rifle and leapt from the cart before her son could even bring the horse to a halt.

"Oh, Yale." Inches from him she stopped and let out a cry at the sight of all that blood.

"Cara?" His eyes couldn't seem to focus. He could see someone standing in front of him, but except for the voice, he had no way of knowing her. "Is it you, Cara?"

"It's me, Yale."

He kept a death grip on the edge of rock, afraid

if he let go he'd find himself sprawled in the dirt. "Why aren't you at the mine?"

"I was worried about you."

He managed a quick smile that tugged at her heartstrings. "No need to worry... Doing just fine." Suddenly his face lost all its color and he felt himself stumble.

Cara made a grab for him, and he leaned his full weight into her. She nearly fell over backwards, but managed to dig in her heels and wrap one of his arms around her shoulders.

"Cody," she shouted. "Bring the cart."

It was no easy matter getting Yale into the back of the cart. He kept stumbling like a drunken cowboy, taking her along with him. But finally, with the help of both her children, Cara managed to settle him into the nest of furs.

He wrapped an arm around her, pulling her close. "...can't see you. But I can smell you." He breathed her in and the grin was back. "...love the sound of your voice. It always makes me think of..." His hand went slack. His eyes seemed to roll back in his head.

Seeing it, Cara felt her heart stop. When she found his feeble, thready heartbeat, she forced herself into action. She climbed up to the hard seat and took up the reins. Turning the horse and cart toward the mine she whipped the mare into a run.

When they reached the entrance to the mine, there was no time to get Yale out of the cart. Instead, she climbed in beside him and tore away his shirt. At the sight of the bloody wound, she gasped in horror.

"I'll need water, Seth. Cody, give me a hand turning Yale. I need to see if that bullet came out, or if it's still lodged in his body."

Both Cara and her son were sweating by the time they'd managed to lift and then turn the unconscious figure. The torn, jagged flesh in his back told her the bullet had gone clear through.

"He must have been shot at close range," she muttered as she began washing away the blood. "I wonder why the shooter didn't finish the job?"

"Maybe he thought Yale was already dead." Cody knelt beside his mother, holding a blackened pot filled with water from their canteen.

Cara lifted her skirts and removed her petticoat, tearing it into strips which she used to bind the wound tightly. Then, lifting Yale's head, she forced several drops of water between his parched lips.

When she covered him with the hide, he lay as still as death.

For several long minutes she watched the uneven rise and fall of his chest, willing him to live.

Then, because she had no idea where Fenner and his gang might be, she led the horse inside the mine where she unhitched the cart. With the help of old Sadie she and her sons struggled for another hour to return all the boulders and brush to the entrance, until she was satisfied that their hiding place wouldn't be visible to anyone riding by.

Little Seth shivered in the gloom of the mine.

Seeing it, Cara wrapped an arm around him. "You're cold, aren't you?"

The little boy nodded.

"And hungry, I bet." Cara drew him close and pressed a kiss to his forehead. "Thank heavens for the deer Yale was able to trap."

She portioned out the venison to the children, then passed around the canteen of water. Afterward she made them a cozy bed using the deer hide to buffer the cold earth, and her shawl and Yale's coat for cover.

As she bundled the children and knelt to kiss them good-night, Cody gave voice to the fear that was in all their hearts.

"Will Yale die, Ma?"

"No, son. He's strong. He'll fight to stay alive."

"Wasn't Pa strong?"

Cara sighed. "Yes, your pa was a strong man. But he was much older than Yale. And his injuries much more serious."

Cody's voice was hushed in the darkness. "Would Pa have lived if we'd found him sooner?"

"We'll never know, Cody. But we can be content with the fact that we did everything we could to find him."

"Just like we found Yale," Cody said.

"Yes." For Cara it was a startling revelation. Had she been thinking about Wyatt when she went in search of Yale? Not consciously, of course. But it seemed reasonable now to concede that his death had been hovering on the edges of her mind. Why else would she have risked her life and that of her children, leaving the safety of the mine to search for him, when he'd expressly told her to stay hidden?

Maybe she thought of this as a second chance. A chance to be in time to save a life.

Later, when the children were finally asleep, Cara climbed into the back of the cart and touched a hand to Yale's forehead. He was burning with fever.

If they were back at her cabin, she would have had so many things to comfort him and speed his healing. Lye soap, to disinfect the wound. Laudanum and whiskey to ease the pain. Chicken broth simmering over a cozy fire. A soft feather bed and even softer blankets, which she'd spun from the wool of a nearby rancher's sheep.

But all of that was lost to her now. All she had was a cold dark mine shaft, and a scant supply of food and water. If Yale's wounds began bleeding she couldn't even tend to them until morning. Now, with what little moonlight managed to filter through the timbers and rocks above, she could barely make out his face. But she could see his grimace of pain, and it twisted a knife in her own heart.

"Oh, Yale." She lay down beside him and brushed damp hair from his forehead. "Please stay with us. We need you." She brushed a kiss over his cheek and felt a sudden rush of tears. "I need you. I've waited a lifetime for you. Now that you're finally here with me, please don't go."

"Not going..." He sucked in a quick breath on the white hot pain and waited until it subsided before adding, "Staying here. Right here. With you, Cara."

"Oh, my darling." She couldn't help herself. Just hearing his voice had the tears welling up and spilling over. "Oh, I'm so glad I went after you."

"Not half as glad as…" The rogue's smile was still on his lips as he drifted back into oblivion.

Cara sat with Yale throughout the night, pressing cool wet cloths to his fevered flesh, soothing him with soft words and whispered promises whenever he moaned and writhed in pain. The worst time for her was when he fell into a deep sleep, struggling for every breath, his pulse thin and reedy. It tore at her heart to see this strong, reckless man so still and quiet. For as long as she'd known him, he had always been in motion. Striding along the main street in Misery, with that cocky, careless attitude that stirred every woman's heart. Or riding bareback across the hills, taking risks no other man would have ever considered.

Now he was barely clinging to life. And there was nothing she could do but watch and wait.

She hated this feeling of helplessness. But the more she railed against it, the more frustrated she became.

Exhausted, she lay beside him.

Drained, she found solace in sleep.

Chapter Twelve

Yale lay as still as death. Every breath burned his throat. Even the simple task of opening his eyes brought a blinding flash of pain behind his lids. His body was on fire.

Hadn't he always known that he'd burn in hell? Why then was he surprised by this? He supposed he ought to accept his punishment as his due. Still, it wasn't in his nature to acquiesce. He was a fighter. And had been all his life.

Despite the stab of pain he opened one eye, then the other, determined to have a look around this den of torture where he'd be spending eternity.

What he saw had his heartbeat speeding up considerably. Lying beside him was Cara. Her long, dark hair was a riot of tangles that spilled over one cheek. Her gown, torn and dirty, had ridden up to reveal a good deal of shapely ankle and calf. The front of her dress was slightly open, revealing the darkened cleft between her breasts. The sight had his eyes narrowing. And though it cost him considerably more pain, he had to reach over and touch her, just to assure himself that he wasn't dreaming.

She lifted her head and was startled to see him awake.

"Yale. Oh, thank heaven. You're alive." She shoved the hair from her eyes and sat up. "I...must have fallen asleep."

"You've been here beside me all night?"

She nodded. "I was afraid to leave you for even a moment. You were burning up with fever." She brought her hand to his forehead. But as she did, he suddenly frowned and caught her hand in his and turned it palm up for his inspection.

His voice was a low growl that might have been pain or anger. "How did you do this?"

She stared at her torn, bloody flesh before shrugging. "It's nothing."

"Nothing?" His tone deepened.

"I had to remove the boulders from the mine entrance before we could go searching for you. Then last night, when we returned, I needed to put them back in place, in case Fenner's gang should come back."

"Oh, my poor Cara." He brought her hand to his lips and pressed a kiss to the palm.

She felt the most amazing rush of heat and snatched her hand away in embarrassment. But it was impossible to hide her feelings. They were there in her eyes. In the high color on her cheeks. In the way her breath hitched once, twice, before she was able to control it.

"You're freezing." He lifted the edge of the fur to share his warmth, but her blush only deepened. It was then that he realized he was naked. His tone warmed with humor. "It appears somebody stole my clothes. Who do you think it could be?"

"I had no choice, Yale." She turned her head, avoiding his eyes. "You were bleeding so badly."

He caught her chin, forcing her to look at him. "I bet you're going to tell me you never looked, aren't you?"

She couldn't help laughing as she pushed his hand aside. "You're the most irreverent man I've ever known. Do you need anything?"

"Cara. Such a question. Especially when you're addressing a man with no clothes."

"Oh." She stood up, shaking down her skirts. "You're incorrigible, Yale."

"Also indecent. But exceedingly grateful to you for all you did." He ran a tongue over his dry lips. "Could I have some water?"

"Of course." Relieved to have something to distract him from his teasing she hurried away and returned with the canteen. Kneeling beside him she lifted his head, pillowing it in her lap, before holding the canteen to his lips. When he signaled that he'd had enough she set it aside.

He looked up, searching her face. Despite his pain, the devil was in his eyes. "Careful, Cara. If you keep on treating me like this, I might learn to like it."

It occurred to her that she might discover the

same thing. The nearness of this man had her heart working overtime, and her imagination, as well.

"Are you in pain, Yale?"

He gave one slight nod of his head, but it was enough to tell her that he was fighting for control.

Her voice trembled with feeling. "I have nothing to give you. No laudanum, no tea. Not even a drop of whiskey."

"Don't worry, Cara. I'll get through it. As long as you're here."

"Oh, Yale." She touched a hand to his forehead, brushing away the damp hair that curled there. "I was so afraid. Afraid that I'd be too late. Afraid that I wouldn't find you, or if I did, afraid of what I'd find."

"You saved my life, Cara. I kept thinking I'd make it back to you, but I know now that would have been impossible. If it weren't for you, I'd still be lying out there."

She touched a finger to his lips to silence him. "Shh. I can't bear to think of it. Close your eyes now, Yale, and rest."

"I don't think I have a choice."

He did as she asked. But the image of her, honey eyes narrowed with concern, and the touch of her, as gentle as a snowflake, stayed with him as he drifted into sleep.

Yale opened his eyes in the thin light of evening, filtering through the mine's timbers. The moment he did he heard Cody's voice calling, "Ma. Yale's awake."

Cara and her younger son hurried over to kneel beside him.

While Seth and Cody lifted his head, Cara held the canteen to his lips for a long, soothing drink of water.

When he'd had enough he gave them all a smile. "Thank you. I don't know what to make of this. I've never been taken care of before."

"Never?" Cara couldn't hide her shock at such a statement.

He shook his head. "I've always been the one taking care of others. After my ma died, I knew it would be up to me to steal enough food to keep us all alive."

"You stole?" Cody's eyes went wide.

"I'm not proud of it, Cody." Yale felt like squirming, but he knew he had to be honest with these boys. They deserved that much. "We were three kids, hardly older than you and Seth. My brother, Gabe, was too straight-arrow to ever steal, even to save his own life. So I knew it was up to me to do whatever was necessary to keep the three of us alive."

"You didn't have any ma or pa?" the boy asked.

"Our ma died along the trail. Our pa…" He glanced at Cara, then away. "Our pa was somewhere in the Badlands. That's all we knew. But I wasn't about to let my brother and sister die in that wasteland. Not without doing everything I could to save them. So I stole what we needed. Milk, meat. I'd have taken more if there had been more to take.''

"Didn't you have a home?" It was plain that Cody was caught up in Yale's story.

Yale shook his head. "We'd lived with my grandfather for awhile. But when he died, and things got tense between my mother and uncle, we left to find my father. The trail was our home until we came upon an old man named Aaron Smiler. He took us in. My sister, Kitty, still lives there.''

"Why'd you leave?" Cody asked.

Yale glanced once at Cara's face, then away. "It was time. I had to find out what I wanted to do with my life. And I decided that I didn't want to live it in Misery.''

"Did you miss it after you left?"

Yale nodded. "Yeah. More than I'd expected to. And most of all I missed the people. At least some of them.''

Cara's face was flaming as she said to her children, "All right. That's enough questions for now. Yale needs his sleep if he's to heal.''

"Do you need anything?" Cody asked.

Yale smiled. "Nothing. But it's nice to know I have so many good people looking out for me.''

The children were beaming with pride as they left him to his rest.

"How long have I been asleep this time?" Yale had lost track of the number of times he'd awakened.

Each time, Cara and the boys had gathered around him, helping him eat and drink, changing the strips of cloth that bound his wounds.

And each time, he realized, his pain seemed a little more tolerable. Or maybe he was just growing accustomed to it.

"You slept most of the last day and night."

He ran a hand through the rough stubble of dark beard that covered his chin. "What did you and the boys do while I slept?"

"They've done some digging, and pocketed a few more nuggets. I managed to wash your clothes, though I'm afraid the bloodstains were impossible to remove. And we've told plenty of stories."

"Any sign of Fenner's gang?"

"So far there's been none."

He held out a hand. "Help me to sit up."

She shook her head. "It's too soon, Yale. You'll cause your wound to bleed again."

"I can't stay here." He took her hand, forcing her to help him to a sitting position.

For a few moments his vision blurred as the figures before him spun and danced in dizzying circles. Then slowly the images came into focus.

He saw the color riding high on Cara's cheeks and realized that the fur covering had slipped to his hips. He managed to keep himself decently covered, though his chest was bare.

Cara studied the sweat that beaded his forehead, to avoid staring at the hair-roughened chest that had her pulse racing. "You're in pain, Yale."

He nodded. "Some. But I need to start moving, or I'll soon be too weak to get up off this pallet."

"Give yourself a little more time."

"Time." He ran a hand through his hair in frustration. "I managed to send Fenner and his men off on a wild-goose chase, buying us time to escape, and now I've squandered our precious time."

"You can't think of it that way. Thanks to you we're safe for now. That's all that matters."

He saw the fatigue in her eyes and caught one of her hands in his, holding it up for his inspection. "At least the time hasn't all been a waste. I see they're healing nicely."

She nodded and snatched her hand away, feeling the familiar rush of heat at his touch. "They're good as new. Now would you like some meat and water?"

"What I'd like is beef and biscuits and eggs." He frowned. "And some coffee."

For the first time Cara smiled as she got to her feet. "Do you hear yourself, Yale? Now I know you're starting to feel better."

"How would you know that?"

"Because you're beginning to grumble. Men are always helpless babies when they're sick or hurting. But when they start to feel better, they just have to grumble. About the food. About the lumpy bed. Next you'll be telling me that you can't be cooped up in this place much longer."

Yale's smile was back. "I was just thinking that very thing. In fact, I was thinking that tomorrow we might have to leave this miserable tomb and get out into the sunshine.'' He winked at Seth. ''Want to go with me?''

The little boy grinned and turned to his brother.

Cody wasn't as easily won over as his younger brother. ''You're not even strong enough to stand up yet. What makes you think you could walk outside?''

Yale shrugged. ''I've got a gold coin that says I'll walk out of here tomorrow. What have you got to wager?''

''Yale Conover.'' There was fire in Cara's eyes, and a sharp edge to her voice that had both man and boy looking at her in surprise.

''I'll not have my son gambling. Do you hear?''

Chastised, he merely nodded. ''You're right, of course. Besides, you had no chance to win, son. I've been known to do just about anything to keep from losing a bet. Even if it opened up my wound and set me back for another day, I'd have walked out of here tomorrow if we had money riding on it.''

He could see the figures in front of him beginning to blur and shimmer. And though it was frustrating to accept any weakness in himself, he knew he had no choice. Exhausted from his efforts, he settled back down in the fur and closed his eyes. Within minutes he was fast asleep.

Cara wriggled between the boulders and shielded her eyes against the sudden stab of sunlight. Climbing to the very top of the mine, she peered in all directions, looking for any sign of horsemen. When she saw nothing, she returned to the mine.

As she stepped into the gloom and waited for her eyes to adjust, she heard Yale's voice.

"Pick a card. Any card."

Annoyed, she stepped closer, just in time to see Seth take a card from the deck Yale was holding out to him.

"Now you and Cody look at it before sticking it back in the deck."

The two children studied the card, before the little boy tucked it into the deck.

Yale shuffled and began turning over cards. Suddenly he stopped, looked at the card, and said, "This is the one. Right?"

Seth gave a gasp of surprise before nodding.

"How'd you do that?" Cody asked suspiciously.

"Maybe it's magic. Or maybe I just have a special way with cards." Yale shuffled again, then fanned out the cards and said, "Pick one, Cody."

The older boy did as he asked.

"Now you and Seth study that card really carefully."

The two children stared at the card.

"All right. Tell me what it is, then place it here, on top of the deck."

"It's the ten of diamonds," Cody said as he returned the card.

Yale set the deck down and tapped on it lightly, before turning over the top card. Instead of the ten of diamonds, it was the five of diamonds.

Both children looked astonished.

"What did you do?" Cody asked.

Yale grinned. "I think I tapped too hard. I probably knocked off a couple of spots. Let's take a look at the card beneath this one." He turned it up, revealing another five of diamonds. "Yep. That's what I did. Oh, well. Maybe I can clear this up." He turned the card over and tapped again, then flipped it to reveal the ten of diamonds.

By this time even Cara was kneeling beside her children, staring in openmouthed surprise.

"Bet you can't do that again," Cody challenged.

Yale's grin was quick and teasing. "How much would you like to bet?"

"Yale Conover."

At Cara's stern words, Yale's grin turned to a rumble of laughter. "All right. I suppose I can do this for free." He shuffled, before holding out the deck to Cara. "Pick a card and show it to all of us."

She chose the queen of hearts.

"A very good choice." Yale waited while she placed the card on the top of the deck. "But everyone knows that a queen always needs a king." He tapped the cards, then flipped the top one to reveal, not the queen, but the king of hearts.

Cara and the children were wide-eyed with wonder.

"Don't worry. I'm sure the queen is nearby." Yale tapped the deck again, before flipping the card over. It was the queen of diamonds.

He merely smiled. "I'm glad to see I haven't lost my touch with the ladies."

"Do some more," Cody said excitedly, while his little brother nodded in agreement.

"You want more, do you?" Yale glanced over their heads to Cara, who was doing her best to look disapproving. But it was impossible for her to hide her fascination.

"All right. Just a few more." Yale forced his attention back to the cards.

It wasn't easy. Having Cara so close was definitely a distraction.

Now that his wounds were healing, he was finding the close confines of this little mine almost impossible to tolerate. At night, while she and the children slept just an arm's length away, he found himself unable to sleep for the wanting. She had become a hunger in his soul. A hunger he wanted desperately to feed.

He held out the deck to Seth. "Go ahead and pick a card."

After showing it to his mother and brother the little boy placed it in the middle of the deck. Yale shuffled the cards, then began slowly turning them over, one after the other. By the time he'd turned over the last card, they were all watching him with matching looks of puzzlement.

"Hmm. Something strange is happening here," he muttered. "Looks like your card is hiding on us, Seth." Just then he looked up with a little frown. "Don't move."

The little boy's eyes went wide.

Yale leaned closed, and plucked the card from behind Seth's ear. ''Well, here's where it was hiding.''

Delighted, the little boy clapped his hands and Cody said, ''He wants you to do it again.''

''I'll try. But these pesky little cards are just full of tricks.'' With a wink in Cara's direction he began shuffling, before holding out the deck to her youngest son. ''Let's see what happens this time.''

Cara sat back, letting the sound of her children's laughter wash over her. How long had it been since they'd laughed like this?

Oh, the sound was doing the most wonderful things to her heart.

''Wait a minute.'' Yale leaned over and removed the jack of clubs from behind Cody's head, sending the two boys into gales of laughter.

Cara sighed. Despite the sense of danger about him, with that full growth of dark beard and his hair long enough to brush his shoulders, not to mention that roguish smile, Yale was so natural with her children. So relaxed and funny. How she loved him for it.

Love.

She felt her heart hitch at the thought.

She'd loved him all her life. But if she hadn't loved him before this, she would surely fall in love all over again, if for no other reason than because of the tender way he treated her two lonely children. Was it because he'd known that same kind of loneliness in his childhood? He seemed to have a special gift for reaching deep inside himself and knowing just what these two needed.

Or was it because, beneath that tough, irreverent face he showed the world, he simply had a kind and generous heart?

Whatever his secrets, whatever sort of life he'd lived until now, she knew without a doubt that she still loved him. She'd been a good wife to Wyatt. But her heart had always belonged to the wild reckless boy of her childhood.

Now more than ever.

Chapter Thirteen

"Yale." Cara nearly dropped the torch she'd been carrying when she caught sight of him, dressed in his black boots and pants and coat, making his way slowly toward the entrance of the mine. "What do you think you're doing?"

He stopped long enough to give her one of those long, appraising looks that always made her heartbeat quicken. "It's time I got up and moving again, Cara."

"But your wound is barely healed."

"I can't lie in that nest of furs another day. Not that I haven't enjoyed being pampered." He shot her a quick, dangerous smile. "But a man could get a little too accustomed to that kind of treatment. Now it's time for me to test my strength."

"At least give yourself one more day, Yale."

"I'd like to give myself a lifetime of it." He tugged on a dark curl, enjoying the flush that stole over her cheeks. "But it's time, Cara." Though he knew the children were watching, he couldn't resist touching his hand to her cheek for a moment before turning away. "I won't be long."

"Where are you going?"

"Outside to have a look around."

Cody stepped forward. "Can I go with you?"

Yale was about to agree, for he'd enjoy the company. But he saw the fear that leapt into Cara's eyes and took pity on her.

"Sorry, son. I think I'd better handle this first time out alone, just to see what's out there."

Seeing the way the little boy fought back tears he clamped a hand on his shoulder. "Tell you what, Cody. If I determine that it's safe, I'll take you and Seth with me tomorrow." He stuck out his hand. "Deal?"

The light was back in the little boy's eyes as he placed his hand in Yale's. "Yes, sir. Deal."

With Cara looking on, the two shook hands. Then Yale turned to Seth and shook his hand, as well.

Without another word he turned away and slipped between the boulders at the entrance, leaving them alone in the gloom.

The next hours seemed to drag, and it occurred to Cara that she and the children had become spoiled with Yale around to lift their spirits with his card tricks and silly jokes. He was such fun to be around, with his good humor and absurd sense of irreverence. It was easy to see why he had managed to become a larger-than-life figure to all who'd met him. He had such a zest for life.

When had the joy gone out of her own life? Had

it been when Wyatt had died? Or had it been much sooner? It pained her to think about the carefree, happy girl she'd been, and the tired, fearful woman she'd become. She held out her hands, studying the ragged nails, the torn, sun-baked flesh.

Once she had wept over a silly hair comb. Now she had two children whose very lives depended on her. They knew she loved them. But did she take the time to laugh with them? To think about their hopes and dreams for the future?

The future. She sighed. Right now it took all her energy to concentrate on the here and now. But if they should come out of this alive...when they came out of this alive, she mentally corrected, she vowed to spend more time with Cody and Seth.

As the sun climbed higher in the sky, she found all her good intentions fading as she began fearing the worst. What if Yale had come upon the Fenner gang? What if he'd fallen and opened up his wound? He could even now be bleeding to death somewhere beyond their reach. She should have insisted on going along with him. But then she would have had to bring the children as well, putting them at risk.

Maybe she should have permitted Cody to go with him. But her fears would have been doubled, and by now she would be making herself sick with worry.

She stood by the entrance, peering into the distance. Where was he? Oh, why had he left them yet again?

As always, the minute Yale was out of her sight,

the doubts and fears began to creep in. Doubts about his character. He was such a careless man. Careless with his own life, and careless with those who depended on him. Wasn't that how he'd chosen to live his life? Wandering from town to town, indulging his own pleasure? When would she ever learn not to be fooled by that smile, that charming manner?

A shadow fell over the entrance and she looked up to see Yale striding toward her.

"What's this?" As he pushed through the boulders, Cara stared in disbelief as he deposited sacks of flour and sugar at her feet.

"While I was surveying the countryside I thought I smelled smoke. And where there's smoke there's usually food." Yale emptied his pockets of half a dozen eggs and a canteen filled with milk. "So I went to investigate and found a miner's cabin a few miles over the ridge. There was nobody around, which means he was working deep in his mine. But there was a fire burning on the hearth, and so many sacks of supplies in the back room, he'll never even miss these."

"You…stole these?"

"I just borrowed them." He gave her that quick smile and decided not to mention the money he'd left on the miner's bunk. "I'm getting a little rusty. Haven't had to use that particular skill for some time now."

She was staring at the supplies as though they were sacks of gold. And despite her disapproval of the fact that they were ill-gotten goods, she couldn't ignore the hunger pangs.

"Oh, Yale. Flour and sugar. We can have biscuits. And eggs and..." She opened a small parcel and breathed in the wonderful fragrance of coffee beans. "Oh, my." She could have wept with pleasure. "Coffee."

His smile was as wide as hers. "Yeah. I figured, as long as I was helping myself to his things, I may as well go all the way."

"Do you think we can risk a fire?"

"We're going to risk more than that. I think we should eat in the open air, and sleep out there, too." He turned to the two boys who had raced up to stand beside their mother. "How about it? Want to breathe fresh air while we enjoy a picnic, and then sleep under the stars?"

"Can we, Ma?" Cody asked.

She looked from one son to the other, noting that both their eyes wore matching looks of pleading. She turned to Yale. "Do you really think it's safe?"

He shrugged. "There you go, asking me to look into the future again. Who's to say what's safe? In the mine, we're hidden from view. That keeps us safe from outlaws and drifters. But the rotten timbers could always collapse, trapping us inside. Or we could sleep outside tonight, and risk finding ourselves surrounded by Fenner's men in the morning."

Seeing her quick flash of fear he touched a hand to her face. "But if it'll make you feel better, I'll stay awake all night and keep watch."

"You will not." She pulled away. "You're still recovering from a grave wound. If anyone is going to keep watch, it'll be me." She turned to her children. "Gather up the furs and put them in the cart. As soon as we can load up everything, we'll leave this place and…" For the first time her smile bloomed. "…breathe fresh air."

"We're really leaving here, Ma?" Cody hadn't moved.

"Yes, honey. We're really leaving here."

"And we're going to have a…" He struggled to remember what Yale had called it. "…a picnic?"

"We are indeed."

The two boys' smiles rivaled the sun as they raced around the mine snatching up the deer hide and the bearskin, shaking them as their mother always did before folding them into the back of the cart.

Within a short time they had the horse hitched and all the supplies loaded. Yale rolled aside the heavy boulders, while Cody led the horse through the opening. Outside they breathed in the fresh air, before following Yale as he led them across a rocky hill. On the far side was a grassy meadow. They crossed it until they came to a stream.

While Cody tended the horse, Yale and Seth hunted up enough wood for a fire, leaving Cara to sort through her supplies. When the dough was set to rise, she studied Cody and Seth, splashing on the banks of the stream.

They were so happy to be out in the sunshine, free to run and play again. There'd been so little of that in their lives. Since the loss of their father they had known only hard work, as they accompanied their mother each day on the endless rounds of ranch chores. Just the sight of them playing and laughing together had her heart lifting.

It seemed no time at all before the fire was blazing, and the air was perfumed with the delicious scent of eggs sizzling, biscuits baking and coffee simmering. After so many days of nothing but dried meat and water, this was a feast. They sat around the fire eating their fill.

After so many nights spent in a cold dark mine shaft, the heat from a roaring fire, and the warmth of sunlight on their faces had their spirits as high as children at Christmas.

"Well now." Yale bit into his third biscuit and washed it down with a second steaming cup of coffee. He glanced at Seth. "Do you know how lucky you are to have a mama who can cook like this?"

The little boy smiled shyly and nodded. And then, without realizing it, moved closer.

If Yale was surprised he didn't let on. "These are just about the finest biscuits I've ever tasted. And this coffee..." He leaned his back against a fallen log and sipped. "There are men who would give up their ranch and their entire herd of cattle for coffee this good."

Cody gave a snort of laughter. "You're teasing us again, aren't you, Yale?"

"Not this time." Yale looked beyond the boy to where Cara sat, looking pleased and embarrassed.

"Why, I could probably even give up a life of gambling for a woman who could cook like this."

Clearly intrigued, Cody swallowed his last bite of egg. "If you gave up gambling, what would you do?"

"I'd probably just sit around all day eating and drinking until I got so fat I couldn't get up off my chair."

That had Seth and Cody giggling at the image of this lean, muscled man turning soft and plump.

Timidly Seth shifted closer. It seemed the most natural thing in the world for Yale to lift his arm and tuck the little boy close to his side. And just as natural for Seth to curl up against him.

Yale winked at Cara. "And finally, I would just eat so much I'd explode. And everybody would be talking about the time old Yale Conover erupted like a volcano, and bits and pieces of him floated all over town."

"Could that happen?" Cody asked.

Yale shrugged. "I don't know. But if your mama keeps on cooking like this, we may find out soon enough. You might see my ear flying over the Black Hills. My beard floating in the stream. My boots soaring all the way to California."

The children giggled.

"Nobody could ever go that far." Cody sighed. "But I sure would love to see California."

"It's a pretty enough place." Yale drained his coffee. "But it can't hold a candle to the Dakota territory."

"You've been there?" The little boy's attention was suddenly riveted on Yale's face.

"That's right." He smiled. "You thinking of going when you grow up?"

"Yes, sir. I guess I'd do just about anything to see California."

"Why is that, Cody?"

The boy looked pensive a moment. "My pa told me he always wanted to go there. And I thought…" He glanced at his mother, then away. "…I thought maybe I'd go for my pa."

"That's a nice dream, Cody." Yale set aside his cup and leaned back, stretching out his long legs toward the fire while folding one arm behind his head, keeping the other tucked around Seth. "Dreams are good. They make us stretch and grow and try for things we want and don't have. Just be sure it's your dream, and not somebody else's."

"Why?" The little boy wasn't even aware that he had stretched out his legs and folded his hands behind his head, in imitation of the man beside him.

"Because it takes an awful lot of time and energy to chase a dream. And sometimes when we catch it, we find it wasn't at all what we wanted. It can make a body feel downright foolish to realize he's chased the wrong dream, when the one he wanted was within his grasp all along."

"How will I know if it's the right dream for me?"

Yale shrugged. "Everybody has to find his own. Just don't let anybody else tell you what you ought to want. Nobody else can know what's in your heart, Cody. Only you. You remember that.''

"Yes, sir.'' The little boy stifled a yawn.

Cara watched and listened in silence, fighting the lump in her throat that was threatening to choke her. There were so many raw emotions twisting inside her. The thought of her own girlish dreams that had been trampled and tossed to the wind. She'd long ago stopped believing in dreams. Had even forgotten to encourage her own sons to follow their dreams. But here was Yale, reminding her again of the feelings she'd known in her childhood, and stirring hope in her sons' hearts.

Her sons. She'd never believed they could be this relaxed, this carefree again. When she saw Yale pick up a sleeping Seth and cradle him in his big arms, she felt her heart almost bursting with love.

Yale turned to Cody. "How would you and your brother like to sleep right here tonight, under the stars, warmed by the fire?''

"I'd like that.''

"Just unroll the bearskin and we'll have you tucked in before you know it.''

"Yes, sir.'' Cody did as he asked, setting the fur in the grass and settling himself beside his sleeping brother.

Cara crossed to them and knelt to press kisses to their cheeks.

"Good night, Cody,'' she whispered.

"Good night, Ma.'' The boy looked beyond her to the man who knelt beside her. "'Night, Yale.''

"Good night, Cody."

While Cara remained beside them, hearing Cody's prayers, Yale walked to the far side of the fire and pulled a cigar from his pocket. Holding a flaming stick to the end, he drew in smoke, then expelled it, sending a rich fragrant cloud curling over his head.

Cara walked up beside him. "Thank you for today, Yale. It was such a special gift."

"It was special for me, too. I wasn't sure I could take one more night in that cold dark mine."

She smiled. "Truthfully, neither did I. It wasn't just the food and the fresh air that made this so special. I thank you for the kindness you've shown Cody and Seth."

"That's easy. They're wonderful boys, Cara. You've done a fine job with them."

She looked down at her hands, twisting nervously. "They've had a hard life. Especially since losing their father. I feel so badly about Cody. He tries to make it up to Seth. To draw his little brother out of his fears. But I know he's as worried about Seth as I am."

"He'll be fine, Cara. He has a strong mother. And a very brave brother. In time, he'll get his voice back."

"Do you think so?"

He nodded. "I do. We all have to grieve in our own way. When I lost my ma, I was angry. And I started breaking all the rules. Maybe that was how I figured to even the score. Maybe it's the same for

Seth. Maybe he isn't so much afraid as he is angry that his pa's been taken away. This is how he can deal with it. By living in a silent world." His voice lowered. "How about you, Cara? How are you handling it?"

She shook her head. "There's been little time for grief. With Wyatt gone, I just never seemed able to keep up with all the chores. Sometimes I feel as though I haven't taken a single moment to catch my breath."

"Maybe this is a good time to start." He reached into his pocket and held something out to her.

She glanced up at him. "What's this?"

"Soap. I figured, since I was helping myself to so much in that miner's cabin, I might as well take a few luxuries as well." He motioned toward the stream, its water glistening in the moonlight. "Why don't you take some time for yourself, while I stay here and keep an eye on the children."

"You don't mind?"

He shook his head and began slipping out of his coat, draping it around her shoulders. "You'd better take this along. It'll be cold when you step out of the water."

She felt the warmth of his touch and shivered. But when she lifted her face to his her smile was radiant. "Oh, Yale. A bath." Her laughter trilled on the night air as she danced lightly away.

It was such a simple thing, Cara thought as she stepped out of her gown and dropped it into the shallows. A bath was something she'd long taken for granted. But since they'd been on the run, she'd given up hoping for such a thing. And now, with food in her stomach and her children safely tucked into their bed, it had become the finest luxury.

She untied the ribbons of her chemise, and dropped it alongside the gown. Then she sat in the shallows and soaped herself all over, taking time to work up a lather in her hair. She walked into the water, loving the way it lapped at her hips, then higher, covering her breasts. Suddenly she ducked beneath the waves, rinsing her hair until all the soap had floated away. Then, gasping for breath, she came up for air.

Oh, it was so delicious to lie back and float, letting the water take her. She felt weightless. As free as a leaf on the current. The stars overhead were glittering diamonds in a velvet sky. And all of them shining on her. The moonlight cast ribbons of gold across the water, lighting her path.

When she grew tired of floating she rolled over and began to swim in long, smooth strokes toward shore. Once there she soaped her clothes and rinsed them thoroughly before wringing out the water. Then she set them out to dry on low-hanging branches.

Shivering, she pulled on Yale's black coat and held it around her as she danced through the grass toward their camp.

Yale sat with his back against a still-warm rock and exhaled a cloud of rich smoke. He was feeling mellow. A good meal and a cozy fire had a way of doing that to a man.

Of course, it might have something to do with the fact that Cara was back in his life. There hadn't been much time to think about that, until the shooting. While he'd been lying there, in and out of consciousness, there'd been nothing else to do but think.

He was a man who'd never put much stock in fate. He believed that every person had to chart his own course and live with the decisions he made. Good or bad, he'd been living with his since he'd been not much older than Cody and Seth.

But all of a sudden he found himself questioning everything he'd ever believed. What else could explain what was happening here? The woman he'd loved for a lifetime was here with him. They were being given a second chance at happiness. It had to be fated. He'd be a fool not to take advantage of it.

He heard the soft footfall and turned to watch her as she made her way toward him.

Once, on a dare from Gabe, he'd climbed on the back of Aaron Smiler's bull. He'd made it halfway across the field before the bull twisted, rolled, and sent him flying through the air to land with a thud on the hard-packed earth, where he'd had all the wind knocked out of him.

He felt that way now as he watched Cara walk toward him.

Her hair, slick and wet, fanned out around her, dripping with starlight. Though his coat covered her from shoulders to hips, her long, shapely legs were clearly visible. And though she kept one hand at the lapels to hold it closed, he could see the dark cleft between her breasts. His throat went dry at the sight.

"Oh, Yale. I feel so clean and fresh and alive, thanks to you." She kept on walking until she was standing directly in front of him.

She placed a hand over his. "I left the soap on a flat rock on the banks of the creek. In case…" Her voice lowered. "…you'd like to use it."

"I suppose I should." He didn't move. His gaze was locked on hers.

Her eyes sparkled with moonlight. She smelled as fresh as a meadow after a rain.

He leaned close, breathing her in. Filling himself with the scent of her until he could feel his heartbeat begin to speed up.

Without realizing it his hands were in her hair, his fingers tangling as he drew her face close and covered her mouth with his in a kiss so hot, so hungry, it had them both gasping.

And then they were both lost in it. Lost in feelings that carried them along in a sudden flood of memories. Of first love, and a need so compelling, it had them by the throat, threatening to cut off their breath.

He took the kiss deeper, giving her no time to think. And as he did, his hands slipped inside the coat. Skimmed her body. That perfect, beautiful body.

"Yale." She drew back, her eyes wide. She

hadn't been surprised by the kiss. But his touch was another thing altogether. The jolt through her system had her pulling away, afraid of the feelings that were tumbling through her. Feelings that were completely out of character. There was such heat. And this sudden deep yearning for things she had thought long dead.

He lowered his hand. "Sorry."

"No. Don't be." Embarrassed, she touched a hand to the beard that covered his lower face. "It's just that I...I've thought of myself as a mother for so long, I've forgotten how to feel like a woman. But I'm...so grateful to you for reminding me..."

"Grateful?" He jerked back, stung by the words. He didn't want her gratitude. Nor did he want her to confuse that gratitude with something else.

Abruptly he turned away. "I'm going to take that bath now. You'd be wise to crawl into the bearskin with your children. You can leave my coat by the fire. I'll sleep in that tonight."

"Yale, wait..."

He was already striding toward the stream. Leaving her to stare after him in stunned surprise.

Chapter Fourteen

Cara stood as still as a statue as Yale strode off into the darkness. A jumble of emotions assaulted her. What had she done wrong? She was so unskilled in lovemaking. Though she'd been a wife, she'd hardly been a lover. Still, though she might be clumsy and untutored in the art of love, she wasn't mistaken about the way Yale felt about her. He'd made that perfectly clear any number of times.

He wanted her. And she wanted him. But now that they had the opportunity to act on their feelings, he'd rejected her. Had walked away without a backward glance.

She drew his coat around her nakedness and turned to the fire, deep in thought. She should have made it easier. Should have reached for him at the same moment he reached for her. And she shouldn't have reacted when he'd touched her. But she hadn't been able to help herself. The feel of his hands on her body had been pure heaven, igniting a firestorm of emotions that had her nearly leaping out of her skin. Even now, just thinking about it made her tremble.

Could he have mistaken her reaction for a rejection?

That didn't seem possible. Still, what had he said, in that gruff tone? She struggled to recall the words.

Grateful. He didn't want her gratitude. But why not? She was so deeply grateful to him for coming to their rescue at their time of need. It was just another reason why she loved him.

Love. Wasn't that what they both felt? What they both wanted?

She lifted her head as the realization came. Of course. It was what everyone wanted and craved. Even a proud, independent man like Yale Conover. Love. Pure and simple.

Oh, she'd spoiled everything with her foolish words. Now, somehow she had to make him understand that what she felt for him wasn't gratitude but love.

Without any idea what she would say or do she turned away from the fire and hurried toward the stream.

Yale took out his frustration on his clothes, kicking them aside, scrubbing them viciously before tossing them over the branches of a tree. Then he scrubbed his hair, his beard, his body, before storming into the deep water to rinse.

Though the water was growing cool, it wasn't enough to end his torment. What sort of fool had he become that he could believe he had any right to a woman like Cara?

She was all the things he could never be. Honest, decent. Innocent. He'd seen the shock in her eyes when she'd heard the litany of things he'd done wrong in his life. And that had been nothing compared to the shock in her eyes when he'd touched her.

She'd faced the horror of losing her husband, the difficulty of raising two children alone. Now he'd added to her distress by allowing her to confuse gratitude with something much different.

And just what was it he was feeling toward her? Wasn't it mere lust? The thought of finally having the fantasy-woman he'd carried in his memory for so long?

Or was it something deeper?

It didn't matter, he thought as he swam downstream, then back, feeling the anger still smoldering. No matter what he was feeling, he had no right to act on it. Not with a woman as fine as Cara.

He touched bottom and started walking through the water. Suddenly he stopped, his eyes narrowing on the figure standing on the banks.

His tone was harsh with the anger that was still simmering. "I thought you'd be asleep by now."

Cara shook her head, sending her damp hair drifting around her shoulders like a silken veil. Courage, she warned herself. This was no time to run from his anger. "It isn't sleep I want, Yale."

His voice was rougher than he intended. "I don't think you know what's good for you."

"Don't I?"

"What...?" Before he could speak, she tossed aside his coat and started into the water toward him.

To see her as he'd always dreamed of seeing her, naked, perfect, robbed him of speech. All he could do was stare at the high, firm breasts, the slender hips, those long, shapely legs as she walked slowly through the waves until she was standing in front of him.

"What I want is you, Yale."

He was already shaking his head. "You don't know..."

She reached for him. The moment she touched him, the protest died on his lips. "There's so much I don't know, Yale. But I know this. I'm grateful for what you did for us. It was so brave and bold. But then..." Her lips curved in a smile. "...I've always known you to be brave and bold."

"I don't want..."

She touched a finger to his mouth. Just a finger, but he felt the heat race through his body and settle in his loins.

"I haven't come here to offer my gratitude. I'm here because, more than anything in the world, I want to love you. Not long ago you told me that there would come a time when we'd be all alone, and you would show me all the things you were feeling. We're alone now, Yale. Will you lie with me? Will you make love with me? Here? Now?"

His eyes smoldered. "Do you know what you're asking?"

"I do."

He framed her face with his hands, his eyes steady on hers. His voice came out in a sigh that came from deep inside. "I've waited a lifetime to hear those words."

"I know." There was no surprise in her. No hesitation this time as she lifted a palm to the dark beard that covered his lower face. "I've waited a lifetime to say them."

"Cara. Cara." He dragged her roughly against him, his mouth on hers, stealing her breath as he kissed her long and slow and deep, until they were both gasping.

Water lapped at their hips, but nothing could cool the heat spiraling through their veins.

He closed his hands over her upper arms, holding her a little away. "I'm not sure I can be gentle. I'm afraid…I'm afraid I'll hurt you."

She was already shaking her head in denial. "Is this my bold, reckless outlaw? Or are you an imposter? What have you done with my wild, dangerous Yale Conover, who came to my house one night, demanding that I go away with him?"

He laughed then and dragged her close. But the laughter died as he savaged her mouth, letting that one kiss speak of all the longing, all the hunger he'd endured through the years.

He drew the kiss out, lingering over her lips, unable to get enough of the sweet, clean taste of her.

When at last his mouth left hers he ran hot wet kisses along the column of her throat, then brought his mouth lower, to close over her nipple.

She moaned and clutched at him, afraid that at any moment her knees would buckle.

As if reading her thoughts he scooped her up and started toward the shallows. Before he'd taken two steps his mouth was back on hers, like a man starved for the taste of her.

"This is madness." On a quick breath she cupped his face, as eager, as hungry as he. Everything inside her was poured into the kiss.

She could feel the heat of him. The strength. The danger. All excited her, and had her straining for more.

"Then I guess we're both mad." His lips raced over her face, brushing her eyelid, her nose, the corner of her mouth.

"I've been mad for you for all my life, Yale."

"I know the feeling." He was grateful to reach the shallows, where he set her on her feet. And gathered her close to feast on her mouth.

All the while his hands began a lazy exploration of her body. He saw her eyes glaze in the moonlight, and heard her sudden moan as his thumbs stroked her already erect nipples.

She pressed herself against him, urging him to take what she offered.

It was all he could do to resist taking her quickly, to end this hard, driving need that was ripping through him. But he wanted more. So much more. He wanted all she had to give, and then more.

His breath was coming in short bursts, and he cautioned himself to slow down. To taste. To savor. They had both waited so long for this. Too long. If this was all he could give her, it would have to be enough to last a lifetime.

He lifted her off her feet and carried her up the slippery banks of the stream, then slowly lowered her to the grass, where he lay beside her. Calling on all his willpower, he forced himself to go slowly, running soft, nibbling kisses across her shoulder, down her throat, until his tongue circled her breast.

He saw the glitter of starlight in her eyes. Saw them widen, then narrow with concentration, as his hands began moving over her.

"I used to see you like this in my dreams, Cara. I'd imagine you in my bed. The thought of it tormented me."

"It was the same for me."

He shook his head. In the moonlight his dark eyes crinkled with humor even while they pinned her. "I doubt it was the same. You have no idea the things I've wanted to do with you. To you."

"Show me." Her voice had changed. Deepened with passion. With need.

His mouth closed around her breast, nibbling, suckling, while his hands moved over her until he found her, hot and moist, and took her on a wild, dizzying ride.

Startled, she could do nothing more than close her

hands into fists as he took her up, then over. He saw
her eyes darken. Heard her moan. But before she
could recover, his greedy mouth was moving down
her body, taking her into dark, new places she'd
never even dreamed of.

"Yale." She jerked back, afraid, but he was beyond hearing as he took her again until she was
shuddering.

Her breath came out in a gasp as the shocking
climax tore through her. Without giving her a
chance to breathe he rolled them both over so that
she was straddling him, and his greedy mouth set to
work tasting, feasting.

Her body was damp with sweat, straining over
his, setting sparks wherever she rubbed. She was
frantic for more.

"I want you in me." Her voice was a hoarse cry
of desperation as she moved over him.

"Not yet." He turned her yet again, so that she
was on her back in the grass and he lay over her,
his eyes fixed on her with such intensity, she was
certain he could see through to her very soul.
"There's so much more, Cara. I want to show you
all of it. Everything."

Though he could feel himself dangerously close
to exploding, he forced himself to touch, to taste,
until she shared his madness. With lips and teeth
and tongue he drove her higher, then higher still,
keeping relief just out of reach.

Beside them the stream rippled over rocks, splashing, gurgling. Neither of them heard. Overhead the

full moon cast ribbons of gold over them, bathing them in its light. But they were blind to it. Blind to all but the need that had them hovering on the very edge of a high, steep cliff.

The fragrance of evergreen was all around her, filling his lungs, until all he could smell, all he could taste was her. His eyes were focused on her. All he could see was the way she looked, her hair a soft, silken veil drifting around a face softened by moonlight. A face as desperate, as dazed, as his own.

Every breath tore at his lungs as he entered her. With an unbelievable strength she rose up to meet him, her body wrapping itself around his, her arms and legs a silky tangle as she began to move with him, to climb with him.

His eyes were hot and fierce as he lowered his mouth to hers, needing to taste her as they mated.

"I love you, Cara. Always you. Only you."

She whispered his name, or thought she did.

Muscles straining, they stepped over the edge.

And soared.

Cara lay perfectly still, afraid to move. Afraid even to breathe.

Except for the ripple of water in the stream, the night had gone silent. No birds cried. No insects chirped or hummed. It was as if the whole world had slipped away. She was alone in the universe with Yale.

His face was buried in her neck, his breath pumping out in short bursts.

He lifted his face and looked down into her eyes. "Am I too heavy?"

She shook her head. "I like having you here." She lifted a hand to his bearded cheek. "Just here."

"Are you all right?"

She nodded. "I feel…" She sighed. "Is it always like that, Yale?"

"Like what?"

"So…" She struggled for the words. "I saw stars."

"You did?" He thought about that, and found himself extremely pleased. "Was that the first time…I mean…hasn't that ever happened before?"

"No. Never. In fact, I never dreamed it could be like that."

His smile had her heart stuttering. "Then I guess that makes me your first." He kissed the tip of her nose. "I like being the first."

She shivered. The cocky, self-assured rogue was back. Or perhaps he'd never been gone. Maybe she'd just imagined the hesitation, the tenderness, when she'd first offered herself to him.

"You're cold." He rolled to his side and gathered her into his arms.

She wasn't cold. In fact, her skin was still flushed. But she found that she liked being held like this. Loved hearing the steady beat of his heart close to her ear, and feeling the warmth of his breath against her temple.

In fact, if this was all part of lovemaking, she

wanted more of it. It was unlike anything she'd ever experienced before.

"You're incredible, Cara."

She looked up at him, surprised by the tenderness of his tone. "In what way?"

"In every way." He tucked a strand of her hair behind her ear. "I still can't believe I'm actually lying here holding you. For so long now I've fantasized about it. Thought about all the ways I'd love you if I ever had the chance."

She wrapped her arms around his neck, pressing herself to the length of him, and brought her mouth to his. Against his lips she muttered, "And now you've had your chance."

"What do you mean, had?" He drew back, seeing the way her eyes widened. Then he chuckled. A sound that had her looking even more confused. "Did you think we were through?"

"Well, I thought you'd want to sleep."

"Why sleep, when there are more important things we can do?"

"But we've done them." She saw his quick grin. "Haven't we?"

"Cara, my innocent." He ran soft butterfly kisses down the smooth column of her throat and felt the way she shivered. Her reaction had his eyes narrowing with sudden need as passion flared again. "Think of all the hours between now and dawn. My sweet, sweet, Cara, we haven't even begun."

Chapter Fifteen

Cara was having the loveliest dream. She was young and carefree, racing across the hills of her ranch, and into the open arms of Yale Conover. He was laughing. A wonderful rich sound that never failed to thrill her as he swept her up and kissed her before swinging her around and around until she was deliciously dizzy.

She awoke smiling, and turned to find him studying her with that intensity that always stirred her heart.

"Good morning." Her smile grew. "What are you doing?"

"Watching you." He ran a fingertip from her temple to her jaw. "I love watching you. There were so many times in my life when I thought I'd never see you again. And now that you're here, I can't seem to get enough of you."

"I should have thought, after last night, you'd had enough."

That had him grinning. All night they'd loved. At

times their lovemaking had been as fierce as a summer storm. Bright flashes of lightning and all the fury of thunder. At other times they'd come together with a gentleness, a tenderness that brought a lump to her throat and made her almost weep for the sheer beauty of it.

She had never dreamed there could be so many ways for a man and woman to express their love. She felt as if a secret door had been opened. A door leading to a beautiful garden of delights. And like a greedy child, she wanted to taste, to see, to experience everything. And she did. With Yale leading the way, she'd opened herself up to trust him to show her all he could.

Just before dawn he had carried her back to the fire, where they'd wrapped themselves in the deer hide for warmth.

She touched a hand to his cheek. "Did you sleep at all?"

He shook his head. "I was too busy watching you."

"I'd better get up." She started to shift.

He caught her hand, pulling her down beside him. "Where are you going?"

"I want to get dressed before the boys wake."

"They'll sleep for another hour or more." He nodded toward the pale pink ribbons threading the clouds overhead. "It's barely dawn."

"But I wouldn't want them to see me…" She felt the heat rise to her cheeks. "I need to be dressed before they're awake, Yale."

"I understand." There was humor in his eyes as he brushed his lips over hers. "We wouldn't want them to catch you in my bedroll, would we? But just one more kiss, Cara, before you leave me."

She pulled back. "You know where that always leads."

His grin was quick, and went straight to her heart. "That's what I'm hoping."

"You devil." But there was no heat in her words as she offered her lips.

His arms came around her, molding her to him. She realized, too late, that he was fully aroused. And then, as he took the kiss deeper, she felt the familiar curl of desire snaking through her veins. Felt the quick liquid rush deep inside.

"I suppose they'll sleep another hour," she murmured as she gave herself up to the pure pleasure of his lovemaking.

"Ma. Something smells good." Cody rolled out of the bearskin and crossed to where his mother sat beside Yale sipping strong, hot coffee.

She reached out a hand to her son, drawing him close for a kiss. "Good morning, Cody. I thought you were never going to wake up. Look, sleepyhead." She pointed. "The sun's been up for an hour or more."

"I didn't wake up once last night feeling hungry or cold," the boy admitted. "I'm glad we came out of the mine. Aren't you?"

Cara nodded. "Very glad. I hope we never have to go back inside a cold dark mine shaft again."

The boy turned to Yale. "Can we stay out here? Or do we have to go back?"

Yale set aside his coffee. "For now I think we're safe out here." He nodded toward the fire. "Your ma's got biscuits warming, and the last of the deer meat ready for breakfast."

The little boy wrinkled his nose. "Do you think we could eat something for supper tonight besides deer meat?"

Yale chuckled. "We could if you and your brother can catch enough fish."

"Fish?" Cody looked hopefully toward the stream. "Can we fish, Ma?"

She smiled. "I don't see why not. And while you're at it, you can take a bath and swim while I wash your clothes."

The boy was ecstatic as he raced down to the banks of the stream and started peeling off his clothes.

Cara turned to Yale. "You'll stay close to him, won't you?"

He nodded. "Don't worry. I won't let him out of my sight." He brushed a kiss over her lips before sauntering away.

Minutes later Seth awoke. The minute he saw his brother in the stream, he raced off to join him. Even the offer of sugared biscuits wouldn't lure the children from the water.

Cara stood on the banks, watching as Yale rolled

his pants to his knees and joined them. Soon he was tossing them into the deep while they squealed with enthusiasm.

"Again," Cody begged, tugging on Yale's already soaked pantleg.

"Oh. You like flying through the air and doing belly flops, do you?" With a laugh he picked up the little boy and tossed him.

And though Cara brought a hand to her mouth in alarm, she saw the look of adoration on her son's face when he surfaced.

"Again," he cried.

But before Yale could toss him, little Seth was tugging on his arm, indicating that he'd like the same treatment as his older brother.

"Oh, you want to live dangerously, do you?" Yale picked him up over his head, but instead of tossing him roughly, as he'd done with Cody, he dropped the boy ever-so-gently in the water.

Seth was laughing when he surfaced. A sound that had Cara's heart nearly bursting with joy.

As she began washing her children's clothes, she watched and listened as the two boys continued approaching Yale, begging for more. Each time he obliged. And each time they laughed harder, until the air was filled with it.

To Cara it was the sweetest sound she'd ever heard.

Feeling a shadow fall over her she looked up to see Yale heading toward her, wearing that teasing smile. On either side of him were Seth and Cody, wearing matching smiles.

"What are you...?" She started to step back, but Yale caught her and lifted her easily in his arms.

"We didn't want to have all the fun, while you had to do all the work. So we've decided you should play in the water, too." He started wading toward the deep, with the two boys laughing and pointing.

"Yale Conover." Cara tried her most commanding tone, the one she always used with her sons when she wanted their complete attention. "Don't you dare."

"And why not? Afraid of a little water, Cara?"

"I'm fully dressed. I'll get all wet." She looked over at her sons. "Stop that laughing right now. I won't be a party to this..." Her words ended in a scream as Yale tossed her into the deep.

She went under with a splash, then came up sputtering. "I can't believe you..." She brushed strings of wet hair from her cheeks and tried to look dignified as she started toward the shallows. But with the water lapping at her hips, and her gown plastered against her like a second skin, it was impossible.

She started past Yale, who was laughing so hard he was shaking. She moved so quickly he didn't even know what hit him when she suddenly ducked beneath the waves and tackled him around the ankles. His legs went out from under him and he sank like a stone beneath the water.

Moments later he broke the surface. Seeing the way Cara and her children were laughing he gave her a dangerous smile. "Oh, lady. Now you've done it. You just declared war."

He made a flying leap, taking her down into the water with him. When they surfaced, she was still being held in his arms. Without giving her a chance to catch her breath he lifted her in the air, poised to toss her again.

"No, Yale." She wrapped her arms around his neck, determined to hold on. "No more."

Grinning, he glanced at the children. "I'll leave it up to you. Should I toss your mother in the deep?"

Cody looked at his little brother before shouting, "We vote yes."

"Traitors," Cara called.

Yale's smile grew. "You heard what the vote was. However, I'll give you one chance to wiggle out of this."

"How?" Her eyes narrowed with suspicion.

"I'll give you a choice. The water, or a kiss. If you kiss me, I'll carry you to shore."

This had the boys laughing even harder.

Cody suddenly surprised her by shouting, "Take the kiss, Ma."

She looked over at her son. "You want me to kiss Yale?"

The boy shrugged. "It sure sounds easier than being dunked."

Cara turned to her younger son. "What do you think, Seth? Should I kiss Yale?"

The little boy covered his mouth with his hand before nodding.

Yale grinned. "You raised very smart children, ma'am. Now what do you say? A kiss? Or do I toss you in the deep?"

She struggled not to smile. "I ought to tell you to toss me, since I'm already soaked clear to my skin. But... All right." She closed her eyes and puckered her lips. "One kiss."

With her sons clapping, Yale brushed his mouth over hers. And though he kept it light and teasing, they both felt the jolt.

To the delight of her children Yale carried her out of the stream and set her on her feet along the banks. "You see? I'm a man of my word."

"So I see." She inclined her head. "I suppose I should be grateful for small favors."

He leaned close to whisper, "It's a good thing you don't have a looking glass handy. If you could see yourself the way I'm seeing you right now, your face would be the color of ripe apples."

She glanced down and could see the way the wet fabric clung to every line and curve of her body. "Yale Conover, you're shameless."

"Yes, ma'am." He brushed a light kiss over her nose. "And tonight, when we lose our audience, I'll show you just how shameless."

He turned away and splashed through the shallows, tucking Cody and Seth under each arm, much to their delight.

As Cara hurried away to wrap herself in the bearskin and hang her clothes to dry, she could hear the laughter of her sons ringing in the still air.

* * *

"Look, Ma." Cody walked from the stream holding a wriggling fish. His dark hair was plastered to his cheeks, his skin no longer pale but kissed by the sun after a day of play. "Seth caught one, too. Yale's taking it off the hook for him."

Cara turned from the fire, where she had just removed a batch of perfectly browned biscuits. "I can't wait to cook them for supper tonight."

"Yale's going to show us how to clean them."

Just then Yale walked up carrying Seth on his shoulders. The younger boy's face was wreathed with smiles. In his hands was a string of fish.

"Look what we caught," Yale called.

"I see." Cara watched as he lifted the little boy down and began to show the two children how to clean and prepare the fish for cooking.

While Yale and the boys finished their chore, Cara removed their dry clothes from nearby branches and laid them out near the fire. Then she stood watching the easy banter between the man and boys. As she did, she felt like weeping for happiness. This entire day had been like a special gift. One she would hold in her heart forever.

As daylight faded to evening, and the sun hovered just above the mountain peaks, the two children pulled on their dry clothes and sat together on the bearskin, watching as the fish sizzled over the fire.

When it was cooked, Cara filled their plates while Yale retrieved the canteen of cold water from the stream. Then they sat together around the fire, eating and drinking their fill.

By the time Cody and Seth had polished off the last of the sugared biscuits, they could hardly keep their eyes open.

"I think all this play has left the two of you ready to turn in early." Cara lifted her younger son onto her lap and pressed a kiss to his cheek. "Would you like me to tuck you in?"

Cody turned down the edge of the bearskin and crawled in, with Seth following.

As Cara bent to kiss them Cody said, "This has been the best day ever." He glanced from his mother to the man who knelt beside her, tucking the edge of the bearskin around them. "Thanks, Yale."

"I was just about to thank the two of you." Yale brushed the hair from Seth's forehead and clapped a hand on Cody's shoulder. "I can't remember when I've had more fun, without even shuffling a deck of cards."

"Think we can do it again tomorrow?"

Yale shrugged. "I can't say for sure, Cody. I've learned it's best to take things one day at a time. But you sleep now. Your ma and I will be right here if you need us."

"'Night, Ma. 'Night, Yale."

Cara knelt a moment longer, stroking their faces, holding tightly to their hands. It felt so good, so right, to finally see them smiling as they drifted into sleep.

When she finally got to her feet and shook down

her skirts, she saw Yale standing some distance away, watching the sun drop behind the peaks of the Black Hills.

When she approached, he held out his hand.

She arched a brow. "Where are we going?"

"Just to the banks of the stream. I like the peacefulness of it."

She laughed. "Not to mention the privacy."

His smile was quick, and filled with the sort of mischief she'd always seen in him in his youth. "There's that, too. And I am in dire need of some privacy. The sooner the better." He paused and without warning turned her into his arms for a long, lingering kiss. Against her lips he muttered, "Oh, Cara. I've been wanting to do that all day."

"And here I thought you were having such fun playing with the children."

"It was fun. And I enjoyed their company. But now it's you I crave, Cara." He kissed her again, long and slow and deep, until both their hearts were thundering, and their breathing grew ragged.

As his fingers found the buttons of her gown, he whispered, "Now it's our turn to play."

Chapter Sixteen

Cara shivered in the pre-dawn darkness and instinctively reached for Yale. All night they'd loved and laughed and whispered, baring the secrets of their souls. Though they'd given little thought to sleep, she felt more rested, more at peace, than at any time in recent years.

The place beside her was empty.

She sat up, shoving tangles from her eyes, and glanced toward the fire, expecting to see Yale adding another log. He wasn't there.

She turned toward the stream. Perhaps he'd decided to wash and dress early. But though she stood and peered through the darkness, she could make out no trace of him.

Minutes later she heard a footfall and was relieved to see him striding toward her.

She hurried forward to meet him. "You're up early."

He nodded. "With this chill in the air, I wanted

to climb high enough to have a look around. Figured if there was anyone in the area, I'd spot a fire."

"What did you see?"

He saw the flash of fear in her eyes and took her hands in his. "Nothing. Not a trace of Fenner and his men."

"You think they're gone?"

"I'm thinking that, once they went past us, they were afraid to backtrack in case the Federal troops were hot on their trail."

Her smile was back. "We're rid of them for good?"

"I wouldn't go that far. But I think this is the time to consider leaving now and heading toward civilization."

"Oh, Yale." Her eyes danced with unconcealed pleasure. "I'll wake the children. We can get started within the hour."

Before she could turn away, he drew her close and brushed a kiss over her lips. "Are you in such a hurry to leave our own private paradise?"

"It has been a wonderful, magical place, hasn't it? I feel…" She searched for a word. "…as though my soul has been restored here."

"I know the feeling. Being here with you has restored mine, too. I've spent far too much time in the company of thieves and gamblers. This was what I needed. Just this." He heard her sigh and kissed her again. "Now just let me hold you a minute more. Then we'll wake the children and make plans to leave here."

She clung to him, absorbing his strength. When they stepped apart, she took a deep breath before beginning her morning tasks.

"You mean it?" Cody was dancing around, too eager to stand still. "We're going to look for a town? Where are we headed?"

Yale laughed at the boy's enthusiasm. "I'll leave the choice up to you and Seth and your mother. We can head back north and find Crescent Butte about a hundred miles in that direction." He pointed. "Or we can continue to head south and make it to Misery, which is probably a good hundred miles distant."

Cara seemed intrigued. "We could go to Misery?"

Yale shrugged. "It's your call, Cara. Would you like to go back there?"

It took her less than a heartbeat to nod. "Even though my folks are gone now, it's still home. It's where my friends are. And though I've denied it for a long time now, I think it's where my heart has always been."

He smiled. "Then Misery it'll be."

As they broke camp and loaded their meager belongings in the back of the cart, Cara gave a long look around at the stream, at the distant mountain peaks. She would always hold this place close to her heart. For it was here that she and Yale had finally been able to express what they felt for one another.

What they felt.

She knew in her heart that what she felt for Yale was love. She knew, too, that he cared deeply for her. But she refused to allow herself to dwell on the future. He was, after all, a man who had spent a lifetime pursuing his own pleasures. When he tired of her, as he surely would, she had to be strong enough to watch him walk away. Again.

Is that why she'd eagerly embraced a return to her childhood home? If she had to face a future raising her children alone, at least in Misery she would have the support and comfort of those who'd known her and her family for a lifetime. What's more, she would always have the memory of Yale there. The boy he'd been, and the man he'd become.

When the children were comfortably settled in the back of the cart, Yale helped her up to the rough seat before pulling himself up beside her. He flicked the reins and the old horse started slowly forward.

Cara turned for one last glimpse of their campsite. Then she turned her face forward.

She didn't intend to look back, ever again. From now on, she would face the future, whatever it might hold, with the same courage she'd glimpsed in Yale.

He caught her hand and lifted it to his lips.

She smiled. "What was that for?"

"Just for being yourself."

"How could I be otherwise?"

He laughed. "You don't know, do you? So many things in life change. So many people change, as well. But not you. You're still sweet Cara Mc-Kinnon."

"I'm Cara Evans, now, Yale."

His eyes crinkled. "Only the name has changed. But you haven't, Cara. And that's what matters."

He kept her hand tucked in his as the horse and cart ate up the miles of wilderness. And when, in late afternoon, they finally stopped and made camp for the night, he took Cody and Seth with him to hunt. An hour later they returned with four rabbits, enough to make stew to last them for the next several days.

And that night, as he and Cara lay under the stars, their lovemaking was sweet and unhurried. As though they had all the time in the world.

"Let's sing a song." Yale turned to the two boys, who were growing restless in the back of the cart. After endless miles of dust and grime, under a relentless sun, he had proven to be amazingly inventive.

He'd entertained them with card tricks, with jokes, and tales of the towns he'd visited, and the fancy hotels he'd slept in.

"With real feather beds?" Cara couldn't hide her sigh at the thought.

He nodded. "In San Francisco the room had gilt trim around the walls, and a satin bedspread on a bed big enough to hold all of us."

She shook her head. "Now I know you're teasing."

He merely laughed, and began singing a bawdy song he'd learned in a saloon in Montana. Whenever he came to a shocking word or phrase he'd pause a moment, hum, then move on. And because the remaining words made absolutely no sense, Cara and her sons were soon weak with laughter. But his silliness had the desired effect. They found, as evening crept over the land, that they'd passed another perfectly delightful afternoon.

They'd been on the trail for more than a week, and each day had passed more quickly than the previous one. Yale had taken the time to show the boys how to fire the rifle, and both Seth and Cody had bagged squirrels and rabbits for their supper. They'd added to their larder with fish and had even found ripe berries and apples.

To make the heat of day more tolerable, they often stopped at midday to swim in a creek or take refuge in the shade of towering rocks or trees. They had begun to look forward to these long breaks, knowing Yale would make it fun and lively with his amazing store of jokes and tricks. The boys were delighted with his stories. And Cara found herself looking forward to hearing about his travels. Though she'd never been out of the Dakota Territory, she found herself seeing the rest of the country through Yale's eyes.

"Do you ever see your brother and sister?" Cara poured coffee and handed it to Yale as they took a break from the trail near a swiftly running stream.

He shook his head. "Not often. Sometimes, when I find myself in a town near Misery, I drop by Aaron

Smiler's ranch for a few hours.'' His voice lowered with feeling. ''I miss Kitty. I love surprising her with little gifts, and seeing her eyes light up.''

Cara filled two cups with clear water and handed them to her sons before settling herself beside them in the grass. ''What about your brother, Gabe? Don't you miss him, too?''

Yale shrugged. ''Some, I suppose. But we haven't been close for years.''

Cody looked over, his arm around Seth's shoulders. ''How can you not be close to your own brother?''

Yale's eyes narrowed. ''I make him uncomfortable.''

''Why?'' the boy asked.

''We chose different paths in life. Gabe's a lawman. He can't help thinking like one, even when he's with me. And I think he's always been ashamed of the fact that he and I haven't always been on the same side of the law.''

''But you said you're not an outlaw.''

Yale realized that both boys were watching him closely, and listening to every word. He managed one of his charming smiles. ''I'm not an outlaw. But I've done some things I'm not proud of.''

''Like what?'' Cody asked.

Yale leaned his elbows in the grass and looked up at the sky. ''I guess I've broken just about every rule my brother considers sacred.''

Cody blinked. ''Ma told us that rules were made for our own good.''

Yale nodded. "Your ma's right. At the time I broke the rules, I told myself I was just doing what was necessary to survive. But I wasn't being entirely honest. Most of the time, I liked doing what I pleased, without regard to what others thought."

He glanced over at Cody and Seth. "Now that I'm older, I've figured out why. When I found out that my father wasn't the man I'd thought him to be, the noble heroic image I'd been carrying in my mind, I just wanted to take it out on somebody. I suppose, if my mother had lived long enough, I'd have tried to punish her for my father's weakness. But when she died along the trail, there was nobody left to fight except my brother, Gabe."

"But why did you want to fight with him?" Cody asked.

"I didn't. Not really. There was just this anger inside me. And I suppose, somewhere inside my heart, I knew my own brother was a safe target. No matter what I did, he'd still love me. But I pushed him too far. And now, after all these years, we've forgotten how to get back to the way we used to be."

"You forgot how to love your own brother?"

Cody shook his head. "Not really. But there's a...wall we've been building. And with every passing year it gets higher. And I've only now begun to realize that if we let it keep growing, soon we won't be able to climb over it. I guess it's that way with a lot of things that start out small, and keep on growing until they're out of our control."

At his words Seth's eyes had gone wide.

Seeing his little brother's reaction, Cody set aside his water. "When our pa died, Seth stopped talking. Is he punishing us?"

Yale shook his head. "Seth's hurting. He's gone inside himself to heal." He winked at the little boy. "And you're healing just fine, aren't you, son?"

Seth tried a wink, and blinked both his eyes instead before breaking into a wide grin.

Cody gave a hiss of impatience. "Is it going to take Seth until he's all grown up to get his voice back?"

Yale tousled the boy's hair. "I think, when Seth has something important to say, he'll find his voice."

"You think so?" Cody turned to Seth, and the younger boy smiled.

Yale got to his feet, then held out a hand to Cara. "Now I think we'd better get back on the trail. We still have a long way to go before we get to Misery."

"Can we ride up front for awhile?" Cody asked.

At Yale's nod of assent the two boys scrambled up and raced to the cart. When everyone was seated, Cody and Seth took their places on either side of Yale, and were delighted when he allowed each of them to take a turn handling the reins.

From her position beside them, Cara had to swallow back the lump in her throat. These two little boys had been starved for the attention of a man. And Yale was so different from the stern father-figure they'd known. With Yale, everything, even the most mundane chore, was a joy to be savored, or an adventure to be enjoyed. What a wonderful gift he'd been given. And one he was willing to share with others. With Yale, everything in life was, quite simply, fun.

This had started out to be a terrifying flight for their lives. But somewhere along the way it had become this wonderful, carefree adventure.

And all because of this man.

Just then Yale glanced over Seth's head and gave her a smile that had her heart actually fluttering in her chest. And though she continued to clasp her hands in her lap and return his smile, she found herself already thinking about tonight. About the pleasure they would discover in each other's arms, and the passion they would unleash, under the cover of darkness.

Just the thought of it had Cara's heart beating furiously, and her blood heating. Though she'd been raised to be calm and sensible, Yale had the ability, with a single smile, to have her become his willing accomplice in merriment. And she loved him for it. Loved him for teaching her how to laugh and be silly. To be inventive and ignore convention. Best of all, she loved him for the way he accepted her sons, without trying to mold them into some sort of proper image.

She glanced over at his strong, handsome profile and knew with sudden clarity that, no matter what the future held for them, she would always love him. Just as she always had.

Chapter Seventeen

"Yale. Look." As their little cart crested a hill, Cara pointed to cattle grazing on a distant hillside. "There must be a ranch nearby."

"More than a ranch. A town." Shading the sun from his eyes he peered at the outline of buildings in the distance.

At his words the boys scrambled up and stood in the back of the wagon, holding to the wooden seat as they bounced over hills and watched the outlines slowly begin to take shape.

In no time they were rolling along the main street of Bison Fork. After the silence of the prairie wilderness, they found themselves fascinated with so much sound. Men and women strolling along the dusty road, calling out greetings to friends and neighbors. A blacksmith, standing beside his barn, the sound of his hammer beating a rhythmic tattoo as he pounded red-hot steel into the shape of a horseshoe. The tinny notes of a piano as they rode past a saloon, and paused finally outside the two-story hotel next door.

Yale leapt down and hitched the horse, then lifted Cara to the ground. Behind her Cody and Seth climbed down and stared around in amazement.

"Where'd all these people come from, Ma?" Cody asked.

Cara turned to Yale with a questioning look.

He merely smiled. "I guess your ranch was too far from civilization to notice the land rush that's been going on here in the Dakota Territory. There's talk that it'll soon become a state."

"Imagine that." Cara stared around in awe at the women who looked so fashionable in their gowns with matching shawls and bonnets. She couldn't help smoothing down the skirt of her faded dress.

Seeing it, Yale put a hand beneath her elbow and led her toward the doors of the hotel. "Come on. It's time we enjoyed a little luxury."

Cara stopped short and pulled back in alarm. "Yale, we can't go in there."

"Why not?"

She stared down at her soiled gown, her scuffed boots, her torn, ragged fingernails. "It's too fine. Besides, we couldn't possibly afford it."

He merely smiled and closed her hand firmly in his. "I can afford it, Cara. And it's not nearly fine enough for you." He turned to wink at the boys. "What do you say? Would you like to sleep in a real bed tonight? In this big hotel?"

"Yes, sir." Cody answered for both of them.

Then, taking his little brother's hand, he skipped through the doorway.

Inside, as Yale approached the front desk, the boys and their mother stood staring in openmouthed surprise at the lobby decorated with ornate rugs and horsehair furniture. Hanging from the ceiling was a huge crystal chandelier ablaze with dozens of candles.

Yale seemed to take forever talking with the bespectacled man standing behind the desk. There were, it seemed, a dozen or more questions before he finally reached into his pocket and handed over a handful of coins. After signing his name in a book he accepted a key before taking Cara's hand and leading her toward the stairway. The boys trailed behind, running their hands along the polished railing.

On the second floor Yale paused outside a door and turned the key, then stepped aside, allowing Cara to precede him.

Inside she stopped and put a hand to her throat, unable to speak.

"Look, Ma." Cody danced across the room and stared at the big bed with its fancy, rose-embroidered spread.

"I see." Laughing nervously, Cara touched a hand to the china bowl and pitcher that rested on a marble-topped nightstand. Then, because she couldn't help herself, she picked up the pretty soap and breathed in the fragrance of mulberry. "Oh, Yale. Are we actually going to stay here?"

"You are." He gave her a mysterious smile. "The boys and I are next door."

"Next door? But why?"

His grin widened at the look on her face. "Because you don't need us around. I've ordered up a bath. It should be here in a few minutes."

"A bath?" Her eyes widened. "Here in the room?"

"That's right. And while you're indulging yourself, I'm taking the boys with me for haircuts and baths at the barbershop down the street. So you just take your time. And when you're done, we'll have supper in the rooming house at the end of town."

He beckoned to her sons. "Come on, boys. Let's give your mother some privacy."

Cara watched as Cody and Seth raced to the door, eager for the next adventure. Yale paused in the doorway. The look in his eyes sent shivers along her spine. Without a word he was gone.

Like her son, Cara danced across the room and touched a hand to the bed. Then she perched on the edge, enjoying the softness of the mattress. Too excited to remain still, she got to her feet and walked to the window. Down below in the street she could see Yale and her sons just entering the barbershop.

At a tap on her door, she rushed across the room. When she opened the door a housemaid entered, carrying a round tub. Behind her were two brawny youths carrying buckets of water.

Within minutes they were gone, but before Cara could peel off her clothes there was another knock.

Puzzled, Cara opened the door to find another housemaid holding several parcels.

"What is this?"

"Your clothes, ma'am."

"Clothes?" She blinked. "I don't understand."

"Your husband ordered these. He said I was to bring them up for your approval." The maid brushed past her and laid the parcels on the bed, then unwrapped them to reveal a lovely pink gown, with matching shawl, and a pair of fine kid boots. In another parcel were a delicate chemise and petticoats, as well as a pretty jeweled comb for her hair.

"Do you approve, ma'am?"

Cara couldn't seem to find her voice. Feeling tears threaten, she merely nodded.

The housemaid smiled. "Your husband was so sweet. He said I was to tell you that if you wish anything at all, you need only ask."

"I…" Cara cleared her throat and tried again. "I can't think of anything more I could possibly need. Thank you."

When the maid was gone Cara stared at the clothes without daring to touch, for fear of soiling them. She looked around, feeling as though this must be a dream.

Then with a laugh she peeled off her clothes. As she settled into the warm water, she gave a sigh that seemed to come from deep within. None of this seemed real. The room. The warm water. The beautiful new clothes.

But if this truly was a dream, she hoped she never woke up.

* * *

Yale strode into the shop, trailed by the two boys. Almost at once there was a perceptible pause in the conversation.

Ignoring the stares of the cowboys Yale placed a coin in the barber's hand. "We've been on the trail awhile, Finn. The boys and I need haircuts, and I'll need a shave."

"Yes, sir." The barber indicated his chair. "Which one of you fine boys wants to go first?"

Seeing the way Cody and Seth hung back, it occurred to Yale that they had probably never been in such a place before. To alleviate their fears he said, "I'll go first. I'm in a hurry to get rid of this horse's mane that's been growing on my face."

As the barber soaped his beard and began to shave him, Cody and Seth watched in fascination.

"You hoping to play a little poker, Mr. Conover?" the barber asked conversationally.

"Not this trip, Finn."

Cody and Seth saw the way the cowboys seated around the room hung on his every word.

"Haven't seen you in these parts lately, Mr. Conover."

"I've been away."

"We've missed you. The town just isn't the same without you."

"That's nice to know, Finn. I'll be needing a few favors while I'm here. Clothes, for one thing. And a good horse." He reached into his pocket and dropped some money in the barber's hand.

"Anything you need, Mr. Conover, you need only ask."

"Thanks, Finn. I knew I could count on you."

Afterward, as Yale's thick dark hair was trimmed and dropped to the floor, Cody heard two of the cowboys whispering about the fact that they were in the presence of a legend.

Before he could ask what that meant, it was his turn to have his hair trimmed. And though he was nervous at first, he soon came to realize that it didn't feel very different from the way his mother cut his hair. Seeing the way his little brother was watching, he managed to smile, and before long the towel was whisked aside and the barber was saying, "There you go, son. Now let's see to your little brother. Climb right up here, son."

A short time later they were led to the back room of the barbershop. Yale, freshly shaved and shorn, peeled off his clothes unselfconsciously and eased into a tub of warm water, then leaned back and held a match to the tip of a fine cigar. In the tub beside his, Cody and Seth climbed in, splashing and frolicking like two puppies.

Cody looked over to ask, "Why did the barber take us ahead of all those cowboys who were waiting?"

Yale shrugged, too content to even open his eyes. "I guess he just liked the color of my money."

After a few minutes of silence Cody looked up to

see a shopkeeper walking in, his arms filled with parcels.

"Yale." The little boy's tone grew more urgent. "Yale. What's he doing?"

Yale opened his eyes and gave a smile to the man. "Thanks, Jed. You work fast."

"I do for you, Mr. Conover. If any of this doesn't suit you, just let me know."

"I will. Thanks, Jed." He closed his eyes and continued to soak and smoke, all the while looking as contented as a cat in a pool of sunshine.

Finally, when the water began to cool, Yale stood and reached for a towel.

As he dried himself he said, "You boys might want to open some of those parcels."

"Yes, sir." Eagerly Cody and Seth began examining the mysterious packages.

Inside they found dark pants, much like the ones Yale always wore. Only these were scaled to their size, as were white shirts. There were even shiny new boots that were so soft inside, they didn't scratch or rub their toes raw or hurt at all.

By the time they were dressed, Yale was pulling on his brand new black coat, and trying on a broad-brimmed black hat.

He gave the boys a cool appraisal, then started toward the door. "You're looking mighty fine, boys. Come on. I think it's time to fetch your ma."

Cara stayed in the water until her skin resembled a prune. Then, wrapped in a thick towel, she scrubbed her dusty old clothes and hung them around the room to dry.

Unable to wait another minute, she slipped into the elegant new undergarments. They were as soft as a spider's web against her skin. She stepped into the pale pink gown, taking her time buttoning the row of tiny mother-of-pearl buttons that ran from neckline to waist. Then she turned to examine her reflection in the looking glass.

"Oh, my." The words fell from her lips as she stepped closer.

Could the woman in the mirror possibly be real? With that cloud of thick dark curls tumbling to her waist, and that sun-kissed skin, she more resembled a Gypsy than the pale, shy woman she'd always been.

She studied the gown. It had a low, rounded neckline and softly-draped skirt topped by a deep rose sash. She picked up the matching shawl and draped it around her shoulders, feeling like a queen. Then, still studying her reflection in the looking glass, she tucked up one side of her hair with the jeweled comb, and stood back to examine the effect.

At the knock on her door she hurried across the room. When she opened the door, Yale and the boys stood staring at her with matching looks of surprise.

"Oh, look at you," she called. "Don't you look grand."

"The barber cut our hair." Cody danced into the room with Seth right behind him. "And we took a bath in a real bathtub." He bounced on the edge of

the bed, and then, because the excitement was con-
tagious, he and Seth started jumping in the middle
of the bed. "And then a man brought us new
clothes, and called Yale Mr. Conover and said if
there was anything else we needed, he'd get it."

Cara stared at Yale, who hadn't moved. He was
still standing in the doorway, staring at her in such
a way she could feel the heat rising to her cheeks.

"Do I look all right?"

"Oh, Cara." His smile came then. Quick and
dangerous. "You look so much better than all right.
You're…" He shook his head. "You're so beautiful, you take my breath away."

She ran a hand down her skirt. "I've never had
anything this fine before, Yale. It's so elegant. And
I'm so…plain."

"You, Cara? Plain?" He caught her by the shoulders and stared down into her eyes, unable to believe
what she'd just said. "If you believe that, you
haven't seen the woman I'm seeing."

He looked over at Cody and Seth. "What do you
boys think of your mother?"

They stopped jumping long enough to stare.

Cody caught his brother's hand and helped him
from the bed. "We think you look pretty, Ma."

"Thank you." She hurried over to hug them both.
"And I think you look grand."

"Come on." Yale held the door open. "Now that
we're all agreed that we're just about the finest looking folks in this town, I think it's time we thought
about supper."

He offered his arm and Cara accepted. With the boys walking ahead of them they descended the stairs. As they did, they were aware of heads turning, and voices whispering.

Cara felt a thrill of pride at the sight of her sons, looking so clean and happy. And then she glanced at the handsome, dangerous man beside her and her heart nearly burst with love. No wonder people were whispering, she thought. Though she knew it was wrong to be vain, she couldn't help thinking that they looked like such a fine family.

Outside they walked along the street, pausing to look in the windows of the many shops. The barbershop, where cowboys fresh from nearby ranches waited their turn. The mercantile, with shelves neatly lined with bottles and jars, as well as bolts of fabric and even a display of guns. Next door was a dressmaker's shop. And a few steps beyond was a boardinghouse.

When they stepped inside they were greeted by a woman whose white hair was pinned back in a neat knot. Her apron was spotless. And as Cara glanced around, she found the house to be equally spotless.

"Why, Yale Conover." The woman's smile grew. "You never told me you had such a lovely wife." She turned toward Seth and Cody. "And two such fine-looking sons."

Cara waited for Yale to correct the woman, but he offered not a word.

The woman offered her hand to Cara. "I'm Margaret Thistle. And you must be very proud of this man of yours, my dear. Whenever he comes to town he always eats his meals here. I have to tell you. In all the years I've known Yale, I've never known him to be anything but a gentleman. And the other folks in Bison Fork will tell you the same. To the rest of the country he may be a rogue and a gambler, but to us he's a welcome guest. We're always so glad to see him.''

Without waiting to take a breath she said, "Come right in and makes yourselves at home. Supper is almost ready. If you'd like, you can refresh yourselves in the parlor. I'll have some elderberry wine brought in, and some lemonade for your sons.''

She bustled away, leaving Yale to lead the way to the parlor, where a settee and several chairs were arranged around a fireplace, where a cozy fire burned on the hearth.

Almost at once a young woman wearing an equally spotless apron entered the room and offered wine to Cara and Yale, and lemonade to Cody and Seth.

When she was gone Cara moved around the room, her hand trailing the smooth wood of the chair, the soft fabric of a fancy pillow.

Seeing the thoughtful look on her face Yale touched a finger to her cheek. "Are you upset that I didn't tell Margaret the truth about us?"

She shook her head. "Oh, Yale. Don't think that. It's just…" She glanced at the two boys who were lying on the hearth, shoulder to shoulder, leafing through the pages of a book. "It's been so long since I've been in a real house. I'd forgotten what it felt like to smell food cooking, and to see my children happy and clean and dressed in shiny new clothes. I think I'd even forgotten what it felt like to be a family.''

She sipped her wine and felt the way it warmed her. ''Hearing Margaret Thistle speak of you...'' She ducked her head. ''It made me realize that I don't really know you. I don't know anything about the way you've lived your life. I imagined you in dark saloons, drinking with outlaws and...'' She shrugged, not wanting to tell him all the things that had gone through her mind. ''And now, seeing you like this, it all seems so...civilized.''

He couldn't help the grin that touched his lips. ''Our lives are what we choose to make them, Cara. Now.'' He caught her hand and lifted it to his lips. ''What do you say we sip our wine, and then enjoy Margaret's wonderful cooking.''

She returned his smile. ''I'd say that sounds like a lovely way to spend the evening.''

Just then the housemaid returned to invite them to the dining room, where they were treated to thick slabs of roast beef so tender it fell off the bone, along with potatoes swimming in gravy, and tender garden vegetables.

As Cara spread strawberry jam on a biscuit, she glanced at Cody, who was wiping his milky mustache on his sleeve. Just then he caught sight of Yale touching a napkin to his mouth. The little boy did the same, and Yale winked at him across the table.

There was that lump in her throat again, threatening to choke her. But it couldn't be helped, she realized. She was, quite simply, too happy to take it all in. She wanted to hold this moment in her heart forever.

An hour later, as they made their way back to the hotel, Cody remarked, "That was the best supper, wasn't it, Yale?"

Yale nodded. "Especially the apple pie."

"You had two slices," Cody said with a giggle.

"I almost had a third, but then I figured I'd better leave room for my special treat."

The two boys, who were walking ahead, stopped.

"What special treat?" Cody asked for both of them.

Yale gave them a mysterious smile and beckoned them into the mercantile. Inside he led them to the counter, where the man called, "Welcome back to Bison Fork, Mr. Conover."

"Thanks, Jeremy. I think you know what I'm looking for."

"Yes, sir." The man lifted the lid from a jar of striped candy sticks and held it out to Yale.

Yale turned to Cody and Seth. "Which one would you like?"

Their eyes were as round as saucers.

"You mean we can have whatever one we want?" Cody asked.

"That's right. Go ahead and choose."

Yale watched as each of the boys took more than a minute to make a selection. Then he nodded.

"Good choice. Jeremy knows which one I'll take. I always have the peppermint stick." He helped himself to a red and white striped stick, then turned to Cara. "How about you, Cara? What's your flavor?"

She was about to refuse when she saw the looks on her sons' faces. Then she dipped her hand in the jar and chose a peppermint stick.

Minutes later they were strolling toward the hotel, busily licking their candy.

When they finally climbed the stairs and paused outside the door to Cara's room, she waited while Yale unlocked her door and stood aside.

"Are you coming in?" she asked.

He shook his head. "I promised Cody and Seth I'd teach them a couple of card tricks." He glanced down at the two boys, still finishing the last of their candy. "Say good-night to your mother."

She bent down to receive sticky kisses from each of them. As she straightened, Yale surprised her by brushing his mouth over hers.

"Good night, Cara. Sleep well."

"I..." She wondered if he had any idea how endearing he looked, with a peppermint stick in his hand and her sons standing on either side of him. "You, too, Yale. Sleep well."

She closed the door and heard them talking as they moved on to the next room. She undressed quickly, then wearing only her chemise, climbed beneath the covers and felt the softness of the feather mattress beneath her.

It had been the most amazing day. She'd seen yet

another side of Yale Conover. A side she would
have never known, had it not been for the strange
circumstances that had brought him back into her
life.

As silence settled over the town, she fell asleep,
still smiling.

Chapter Eighteen

Cara awoke and lay very still, her mind muddled. What was this softness beneath her? She touched a hand and remembered. The big feather bed.

She opened her eyes. The bright sunlight outside her window told her it was already morning. Had she slept the entire night away? She couldn't even remember falling asleep. But here it was, a new day.

She climbed out of bed and washed herself, then dressed in the new gown and soft kid boots. Then she rolled her old clothes, which were now dry, into a bundle.

Before she could decide whether or not to go looking for Yale and the boys, she heard a knock on the door.

She opened it to find the objects of her thoughts standing in the hallway, all wearing matching smiles of excitement.

"Good morning." Yale stood behind Cody and Seth. "How did you sleep?"

She was nearly dazzled by the sight of him. So

tall and handsome and elegant in his black suit and boots, the wide-brimmed hat in his hand. Gone was any trace of the tough, bearded hero who had saved them from so many disasters along the trail. He looked, instead, like a man who'd been born to wealth and comfort.

"I don't remember a single thing after my head touched the pillow."

"Good." He gave her an admiring look. "That's what you needed."

"And you two?" She bent to kiss her sons. "Did you sleep at all? Or did you keep Yale awake all night pestering him for more card tricks?"

"We slept some," Cody admitted. "But we learned some really neat card tricks. Can we show her, Yale?"

"Maybe later. Right now I think we ought to load our things in the cart before seeing what Margaret Thistle has for our breakfast."

Again Cara took Yale's arm and felt the stares from those gathered in the hotel lobby as they passed through. When they stepped outside Yale placed the bundles of clothes in the back of their cart.

Cody pointed to a beautiful black stallion hitched alongside their horse and cart. "Yale took us to the stable this morning, where he bought Jackpot."

"Jackpot?" Cara halted. "You bought a horse?"

"Not just any horse." He smiled when he took her arm. "With a name like that, I figure he was meant to be mine."

As they continued along the street, Cara glanced back over her shoulder to see the stallion toss his head. She was forced to admit that the horse seemed to suit the man. Larger-than-life. Mysterious. Spirited.

At the boardinghouse they were greeted by a smiling Margaret Thistle. "Good morning. I was hoping I'd see you for breakfast." She stepped aside. "Come in."

Again Cara was swamped by the wonderful smells of meat sizzling and breads baking. Smells that would always remind her of her own childhood.

They were ushered into the dining room where the boys were offered cold milk and Cara and Yale were served hot, strong coffee. Over a breakfast of bacon, sausage and beef, eggs, potatoes and biscuits, Cody regaled his mother with tales of their nighttime antics.

"I can make a card disappear, and Yale says if I practice, I should be able to shuffle the cards like him in no time."

"An admirable goal." Cara couldn't help smiling as she said it.

Just then Margaret Thistle bustled in to serve slices of her sugared coffee cake. "Will you folks be staying on in Bison Fork another day?"

Yale shook his head. "I'm afraid not. We leave right after breakfast for Misery."

"Ah." She filled his cup and for good measure placed a second serving of coffee cake on his plate.

"You've a lovely day for traveling. You should be in Misery well before supper."

A short time later they shoved away from the table and made their way to the front door.

When Yale had paid Margaret Thistle for their meals, she offered her hand. "I hope the next time you're passing through Bison Fork you'll bring your wife and lovely family."

Cara thought again about correcting her. But it was such a lovely myth. It seemed the most natural thing in the world to merely smile and wave goodbye as they walked down the porch steps and started toward their waiting cart, with the boys giggling behind their hands.

Yale tied his horse behind the cart before helping her up to the seat. With Cody and Seth tucked in the back, he climbed aboard and flicked the reins.

Cara turned for a last glimpse as they rolled out of town and started across yet more prairie wilderness.

Yale caught her hand. "Sorry to be leaving all that luxury behind?"

She shook her head. Her eyes danced with unconcealed excitement. "How can I be sorry when I'll soon be home?"

The lowing of cattle alerted them that Aaron Smiler's ranch was near. In the distance Yale saw the simple shack that had been home to him in his childhood. And though he told himself it didn't mean that much to him, there was no denying the way his heartbeat quickened when he caught sight of the old man seated on the porch.

As their horse and cart rolled to a stop, Aaron reached for a cane and got slowly to his feet. He'd barely gone two steps when Yale leapt from the cart and raced toward him.

He stopped. Stared as if seeing a ghost. "Yale? Is it really you, son?"

"It's me, Aaron." Yale opened his arms and the old man hugged him fiercely.

When they stepped apart, Aaron studied him for a long, silent moment. Then he put his fingers to his lips and gave a whistle that would carry for a mile.

Within minutes a buckskin-clad creature came galloping up on the back of a mustang. Horse and rider looked as though they might plow right into the two men. But just inches before the collision, the horse stopped abruptly and the rider leapt from the saddle.

Yale grinned broadly. "Hey, Kitty. Where's my kiss?"

"Yale?" With a screech, she launched herself into his arms with such force she would have flattened a lesser man.

He laughed and swung her around and around before setting her on her feet. Then he stood back and studied her. "When did you get all grown-up and pretty?"

"While you were off doing whatever it is you do in all those saloons."

"I gamble." His smile widened. "And I happen to win more often than I lose."

She nodded toward the woman and boys who were watching in silence from the cart. "You win them in a poker game?"

He walked to the cart and offered a hand to Cara. When she and her sons were standing beside him he said, "You used to know this pretty lady years ago as Cara McKinnon. Now she's Cara Evans. And these fine boys are her sons Cody and Seth." He led them closer. "This old coot is Aaron Smiler, the closest thing I ever had to a father. And this wild woman is my sister, Kitty." He winked at Cody and Seth. "Better watch her, boys. She can out-ride, out-shoot and out-fight most men. Except me, of course."

"A dandy like you?" Kitty gave a snort of laughter. "After all those years sitting in a saloon doing nothing more challenging than shuffling a deck of cards, why, I bet even these two boys could take you in a fight."

That had Cody and Seth giggling behind their hands.

Aaron stepped forward to take Cara's hand. "Welcome to our ranch, Mrs. Evans."

"Please." She smiled. "Call me Cara."

He nodded. "I knew your father and mother, Cara. And I remember hearing that you'd returned to Misery to nurse them through their illnesses. I was sorry to hear about their ranch."

Cara felt the heat rise to her cheeks and was grateful when Yale smoothly changed the subject.

"Is that a new barn and corral?"

Kitty nodded. "I needed more room for my mustangs." She turned to the little boys. "Would you like to have a look at my latest herd?"

"Yes'm." Cody nudged his little brother, who nodded.

With her arm around her brother's waist Kitty led the way toward her corral, with Aaron and Cara trailing more slowly.

When Cody started to climb up the rail fence that surrounded the corral, Kitty put a hand to his arm to stop him. "These are wild critters, son. They'll take any opportunity to charge you and stomp you. So you have to be very careful around them. You'd best keep well back from the fence."

She pointed. "So far I've only broken half a dozen to saddle. But I hope to break the rest of them before the soldiers return."

Yale's head came up. "What soldiers?"

She shrugged. "Had a troop of them come through Misery about a week or more ago. I brought one of their officers out here to see my herd, and he said he'd buy all I had, as long as they were broke to saddle."

"Did he say when they'd be back?"

She shook her head. "I guess whenever they do what they came to the Territory to do."

She saw a look pass between Cara and her brother. "You in some kind of trouble, Yale?"

He tugged on a yellow curl. "Are you always going to believe the worst about me?"

She turned to Cara. "Maybe I'll get a straight answer out of you. Is my brother in some kind of trouble again?"

Cara shook her head. "To my sons and me he's a hero. Yale saved us from a gang of outlaws. If it hadn't been for your brother, we wouldn't be here now."

"Well." Kitty's smile grew. "Maybe you really do know how to do something besides shuffle a deck of cards." She turned toward the shack. "How about some coffee, and those hard rocks Aaron calls biscuits?"

Cara saw the affection between this young woman and the old man, and recalled the story she'd heard as a child, about how he'd opened his heart and home to three orphans who had wandered in from the Badlands.

She liked him instantly. And liked, even more, the bond of love she could see between Kitty and Yale.

"I'd love some."

"Have you come back for a visit?" Aaron sat in the rocking chair on the porch, with Yale and the boys sitting on the steps, while Kitty and Cara sat on wooden chairs brought from the kitchen. "Or are you back to stay?"

When Yale said nothing, Cara set down her cup

of coffee. "I think I'd like to settle in Misery. I'd like my boys to grow up here, the way I did."

Aaron nodded in understanding. "Will your husband be joining you?"

"My husband is dead."

Out of the corner of her eye she saw Kitty look over at her brother.

"I'm sorry to hear that," Aaron said softly. "You said Yale saved you from a gang of outlaws?"

She nodded. "The Fenner gang."

At that both Aaron and Kitty shared a knowing look.

Kitty cleared her throat. "Gabe got word that you were running with the Fenners, Yale."

"For awhile."

Seeing that Yale wasn't about to explain, Cara said, "Your brother saved the life of one of the gang members. When he was invited to join them, he thought one of them might know something about your father."

Kitty jumped up, her face animated. "Oh, Yale. What did you learn?"

He saw the light of excitement in her eyes and hated that he had nothing more to offer her than empty words. "Nothing, Kitty. Nobody's ever heard of him." He looked up at the fading sunlight. "I think we'd better get started toward Misery before it gets too dark."

He reached into his pocket. "I almost forgot. Aaron, these are for you." He handed the old man a box of fine cigars.

Aaron accepted them as though they were gold. "Thanks, Yale. You always know just what pleases me. I'm mighty grateful."

"What did you buy for me?" Kitty was beaming like a child.

"What makes you think I bought you anything?" Yale was grinning from ear to ear.

"Because you always bring me a gift. I just hope it's not another gown."

"You didn't like the **gown** I bought you?"

"It was beautiful. And it's still in the wrappings, up in my loft." She looked down at her buckskins. "Can you imagine me in a dress, trying to work this ranch and break those mustangs?"

"There must be some place you can wear a brand-new gown."

She shook her head, sending yellow curls tumbling around her face. "Don't bother much with that visiting preacher. And when I do, it's usually after I've tended to a dozen or more ranch chores first. And there's no one beating down the door to ask me to a town dance."

"Maybe that's because you've never bothered to put on that gown." Yale walked to the cart and removed a parcel. "Well, let's see how you like this."

She tore off the wrappings, then gave a squeal of delight. "Oh, Yale. Peppermint sticks. There must be a dozen of them."

"Two dozen. I figure that ought to fill your sweet tooth for a few days."

"Oh, I love them." She wrapped her arms around his neck and kissed him soundly.

Pleased, he kissed her back and swung her around before setting her on her feet. Then he crossed to Aaron and the two men shook hands before embracing.

In his courtly manner Aaron caught Cara's hand between both of his. "I'm so glad you've returned to Misery, Cara. I hope you and your sons will come to visit often."

"I'd like that, Aaron. Thank you for your hospitality."

She turned to Kitty. "Will I see you in town?"

"Not very often." Kitty walked with Cara to the cart and watched the way her brother gently lifted this woman, allowing his hands to linger at her waist. If she hadn't been certain of his feelings before, she had her answer.

She shaded the sun from her eyes as her brother climbed up beside Cara and picked up the reins. "I hope you intend to have a visit with Gabe."

Yale shrugged. "He won't be happy to see me."

"Gabe's changed, Yale. He has a wife now and…"

"A wife?" Yale's jaw dropped. "Gabe is married?"

Kitty nodded. "Her name's Billie. She cooks at the Red Dog."

Yale couldn't hide the grin that curved his lips. "My brother, the straight-arrow lawman, is married to a girl who cooks in a saloon?" He threw back his head and let out a roar of laughter. Then he flicked the reins and called over his shoulder, "I guess I'm going to have to pay a call on brother Gabe, just so I can meet the woman who could put up with him."

"Welcome to Misery," Yale muttered as the horse cart rolled along the dusty main street.

"It's grown so much." Cara felt a wave of nostalgia as she studied Swensen's Dry Goods, and caught sight of Inga and Olaf Swensen inside. There was the giant, Eli Moffat, the blacksmith who owned the town stable, his boots caked with mud and manure, his big hands holding a piece of molten steel to the fire. Further along the street she saw Jesse Cutler, still rail-thin, with his hawkish, angular face and a cap of monk's hair surrounding a shining bald head. Two of his sons were sweeping while he was brandishing his scissors to a cowboy's mop of hair.

As they rolled past Doc Honeywell's surgery they saw the doctor mopping sweat from his forehead while he bent over a blanket-clad figure on the table.

"Oh, my. Look at all the additions." Cara pointed.

There was a small cabin with a sign that read Rescue Mission, though she had no idea what that meant. And at the end of the street, she was astounded to see that the jail had been enlarged. Beyond the jail was a large cabin with several buildings and pens surrounded by fencing.

At least half a dozen more buildings were under

construction. The town appeared to be a beehive of activity.

When Yale reined in the horse in front of the Red Dog Saloon Cara shot him a look of surprise. "Why are we stopping here?"

"There's no boardinghouse in Misery. We'll have to sleep here tonight."

She glanced at her sons in the back of the cart. "Yale, I can't have my boys sleeping in a saloon."

He touched a hand to her shoulder. "It'll be all right. Trust me, Cara."

After the bright sunlight outside, it took Yale a moment for his eyes to adjust to the gloom of the saloon. Spotting a woman just walking through the deserted room he called, "Where is everybody?"

She turned and he could see that she was prettier than most of the women Jack Slade usually employed. Things were definitely improving in Misery.

"Sorry." Her voice sounded breathy, as though she'd been rushing around. "If you're looking for a game, I can find Mr. Slade. He's always happy to oblige. If you're here for supper, you're early. It won't be ready for another hour."

"I was thinking of getting a couple of rooms. Where's Roscoe Timmons?"

"Oh." She nodded in understanding. Roscoe Timmons was not only the bartender, but handled room reservations for those men looking for female companionship. "I think he's upstairs. I'll have to find him. Who should I say is looking for him?"

"Yale Conover."

She'd been rushing toward the stairs. But hearing his name she stopped dead in her tracks. Turned. "You're...Yale?"

"Yeah." He smiled. "You've heard of me?"

She nodded. Instead of continuing up the stairs she walked back down and paused in front of him, rubbing her palms on her skirt before offering her hand. "I guess that makes us related. I'm Billie. Billie Conover. Your brother Gabe's wife."

Chapter Nineteen

"**Y**ou're Billie?" Yale continued holding her hand, studying her with an intensity that had her blushing.

"Well." She pulled her hand away. "I'd heard you were a dandy. I just hadn't expected you to be so…good-looking."

His grin was quick. "Thanks. I might say the same for you. I never expected Gabe to marry. But especially someone as pretty as you."

"I guess we're just full of surprises." She looked up at him. "Does Gabe know you're here?"

He shook his head. "We just got in."

"We?" She glanced around.

"Some special friends. A woman and her two sons. And since there isn't a boardinghouse in town, I figured I'd need a couple of rooms."

"I see." She linked her arm through his and started toward the swinging doors of the saloon. "Since dinner's cooking, I have time to take you home. Come on. It's time you saw your brother."

"Won't he be at the jail?"

"Not right now. Lars Swensen is there until after supper."

"Lars?" Yale laughed. "Is he old enough to work at the jail?"

Billie smiled. "You've been gone too long. Lars is deputy now, and married to a sweet girl. They have two children."

"Lars?" Yale's laughter deepened. Then he merely shook his head in wonder. "You're right. I've been gone way too long."

Outside he led Billie to the cart and said, "Cara, this is my sister-in-law, Billie. Billie, this is Cara Evans. And these are her sons, Cody and Seth."

"Nice to meet you." Billie climbed up and settled herself beside Cara.

When Yale climbed aboard and picked up the reins, he turned to Billie. "Where do you and Gabe live?"

She pointed to the fresh new cabin beyond the jail and said with a note of pride, "That's our place."

"Oh." As they drew near, Cara let out a sigh. "What a nice home, Billie."

"Thank you." Billie was flushed with pleasure. "The town built it for us, to make certain Gabe wouldn't leave."

"They must think the world of him."

Billie nodded. "They do. And so do I."

Yale helped her down, then reached for Cara, tucking her hand in his as he started toward the front door. Not for courage, he told himself. Certainly not for courage. But the thought of seeing his stern-faced older brother had something twisting inside him. He found himself remembering his Uncle Junior, with his quick temper, and the tyrannical demeanor of his grandfather and his litany of rules to be followed. He didn't want any reminder of his past.

"Gabe," Billie called, "come and see who's here."

At her shout the door opened, and Gabe stepped out. For the space of a full minute he merely stared at the brother he hadn't seen in more than a year.

"Hey, Gabe." Yale released Cara's hand and stepped forward.

"Yale?" Gabe seemed frozen to the spot for a moment, before awkwardly extending his hand.

"I met your wife. She's beautiful."

Gabe almost smiled. "Yes, she is." He drew an arm around her shoulders. "What're you doing in Misery, Yale?"

"I brought Cara home." Yale released her hand. "You remember Cara McKinnon, don't you? Now she's Cara Evans. And these are her sons, Cody and Seth."

"Cara. Cody. Seth." Gabe touched the brim of his hat.

Yale cleared his throat. "Billie says the town built you this place."

Gabe nodded and, needing something to do, waved an arm. "Want to have a look around?"

"Sure."

Billie took Cara's hand. "Let's let the men look around, while you and the boys come inside with me and have something cool to drink."

"That would be nice. Thank you, Billie." Cara herded her sons inside, leaving the two men alone.

Gabe and Yale remained a good distance apart as they walked to the small fenced-in enclosure.

"What's all this?" Yale studied the hens scratching in the grass. "You're raising chickens now, Gabe?"

He couldn't help grinning. "It's Billie's doing. She has more energy than ten women. I swear, if ambition has anything to do with it, she's going to be the richest woman in the territory. She cooks at the Red Dog, and sells eggs to the ranchers, and now she's planning to start serving chicken suppers once a month after Sunday services. Besides that, she's raising bees, and starting to sell the honey. Every morning she wakes up with a new idea."

Yale chuckled. "You don't sound very upset about it."

"Hell." Gabe's laughter rumbled. "She's just so cute. How can I get mad at anything she wants to do?"

Yale stared at his older brother, seeing a side of him he'd never before revealed. Had he always had this softness inside him? Or had marriage to this amazing woman given him a new dimension?

"Besides," Gabe admitted gruffly, "she's already making more money than I do as sheriff."

"You don't say?" Yale leaned on the fence and

listened to the clucking of the hens. "It looks to me like you've made a good life for yourself here."

"Yeah." His brother turned to face him. "How about you, Yale? The last I heard you were running with the Fenner gang."

Yale's smile was wiped from his mouth. His eyes grew hard. This was what he'd expected from Gabe. Accusation. Condemnation. "I was, for a while. I'm not proud of it. But I thought they'd be able to tell me something about Pa."

Gabe straightened. "Did you learn something?"

Yale shook his head. "None of them ever heard of him. I'm beginning to think he never even made it to the Badlands. Otherwise, you'd think someone would have known his name."

Gabe's eyes narrowed. "Is that why you started hanging around the Badlands? You were trying to find our pa?"

Yale shrugged. "I suppose that was part of it. A big part of it, in fact."

Gabe gave a sigh and surprised himself by dropping an arm around his brother's shoulders. "The not knowing is hard."

"Yeah." But it occurred to Yale that just having someone who shared the same pain made it more bearable. "Come on. Show me the inside of your place."

"You'll like it. Billie's made it real nice."

When they stepped inside, they found Billie and Cara sipping lemonade, while the two boys nibbled biscuits spread with some of Billie's special fruit conserve.

Billie looked up. "I've invited Cara and the boys to stay here with us, Gabe. And I want you to stay, too, Yale."

Yale was already shaking his head. "That's too much work, Billie."

"Not at all. We have the room. And Cara has already said she'd give me a hand over at the Red Dog cooking."

"At the Red Dog?" Yale's smile returned. As well as a glint of teasing humor in his eyes. "You're going to cook in a saloon, Cara?"

She flushed. "Billie said it's not like working in a saloon at all. I can stay in the kitchen, and she'll handle serving the tables."

"What about the boys?"

Billie waved a hand. "I'm going to show them how to feed the chickens, and they can save me that chore while they're here. I'll bet, if they ask around town, they can find a few more jobs as well, to keep them busy while their ma's busy at the Red Dog. And if Gabe gets me that heifer I've been wanting, I'll show them how to feed her and…"

Gabe rolled his eyes and nodded toward the back door. "I think I've got a couple of cigars around here someplace. Let's go sit out back and smoke."

The two brothers were chuckling as they slipped away, leaving the women to their plans.

Yale stood by the window of the tiny room he was sharing with Cody and Seth. The house had gone still and quiet. The boys had long ago fallen asleep. As had his brother and wife.

He let himself out of the room and walked down the hallway, past the closed door where Cara was sleeping. He longed to go to her. Needed to feel the press of her body to his. But it had been a long journey, and she had looked so overwhelmed by all that had transpired in the space of a single day. Determined to do the right thing, he kept on walking until he came to the back door.

When he stepped outside he saw Cara. She was wearing one of Billie's nightgowns. A prim cotton thing buttoned clear to her throat. The hem billowed in the breeze, revealing her bare toes. Draped around her shoulders was a blanket.

She had her back to him, and was leaning on the fence, staring at the crude chicken coop.

"I thought you'd be asleep by now."

She whirled, hand to her throat, then relaxed when she saw him. "I'm too excited to sleep. I didn't realize how much I've missed this town until I came back here."

He stepped up beside her and draped an arm around her shoulders. "I guess this means you aren't sorry you came back?"

"Oh, Yale." With a sigh she rested her head on his shoulder. "I want this."

"This chicken house?"

She laughed. "This." She lifted her hands. "A simple cabin and some land, with room for my boys to grow and become all they can be. I feel…'' She took in a deep breath. ''I feel so many emotions twisting inside. I'm happy to be back here, but so angry at Wyatt for losing all my family had worked for.''

''Shh.'' He turned her toward him and pressed a finger to her lips. ''You have to let the past go, Cara. Otherwise that anger will just fester inside you until it eats at your soul. I ought to know. I'm a master at chasing after ghosts that are better left alone. But I think I'm finally learning how to give it up.''

She looked up at him. ''I hope you're not ready to give up everything from your past.''

He grinned. ''Why, sweet little Cara. Are you trying to seduce me again?''

Her smile was back. ''It seems a shame to waste all this moonlight.''

''You're right.'' He gathered her into his arms and kissed her until they were both sighing.

Then he caught her hand and started leading her toward a grassy hill. ''Good thing you brought a blanket. I think we can put that to good use.''

''Have another of Billie's biscuits.'' Gabe passed the basket to his brother, grinning at the amount of food they'd managed to put away for breakfast. ''I swear they're lighter than air.''

Yale shook his head. ''I couldn't eat another thing. But I can see now why Jack Slade doesn't want to lose you, Billie. That's just about the finest cooking I've ever tasted.''

"You said the same thing about Ma's cooking," Cody said over a mouthful of eggs.

"You're right. I did." Yale chuckled. "It's just that I've spent half my life eating in saloons. I'd forgotten how good home-cooking can be."

Gabe pressed his wife's hand as she topped off his coffee. "Then maybe it's time you gave up the saloon life, so you could enjoy this sort of treatment every day."

"I've been thinking that very thing."

At his words Cara sloshed coffee over the rim of her cup and was forced to set it down very carefully. When she looked up, she saw Yale watching her.

"Sheriff." Lars Swensen popped his head in the door after a perfunctory tap. Seeing the others he whisked his hat from his head. "Sorry to bother you, but you're needed at the jail."

"Trouble?" Gabe asked.

"Yes, sir. Not here in town. But trouble all the same."

Gabe pushed away from the table and gave his wife a kiss before picking up his gunbelt and rifle and following his deputy out the door.

"Well." Billie watched them go with her hands on her hips.

"Aren't you curious about the trouble?" Cara asked.

She shook her head, sending red hair dancing. "With Lars, it's always something big. Then Gabe comes home to tell me it was a run-away bull, or a drunken cowboy over at the Red Dog who shot himself in the foot.''

The others were laughing as she began rushing around, filling a basket with eggs, searching for her shawl. "I'd better run."

"Where are you off to?" Yale asked.

"I have eggs to deliver to Inga Swensen. And I left a list of supplies I'll need for today's supper with her. Inga said she'd have them ready this morning."

Yale pushed away from the table and got to his feet. "The boys and I have nothing to do today. Why don't you let us deliver the eggs and pick up your supplies? That way you can stay and visit a while longer with Cara."

She skidded to a halt. "You wouldn't mind?"

"Billie, it's the least we can do to return all your fine hospitality." Yale turned to Cody and Seth. "What do you say, boys? Want to lend a hand?"

Two heads bobbed in unison.

"You see?" Yale took the basket from Billie's hands and surprised even himself by bending to the chair to brush a kiss over Cara's cheek.

She blushed clear to her toes before asking, "What was that for?"

He gave her one of those killer smiles that had her heart tumbling in her chest. "For home cooking. And...other things."

He started out the door, with the boys eagerly trailing.

As he walked along the street, Yale took his time,

pausing to admire how much the town had grown since he'd last seen it. It would seem, if the territory actually became a state, that Misery was poised to make its mark on the prairie.

He'd often thought it a dreary, dusty spot on the landscape. And when he'd left, he told himself he'd never look back. But now he was seeing it through new eyes.

Cara's eyes, he thought with a smile.

Maybe it wasn't the town that had changed. Maybe it was him. He'd been changed by love.

Love. Even as the word took shape in his mind, he felt a moment of panic. He'd been footloose for so long now, he wasn't sure he could ever settle down. Could he turn his back on the thrill of the game? Could he walk past a saloon and ignore the itch to step inside? Could he walk the straight, narrow road his brother walked? Or would he always feel as though something was missing from his life?

"Look, Seth." Cody stood, nose pressed to the window of Swensen's, pointing at the jar of peppermint sticks in a big jar on the counter.

Yale stopped in his tracks, watching the look on their faces. When he looked at these two boys, he felt a fierce protectiveness toward them.

Wasn't that also love? He didn't think he wanted to probe these feelings too deeply.

He was whistling as he walked into the store and set the basket of eggs on the counter. As he did, half a dozen women turned to gape in openmouthed surprise.

Inga Swensen stepped behind the counter. "Yale Conover. So it's true. You're back."

"Yes, ma'am."

Women young and old suddenly seemed engrossed in the supplies stocked closest to the counter. They crowded around, hoping it wasn't too obvious how eager they were to watch and listen.

"And you're delivering eggs these days, Yale?"

He grinned, setting hearts aflutter. "My sister-in-law Billie sent these. And said I'm to pick up her supplies."

"I have everything ready." Inga studied the two little boys. "Could these possibly be Cara's sons?"

"That's right. This is Cody and this is Seth."

The older woman leaned over the counter. "I saw you both the last time your ma was in Misery, to take care of her folks. You were just little tykes then." She straightened. "There's Billie's supplies, Yale. Is that all you wanted?"

"Not all." He reached into his pocket and removed a coin, which he set on the counter. "We'd like three peppermint sticks, please."

Inga laughed as she held out the jar. "Yale Conover. You just never change, do you?"

"No, ma'am." He waited until Cody and Seth reached in, then he tucked his own candy stick in his pocket before hefting the sacks as easily as if they weighed nothing at all.

"You tell Billie I'll have her egg money here whenever she wants it."

"I'll tell her."

As he left the store Cody and Seth seemed puzzled by the reaction of the women, who were seen sighing and fanning themselves, before huddling around the counter to giggle and whisper. But when they looked at Yale, he seemed completely oblivious to all that had just transpired.

Chapter Twenty

With the boys trailing in his wake, Yale carried the sacks across the dusty road and around to the back door of the Red Dog Saloon. Inside Billie was busily kneading bread dough.

For a few moments Yale leaned against the doorway and watched in fascination as she pounded the dough, turned it and pounded again and again. She was a whirlwind of activity. All the while she beat on the dough, her red hair danced on her shoulders and her face, dusted with flour, wore the sheen of exertion.

"Don't you ever stop?"

At his words she looked up, then laughed. "That's what Gabe always asks me. I guess I just love my work."

Yale indicated the sacks. "Where would you like these?"

"Right over here." She wiped a cloth over a low wooden shelf, and Yale noted that the entire kitchen was spotless.

He deposited the sacks, then took the peppermint stick from his pocket and broke it in two, offering half to her.

She dimpled at the sweetness of the gesture. "Thanks."

They walked out on the back stoop, to escape the heat of the kitchen and sat on the top step, licking their candy.

"Inga said she has your egg money over at her place whenever you want it."

Billie nodded. "I appreciate it, Yale."

"Gabe says you make a good living here."

"I do. And I intend to make a whole lot more. I'm hoping for some hogs next year. Right now I have to trade eggs and honey for hams from Jeb Simmons, a hog rancher outside of town. I'd rather raise my own. And then I need some cows, for milk. And some…"

Laughing, Yale held up a hand. "You'd better stop. You're making me dizzy."

She smiled shyly. "You sound just like Gabe." She ducked her head. "He's so happy to see you."

Yale licked the last of the candy from his fingers. "That's nice to know, Billie. To tell the truth, I wasn't exactly looking forward to seeing him. We've never hit it off too well."

"You're wrong, Yale. You're family." She got to her feet, shaking down her skirts. "Nothing can ever change that. No matter how many disagreements you and Gabe have." She looked up and smiled. "Thanks for the candy. I always did have a sweet tooth. Now I've got to get back to work. I'll see you at home later.''

She brushed a kiss over his cheek, then hurried inside.

Yale beckoned to the boys. "I think we'd better start back now. Along the way we'd better stop at a horse trough and get rid of this sticky mess, or your ma will skin all of us.''

They were still laughing when they paused outside the hitching post of the Red Dog to dip their hands in the trough. As they did, voices from inside the saloon drifted through the swinging doors.

A man's voice, loud and boasting, silenced the others. "There's nobody good enough in these parts to beat me, gentlemen. So you might as well just empty your pockets right now and hand over your money. Old Buck Reedy came to town today to win.''

Yale straightened, his eyes narrowed in concentration. Last night he'd tried to comfort Cara as she'd talked about the loss of everything she'd held dear. And now, look who was being dropped into his arms like a gift from the gods? There was no denying it. He was being given the chance to avenge Cara's loss, with the very one who'd taken it all away from her.

"What's wrong, Yale?" Cody asked.

"Nothing. You boys run on home.''

"What about you?" Cody saw the way Yale was staring at the doors to the Red Dog. His heart gave a funny little hitch. "Aren't you coming with us?''

Yale shook his head. "I've got something I have to do." He took out a clean handkerchief and dried his hands, then returned it to his pocket, leaving the little points dangling from his breast pocket like a dandy.

When he walked up the steps of the saloon he looked different somehow. There was a swagger to his walk. A cocky tilt to his head. And though the self-assured grin was still on his lips, there was a steely look in his eyes that was almost frightening to see.

Alarmed, Cody caught hold of Seth's hand and started running.

When Seth held back Cody tugged on his arm. "Come on." The older boy was close to tears. "We've got to get back to Ma. Right now."

Jack Slade deftly shuffled the cards and dealt out the hands. Like Buck Reedy and the cowboys seated around the poker table, Jack couldn't take his eyes off Yale, looking as fine as if he were sitting in a pleasure palace in San Francisco.

Jack had figured that he'd never again get the chance to watch a true legend in action. But here he was, Yale-by-god-Conover, sitting in the Red Dog, barely glancing at his cards before tossing another gold coin in the center of the table.

Jack had known Yale when he'd been nothing more than a rough-and-tumble kid, dressed in shabby clothes, breaking hearts while breaking every rule in the book. Something of that boy remained in the man seated in their midst. But Yale had come back to Misery changed in many ways. The black suit and hat were obviously new and expensive. As were the shiny black boots. It was apparent that gambling had been very good to Yale Conover. And there was, beneath the expansive smile and air of success, a barely-concealed edge of danger.

Jack Slade had the sense that this was much more than a casual game of poker to Yale Conover.

"Whiskey?" Roscoe Timmons walked up to the table with a tray of glasses.

"Thanks." Yale accepted a tumbler and set it beside his hand.

Buck Reedy helped himself to a tumbler and drained it, then took a second and sipped it more slowly while the cowboys around the table added to the pot.

Buck discarded. "I'll take three cards."

He picked up the ones Jack dealt him and couldn't hide the gleam of triumph in his eyes.

"How about you, Yale?" Jack sat poised, ready to deal.

"I'll take three." He discarded.

Jack dealt three cards, then moved on, dealing to the cowboys, before he glanced around the table. "All right, gentlemen. Let's see them."

Buck Reedy dropped his pair of aces and chuckled. As he reached toward the pile of money Jack called sharply, "Don't get greedy, Buck. We haven't seen the other hands yet."

"You think anybody can beat my aces?" He grinned foolishly. And though it wasn't yet noon, the whiskey was already beginning to take effect.

Without a word Yale set down his hand, showing three deuces.

Reedy scowled as the money was shoved toward Yale. "I'd like to see you act this cool if we were playing for some real money."

Yale barely flicked him a glance. "What do you consider real money?"

"How about a hundred dollars a hand?"

Yale looked bored. "I thought you were talking about high stakes."

Reedy choked in embarrassment when he saw the cowboys grinning. "What do you consider high stakes, Conover?"

Yale tapped a finger on the table, as though considering. "You still own that ranch outside of town. The old McKinnon ranch?"

Buck's eyes narrowed. "Of course I do. Why?"

"What do you think it's worth?"

Buck began mentally calculating. The cabin had burned down more than a year ago. The barn, such as it was, was still standing. As for the land, the fields hadn't been plowed in years and had gone to weed. In this part of the Territory, there was an abundance of land. He considered it worth little more than a couple of hundred dollars, but there was no reason to make that fact known. "Five hundred dollars."

Yale nodded. "All right." He reached into his

pocket and peeled off the money, while the men around the table gasped. Passing it over to Jack Slade, he said, "My five hundred against the deed to the old McKinnon ranch." He turned to Buck Reedy. "Agreed?"

Reedy had never dreamed it would be this easy. He'd anticipated at least a little dickering before the price was set. He rubbed his hands together. "I don't have the deed with me."

"No need." Yale glanced at Slade and the others. "Just sign a paper saying you're putting up the land against my money. These men can witness it."

A paper was produced, and Jack Slade listed the terms of the agreement before passing it to Yale to approve. With a nod of his head Yale passed it to Buck Reedy, who signed with a flourish before passing it around the table for the rest of the signatures.

Reedy signaled for another whiskey, then turned to the saloon owner. "Hurry up, Slade, and shuffle those cards. I can't wait to count my money."

Jack Slade dealt out the cards, trying to read their faces as the two men studied their hands. Buck looked pleased with his cards. As for Yale, it was impossible to tell. He seemed to wear the same mask no matter what the hand.

"Would either of you gentlemen care for a card?" Slade asked.

Reedy discarded before saying, "Two cards."

He picked up the cards and placed them in his hand, then positively beamed.

Slade turned to Yale. "Cards?"

Yale shook his head. "I'll play these."

Reedy looked annoyed. "You don't want any cards?"

Yale didn't bother to reply. He merely shot him a challenging look.

Buck lay down his hand and the cowboys around the table were scratching their heads in amazement. "Three kings. It doesn't get much better than this. Now let's see you beat that, Conover."

Yale hesitated, and everyone leaned forward, watching intently. Without expression he set down his cards, face up.

Jack Slade spoke almost reverently. "Now doesn't that beat all. A full house. Queens and aces."

Savoring the expression on Buck Reedy's face when he realized he'd been beaten, Yale finally allowed a small smile. "The ladies have always been good to me."

"Why you..." Reedy leapt to his feet and reached for his pistol.

Before he could draw, Roscoe Timmons was right behind him, restraining him in a bearhug that had his arms pinned at his sides.

"You have two choices, Buck," Jack Slade said softly. "Get on your horse and head home, or spend the day over in the jail. We all know it won't be the first time."

Reedy swore. "You owe me another chance, Conover."

Yale gave a slight nod of his head. "Whenever

you say, Buck. Would you like to play for the deed to your own ranch now?''

Knowing he had no chance against this gambler, Reedy flushed and lowered his head.

Roscoe released his hold on him and escorted him to the door. When the bartender returned, Yale got to his feet and stopped beside the owner of the Red Dog.

''I'll take my money, Jack, and the paper Buck signed.''

''With pleasure.'' Slade handed them over, then offered his hand. ''It was a real pleasure to watch you play again, Yale.''

''The pleasure was all mine.'' Yale was smiling as he turned around.

The smile died on his lips when he saw the three men who had just stepped inside the Red Dog. All were holding guns. All the guns were aimed at him.

Will Fenner's voice was warm with laughter. ''Well now, boys. What did I tell you? If you want to find a gambler, just look in a saloon.''

He walked up to Yale and pressed a pistol to his chest. ''You just saved us the trouble of hunting for you, Conover. Now the first thing I want you to do is unfasten that gunbelt.''

With one hand Yale released his gunbelt and let it fall to the floor. Fenner kicked it across the room, where Justin Greenleaf bent and retrieved it.

Fenner nodded toward Slade and the cowboys who were seated around the table. ''If you're wise, you'll take yourselves out of the range of fire. You see, my boys and I have a score to settle with this traitor. And we're not leaving until he's paid up.''

Slade and the others shoved away from the table and backed up, leaving Yale alone to face his fate.

Cara strode through the town with fire in her eyes. If what Cody told her was true, Yale had returned to his old ways.

How could he do such a thing? Especially in front of her sons? Drinking. Gambling. In the very saloon where his sister-in-law was the cook. In the town where his own brother was the respected sheriff. By tomorrow, everyone would know. And they'd all enjoy gossiping about the wild, reckless Yale Conover, who still didn't have a lick of sense.

Not that she cared, she told herself, blinking back tears. What Yale did with his life was his own business. But he had no right to display such a weakness in front of her sons. They deserved a better example than that from a man they admired.

Admired. He didn't deserve their admiration. What he deserved was their contempt. And she was going to let him know as much. Right now. In front of everyone in that wicked, terrible place.

Though she'd never set foot in a saloon before, she stomped up the steps and shoved her way through the swinging doors. It was then that she realized her sons had followed her.

''Ma,'' Cody shouted.

She went through the doors before turning to him.

"You get on home now. I don't want you in this place."

"Ma…" Cody was staring beyond her.

She turned. As her eyes adjusted to the dim light she saw Yale standing near the poker table. In quick strides she crossed the room and pushed past the man beside him to poke a finger in his chest.

"How dare you leave my sons in the street while you come in this…this saloon."

His voice was deadly quiet. "Go home, Cara."

"Oh, you'd like that, wouldn't you? Send me home to be a good little woman while you…drink and gamble like some…"

"Gambler," he said softly. "That's what I am. What I'll always be. Now go home, Cara. And take the boys with you." His tone deepened. "Right this minute."

At the harsh look in his eyes she backed up a step. Then finding her courage she wagged a finger in his face. "Oh, yes. I'll go. I certainly have no intention of staying in this filthy place. But know this, Yale Conover. I don't ever want to see your miserable face again. Do you understand me? Whatever I thought…." She swallowed, fighting back the emotion that was threatening to undo all her courage. "Whatever I was beginning to believe about you was all a lie. I know that now. A skunk can't be tamed into a housepet. And neither can you. All you'll ever be is a no-good drinking, gambling fool. My pa was right about you. You're not good enough for me. You weren't when we were young, and you aren't now. So just stay away from my boys and me. Do you understand?''

"I understand.'' His hands fisted at his sides. His voice remained completely unemotional. "Go on now. Get out of here.''

Her jaw dropped. And though tears threatened, she managed to blink them away. "That's it then? That's all you're going to say? You're just sending me away, never to see you again, and all you can say is get out of here?''

He started to reach for her, then thought better of it and merely stared at her with a mixture of pain and fury. "That's right. Now go. Get out.'' He glanced over at her sons, who were cowering near the door. "Take your mother home now. You hear me?''

"Yes, sir.'' Cody hurried over to catch her hand.

In a state of shock she allowed herself to be led out of the saloon.

As she walked through the swinging doors she heard a voice say, "That was good. You're real smooth, Conover.''

She froze. She'd heard that voice before. At her ranch, when he'd shouted his threats. And then again when they'd taken refuge in the mine shaft. And though she'd never seen his face, she would never forget that voice.

Will Fenner.

And those men standing in the dim shadows hadn't been drinking and gambling in the Red Dog. They were part of his gang.

Catching her sons' hands she began running toward the jail. Their only hope was to summon Gabe as fast as possible. Knowing Fenner's temper, he wouldn't waste any time before taking his revenge on Yale.

Sweet heaven. Hadn't Yale warned her that Fenner would take this personally? He saw Yale as his enemy. The man who'd betrayed him. And he wouldn't rest now until he'd exacted the ultimate price for that betrayal.

Chapter Twenty-One

By the time Cara reached the jail her breath was burning her lungs. As she stood in the doorway she called to a boy of about six, "The sheriff. We need him right away."

"Sorry, ma'am." The little boy smiled. "The sheriff and my pa, Lars Swensen, got word that a gang of outlaws were a few miles outside of town. That's where they've gone. To arrest them."

"Can you go after them?"

The boy shrugged. "I don't think they'd like that, ma'am. My pa told me to wait here for them."

"Listen to me." She struggled for breath and had to keep herself from shaking the boy into submission. "You have to find them and bring them back right away. The gang of outlaws isn't out there beyond the town. Those men are right here. In the Red Dog."

At her words the boy's eyes widened. "You sure of that, ma'am?"

"I am. And if you don't fetch the sheriff right away, his brother will die."

He brushed past her and pulled himself onto the back of a pony. "I'll go as fast as I can, ma'am."

Desperate, Cara looked around, then seeing a locked wooden cabinet containing several rifles, she grabbed up the broom from a corner of the room and began prying open the door of the cabinet.

"Ma. What are you doing?" Cody grabbed at her arm but, like a crazy woman, she brushed him aside and continued battering the cabinet until the door finally gave.

She reached in and snatched up a rifle and a pouch of ammunition. Her hands were shaking so badly she fumbled and dropped several of the bullets before finally managing to load the rifle.

Turning to her son she ordered, "Cody, stay here with your brother."

Then she started running toward the saloon, praying she wouldn't be too late.

Will Fenner's eyes were hot with fury as he faced the man who had fueled his festering anger across a long and tedious trail.

"When Justin first brought you to us in the Badlands, I had a funny feeling about you, Conover. You were too smooth. Too polished. And you had way too many questions. I thought you might be the law. There've been lawmen in the past that tried to pass themselves off as outlaws hiding in the Badlands in order to arrest entire gangs. I figured you for one of them.'' His teeth peeled back in a snarl. ''You'll never know how many times I've wished I'd followed my first instinct about you and just shot you where you stood.'' He glanced at his gang members. ''There's a lesson to be learned here, boys. Next time, shoot first and ask questions later.''

Rafe threw back his head and roared. ''I'm with you, Will. Now how about some whiskey? We've been on the trail a long time.''

Fenner nodded. ''Bartender. Get over here and pour us some whiskey.''

Roscoe Timmons slunk out of the shadows in the corner and stepped behind the bar, pouring the contents of a bottle into three glasses. Then he walked among the men, handing them out.

Before he'd even given away the last glass, the first ones were already emptied, and he was forced to retrieve the bottle and pass among them refilling their glasses. Rafe grabbed the bottle from his hands and lifted it to his lips, completely ignoring the whiskey that trickled down the front of his shirt.

Fenner drained his glass and wiped his mouth on his sleeve, all the while keeping a narrowed gaze on Yale's face. ''You're real smooth, Conover. With that pretty-boy face and those soft gambler's hands. I bet you've never done a lick of work in your life.''

Yale gave a slow, easy smile, hoping to keep this outlaw talking, while he figured out his next step. ''Work is for suckers. I found out early in life a better way to make a living.''

Fenner chuckled. ''Me, too.'' He turned to his

men. "Didn't I, boys?" Out of the corner of his eye he saw Yale take a step forward and swung his head back, jamming his pistol in Yale's chest. "But I'm no fool, pretty boy." His eyes narrowed. "You think you can take on me and my gang and walk out of this place alive?"

Yale met his stare with cool appraisal. "You call three men a gang? What happened to the rest?"

"Thanks to you, the rest are either dead or ran off in the night, afraid of what might happen next." He gave Yale a chilling look. "But I don't need any help killing you. It's going to be a pleasure. And this time, you're not going to wiggle your way to freedom, are you?"

"I could if you'd give me a fighting chance." Yale nodded toward his gunbelt, in the hands of Justin Greenleaf. "Just toss me one of my guns, and I'll show you how."

"Now I know you take me for a fool. Maybe all that sweet-talking nonsense works on the ladies, but you're dealing with men now."

Yale's voice was pure ice. "No. I'm dealing with cowards. Men who plot and scheme to use their violence on a helpless widow and her children."

Fenner's eyes grew hot with fury. "It was a good plan. And it would've worked if you hadn't spoiled everything."

A voice in the doorway had everyone turning. "If you and your men had your way, my ranch would have become your hideout. And my boys and I would be dead. It's only because of the goodness and courage of Yale Conover that we got through that ordeal safely. Now drop your guns.''

For the space of several seconds the saloon went deadly quiet as everyone studied the slender figure in the doorway, looking incongruous in her delicate pink gown, taking aim with a rifle. A rifle pointed at Will Fenner.

Fenner turned to his men. ''Are you just going to stand there and let one skinny woman give us orders?''

''If either of you takes a single step toward me, I'll shoot your leader.'' Though Cara's legs were trembling beneath the long skirt, her voice sounded strong and steady.

A feral smile curled Fenner's lips. ''Well now. Isn't this interesting?'' He kept his pistol aimed at Yale. ''I see you've sweet-talked your way into another female's heart. And probably into her bed, didn't you, Conover?'' He lifted his head. ''I say the lady's bluffing. But just to guarantee that she doesn't get away with this, if she shoots me, I'll see that this traitor dies with me.'' He gave a chilling laugh. ''Now what do you say, woman?''

Taking advantage of her momentary hesitation, Rafe started toward her, causing her to back up.

''You see?'' Fenner challenged. ''Take her gun, Rafe.''

As the burly outlaw reached for her rifle, a small figure stepped through the swinging doors. A quavering voice called, ''Don't you touch my ma.''

Cody stood there, taking aim with a rifle he'd

taken from the sheriff's cabinet. And though his hands were shaking, he stood his ground.

"You going to let a scared kid stop you?" Fenner demanded.

"I am when his rifle's pointed at me." Rafe stood still, assessing the situation.

Fenner's patience snapped. "You do as you're told."

As Rafe stepped closer, little Seth darted underneath the swinging doors and scrambled to his feet holding a rifle that was bigger than he.

Now it was Rafe's turn to back up, with three guns pointed at him.

Seeing it, Fenner gave a hiss of frustration. "I suppose this scrawny brat's going to tell me he can shoot that gun." When Seth said nothing, Fenner taunted, "What's the matter, boy? Too afraid to even get a word out?"

Cody took a protective step closer to his little brother. "Seth can't talk."

"A mute?" Fenner threw back his head and laughed as Rafe, finding his courage, started forward again. "Isn't this rich, boys? The only thing keeping us from getting our revenge against this traitor is a poor little widow and her two useless sons. It's time to teach these fools a lesson. Take their guns, Rafe."

The scar-faced outlaw grinned. "As easy as swatting flies, Will."

Rafe swept a hand out, knocking the rifle from Seth's hands. In that same instant Cody squeezed off a shot, and the outlaw let out a howl of pain as he grabbed his shoulder and dropped to the floor.

Cara, seeing Justin Greenleaf aiming his gun at her son, took aim and fired, sending him whirling backward against the wall, where he slid to the floor, looking dazed and helpless.

Yale used that moment to lunge forward, pressing Fenner up against the poker table as he wrestled desperately for the outlaw's gun.

Cara and her sons were forced to stand by and watch helplessly, knowing they could just as easily shoot Yale as the outlaw.

There was a roar of gunfire, and Yale seemed to stiffen, before his arm, dripping blood, dropped uselessly by his side. Using him as a shield, Fenner wrapped a beefy arm around his throat and ordered Cara and her son to drop their guns. Cody looked to Cara for guidance.

Seeing her hesitation, Fenner lifted his pistol to Yale's temple. "If you don't drop them right now, I'll blow this gambler away right before your eyes. Is that what you want?"

Through a blur of pain Yale shook his head. "Don't do it. He's going to kill me anyway. Those weapons are your only defense."

Cara's voice trembled with emotion. "Promise me you'll spare his life if we throw down our guns."

A grinning Fenner lowered the pistol. "I give you my word."

When they dropped their rifles, Fenner motioned to Justin Greenleaf, who was sitting weakly against the wall, still holding Yale's gunbelt in his hand. "If the woman or her brats make a move, shoot them."

He stepped away from Yale. "Now, traitor, you'll taste my revenge. And I promise you, it's going to be slow and painful."

Cara let out a cry of horror. "You gave me your word you'd spare his life."

The outlaw gave a chilling laugh. "You've just learned a valuable lesson, woman. Never trust the word of an outlaw."

Slowly, deliberately, he fired a second shot into Yale's shoulder.

The force of the bullet drove Yale backward, against the poker table, where he clutched the edge before sinking slowly to the floor.

Across the room Cara dropped to her knees, sobbing. Her two sons seemed frozen in place as they watched the scene unfolding before them.

Fenner stood smirking as blood streamed through Yale's fingers and spilled in an ever-widening pool on the floor around him. "When I'm through with you, pretty-boy, no one will even recognize you. Now you're going to learn what it means to cross Will Fenner."

He lifted the pistol again and took aim. As he did, little Seth launched himself across the room shouting, "No. Don't you touch him."

Cara and Cody were so startled, it took them a moment to react. Then, seeing Seth throwing himself at the outlaw's back, they raced across the room to stop the little boy before he could be harmed.

Furious, Fenner tossed the boy to the floor in a heap. Then seeing Cody and Cara heading toward him, he took aim at them. "Stop right there or I'll kill all of you."

Through a haze of pain Yale realized that Cody and Cara had no chance against the outlaw's gun. Through sheer force of will he staggered to his feet and stumbled forward, determined to put himself between them and the line of fire.

Just as he did, Fenner turned toward him and took aim. There was a tremendous explosion of sound. Yale looked up, wondering why he was still standing. Then he realized the shot hadn't come from Fenner's gun, but from somewhere across the room. He looked over to see Justin Greenleaf, looking grim as death.

"You once saved my life, Conover," he said softly. "Now we're even." He turned to Rafe, who, though still alive, was too wounded to stand. "I don't know about you, but I've seen enough killing to last me a lifetime."

Cara and her sons crowded around Yale, who had slumped to the floor.

"Oh, my darling." Cara stared at the pool of blood and lifted his head to her lap. "Please don't die, Yale."

He managed a slight smile, before the pain rocked him. "...don't want to die, Cara. ...want to live for…'' He touched a hand to Cody's face, then Seth's. "You were both so brave."

"You taught us how," Cody said.

His hand lingered on Seth's cheek. "You picked a good time to have something to say, son."

Seth burst into tears.

"I'm so sorry for the things I said earlier, Yale." Like her son, Cara's tears rolled down her cheeks, splashing on his blood-spattered coat. "I feel so ashamed."

"Don't." He could feel himself beginning to fade, and fumbled in his chest pocket for the blood-stained paper, which he handed to Cara. "You were right, Cara. I'm nothing but a low-life saloon gambler. But I came in here for a reason today. I wanted to win this for you."

She read the signed paper, then looked at him in astonishment. "You…won back my father's ranch?"

"You said you wanted a place where your boys can grow and learn." He was babbling, he knew, but there was so much he wanted to tell her. "I figure Misery's as good a place as any. At least it was good for us."

"Oh, Yale. How can I…?" Cara's voice trembled with emotion. "How can I ever thank you?"

"You can marry me."

"Marry…?"

He lifted a finger to her lips to still her words. "I know I'm no prize. I'm just a no-good drinking, gambling fool."

"I said that in the heat of anger. Besides, you're *my* no-good drinking, gambling fool."

His eyes took on that blank look that brought terror to her heart. He was slipping away. She could feel it. Her tears were falling faster now as she clutched at him. "Oh, Yale. Please stay with me. Don't leave me now that you've finally said the only thing I've wanted to hear. Please don't leave me, Yale. I love you so much. I've always loved you."

But Yale was beyond seeing or hearing anything. He'd slipped into that long, dark tunnel of unconsciousness.

That was how Gabe and his deputy found them when they stormed into the Red Dog, with a long line of soldiers trailing behind them. Jack Slade and the others were all shouting at once, trying to explain about the outlaws, one of whom was dead and two wounded.

But all Gabe saw was his brother, lying in a pool of blood, while Cara and her two sons knelt by his side, refusing to leave even when old Doc Honeywell arrived with his black bag and ordered Yale carried to his surgery down the street.

Yale sat on a wooden bench on the back porch of his brother's cabin, watching the sun setting behind the peaks of the Black Hills. He was surrounded by pillows, at Cara's insistence. In his hand was a glass of whiskey, which the doctor himself had said would help ease the pain.

Cody and Seth were in a small, fenced enclosure

with Billie, examining a young heifer she'd just acquired from a rancher.

Yale turned to his brother. "Looks like your wife's going to start that herd of cattle sooner than expected."

Gabe merely smiled. "There's just no stopping my Billie." He paused a moment, then decided to take the plunge. "I had a long talk with Justin Greenleaf, over in the jail, before the soldiers took him away. He told me how you saved his life, and how he introduced you to Fenner and the gang in the Badlands. He admitted that you were never considered part of the gang. He claims that you never participated in any of their crimes. And the reason Fenner came after you was because he considered you a traitor."

Yale tensed, waiting for what was to come.

For the first time Gabe smiled. "I just came back from talking to Judge Hathaway. He sees no reason to prosecute you, since every man in the Red Dog heard Fenner claim you weren't part of his gang." He climbed the porch steps and extended his hand. "You're a free man, Yale. The past is where it belongs, in the past. I'm really glad you're back. I hope this time you're home to stay."

Yale clasped his brother's handshake. "Thanks, Gabe. That means a lot to me."

When Gabe walked away Yale stared down into the amber liquid in his glass, wondering at the powerful emotions swirling inside him. Whatever resentment he'd once felt for his straight-arrow brother had dissolved. The feelings that had surfaced were so strong, so new, he couldn't define them. But this was much more than friendship. It was the sort of family love and loyalty his mother had urged, before her death so many years ago.

Cara stepped outside and walked over to sit beside him, touching a hand to his forehead. In her eyes was a look of concern. "How are you feeling, Yale?"

He took her hand in his and lifted it to his lips. Keeping his eyes steady on hers he whispered, "I can't remember when I've ever felt better."

"The pain of your gunshots...?"

"It's unimportant. But there's something we need to settle." He saw the look of uncertainty in her eyes and gave her one of his heart-stopping smiles. "I seem to recall asking you to marry me, but I can't remember your answer."

She flushed. "I was afraid when you were recovered, you might regret your impulsive behavior."

"Cara, I've been impulsive and reckless all my life. And I'll admit to being regretful over some of the things I've done. But asking you to marry me isn't one of them. We've lost so much time. I don't want to waste another day. Can you find it in your heart to forgive all the wild things I've done and consider marrying me?"

She could feel the tears welling up and blinked hard to hold them at bay. She didn't want tears to mar this special moment.

She leaned close, brushing her lips over his. "I

was never permitted to be impulsive. All my life had to be carefully planned. But who's to say this isn't part of some grand plan? What else could explain the strange twist of fate that brought us back together after a lifetime of separation? Oh, Yale. We've been given a second chance. And this time, I won't let anyone stop me.'' She wrapped her arms around his neck and hugged him fiercely. ''I love you. Only you. And I want to be your wife.''

He gave a sigh that seemed to well up from deep inside. ''I was so afraid I'd made a terrible mess of things.''

She framed his face with her hands. ''Let's tell the boys. They'll be so happy.''

As she started to pull away he drew her back, covering her mouth with his. ''We'll tell them. In a minute. For now, just let me hold you, Cara.''

It occurred to Yale that he'd carried her image in his heart for a lifetime. And now, at last, they could look to the future. Together.

Together. What a beautiful word.

He wondered if this was how that Prodigal Son had felt when he'd returned home after a lifetime of wandering. Aware of what he'd almost lost, and finally, completely at peace with himself and the world around him.

Epilogue

❦

"Figured we'd find you out here." With Aaron beside him Gabe stepped around back of the crumbling barn that stood on the property that had once been known as the McKinnon ranch. Now it was called the Conover place, and a neat new cabin had been built. The yard was teeming with townspeople who had come for the wedding of two of the town's leading citizens.

"There's been a lot of talk lately about how free you've been with your money." Gabe studied his younger brother, standing in the midst of a crowd of men, wearing a brand-new black suit and wide-brimmed hat.

"That so?" Yale's head came up.

"The story I heard is that you loaned Olaf Swensen the money to add on to his store, and build a cabin for Lars and his wife and family."

Yale shrugged. "That's no risk. They're good for the money."

"There's another rumor going around. It seems

Cody and Seth got an assayer's report back, and some nuggets they had in their pockets tested for gold. Some folks say you've already staked a claim on their behalf up in the Black Hills.''

Yale gave one of his famous grins. ''Just my luck to be adopting a couple of rich little boys.''

Gabe arched a brow. ''The rumor is that you might become the bank of Misery.''

At that Yale laughed and slapped his brother's back. ''Maybe I will. After all, gambling's been good to me. I don't mind lending it. But my real job is going to be as a gentleman rancher. I gave my word to Cara and the boys. Come on now. Help me celebrate my big day.''

Jack Slade and his regulars from the Red Dog were passing around a jug, and enjoying the fine cigars from a box that Yale had set on a bale of hay. He handed one to his brother, and one to Aaron Smiler.

''You're looking real fine, Yale.'' Aaron leaned forward as the groom-to-be held a match to his cigar. Then he blew out a wreath of smoke and accepted a tumbler of whiskey from Jack Slade. ''How're your nerves holding up?''

Yale held out a hand. ''You're talking to a gambler, Aaron. I've got nerves of steel.''

Just then the match burned his fingers and he let out a yelp before dropping it to the ground. ''All right. I'll admit, I've never been in a game as important as this one.''

Aaron and Gabe burst into gales of laughter.

"Does he remind you of anybody?" Gabe asked.

"You bet. You, on your wedding day." Aaron turned to Yale. "Your brother was like a bear in a briar patch that day. I thought he was going to take off someone's head."

Yale turned to Gabe. "What did you do to settle down?"

Gabe smiled and flicked ash from the expensive cigar. "That's easy. I went to see Billie."

Yale's brows shot up. "She let you?"

"Hell." Gabe gave a grunt of laughter. "She had no choice. After I bullied my way through the line of females surrounding her, I was ready to take on a gang of outlaws. But one look at Billie, and I knew I'd live through the rest of the day, no matter how many people I had to meet and greet."

Yale was shaking his head. "Why do women have to make such a big thing out of a wedding?"

Aaron chuckled. "Son, it's been going on for as long as there were men losing their hearts, not to mention their common sense, to women." He glanced over. "Not having second thoughts, are you?"

Yale seemed genuinely surprised by the question. "I've loved Cara for a lifetime. I'd walk over hot coals in bare feet for her. Hell, I'd even give up drinking and gambling for her."

Aaron shared a laugh with Gabe. "I'm sure she'll be bringing that up very soon now."

Yale stubbed out his cigar and refused an offer of

whiskey before beginning to pace. Suddenly he stopped and turned away, heading toward the cabin.

"Where're you going?" Gabe called.

Over his shoulder Yale said, "If it worked for you, I'm hoping it'll work for me. I need to see Cara. And I need to see her now."

"Ten dollars says the women from town won't even let him inside the cabin." Jack Slade reached into his pocket and withdrew a roll of money.

Within minutes the others were making bets.

He turned to Gabe and Aaron. "Want some of this action?"

Gabe shook his head. "You're talking to a man of the law. You know I never engage in gambling." He started toward the cabin. "I think I'll tag along and see if my brother's sweet-talk can work this time."

Moving by his side Aaron whispered, "A dollar says he can."

Gabe grinned. "You're on, old man." He threw his arm around Aaron's shoulder. "Let's see who wins."

"Oh, Cara." Billie finished fastening the tiny row of mother-of-pearl buttons that paraded down the front of the pale pink gown, then stood back to admire the beautiful bride.

On Cara's feet were soft kid slippers. Instead of a veil she had pinned Yale's beautiful jeweled comb in her thick cloud of dark hair.

"Why didn't you accept Inga Swensen's offer of a white gown and veil?"

"Because this is the gown Yale bought me." She touched a hand to the comb in her hair, remembering that heart-wrenching night of her youth, when Yale had walked out of her life. "And this has very special meaning to us both."

"You look just like you did when we were little more than children." Kitty, in her usual buckskins, stood to one side. "No wonder Yale loved you all these years."

"You knew?" Cara looked up in surprise.

Kitty grinned. "I think everybody in Misery who had any sense at all knew he was sweet on you."

Billie walked to the window to watch as more wagons rolled into the yard. "I can't believe the women of Misery wouldn't let me fix your wedding supper."

"That's because you work so hard, Billie." Cara kissed her cheek. "They wanted you to have the whole day to relax with your family. You deserve it."

Billie shrugged, knowing Cara was right, but wishing she could take charge as she always did. Planks set across saw horses groaned under the weight of hams and pheasants and pot roasts, as well as cakes and pies and fancy cookies.

Children played tag around the wagons and carriages parked in front of the cabin while the older boys and girls grinned and teased and flirted. The men of Misery wisely got out of the way, while the womenfolk took over the day.

While she watched, she saw Yale striding up to the porch. On his face was a look she'd come to recognize.

Billie hurried across the room to bar the door, but was too late.

The door was thrown open, and Yale stood in the doorway, looking so fierce, both she and Kitty backed up.

"You don't belong here," Billie said.

"That's right." Kitty took a step forward. "Go wait with the men until your bride is ready to be seen."

"Kitty." Yale picked her up and swung her around, kissing her soundly. "I love you. You're my little sister. But right now, if you don't get out of this room, I'll have to throw you and Billie out." He set her on her feet and gave her a steely look. "Do you understand?"

The two young women glanced at Cara, who merely smiled and nodded her head.

"All right." Kitty laid a hand on his arm. "But the preacher is already fretting about the time."

"We'll worry about the time." He winked at Cody and Seth, dressed in brand-new black pants and crisp white shirts, who had come bounding into the room when they'd caught sight of him. "It's our wedding day, not his."

"Are we getting married, too?" Seth asked innocently.

"You bet."

Yale watched until the two women walked from the room, then beckoned the two boys inside before closing the door and leaning against it.

Cara took a halting step toward them, then stopped at the look on his face. "Is something wrong?"

Yale shook his head, his gaze never leaving hers. "Everything is so right now. I just needed to see you. To prove to myself this was really happening. I woke up this morning wondering if this was another dream. I've had so many through the years. And always, when I woke to the reality of my life, the loss would be so much worse." He stepped closer, to touch a hand to her cheek. "I couldn't bear losing you again, Cara."

She reached up to cover his hand with hers. "I'm not going anywhere without you, Yale."

"How about us?" Cody tugged on his sleeve for attention.

"We're about to become a family, son." Yale's voice was low with passion. "You know what that means?"

"I...think so."

"It means that from now on we stick together. No matter what."

"Can we..." Seth paused, summoning his courage. "After today, can we call you pa?"

Yale knelt down, so that his eyes were level with the little boy's. "You don't have to. You already have a pa in heaven. But if you'd like to call me that, I'd consider it quite an honor.''

Seth circled his little arms around Yale's neck, and Yale gathered him close to his chest as he got to his feet, keeping hold of Cody's hand.

Seeing them, Cara felt her heart hitch.

Cody looked up at his mother. ''Ma, what's a legend?''

''A legend.'' She thought a minute. ''A myth. Something that's been told and retold until it becomes famous. Where did you hear that word, Cody?''

''The first time was in the barbershop in Bison Fork. I heard a cowboy say that when we walked in. Today, while Seth and I were chasing some boys in a game, one of them said it again. He said that our new pa is a legend. Is he, Ma?''

She turned to the man beside her, and felt her cheeks grow warm at the way he was watching her. Then she wisely shook her head. ''He's just a man, Cody. A funny, irreverent, reckless man, who has taught us all the meaning of love.''

Yale winked and caught her hand in his, lifting it to his lips. ''I'm the one who's been learning about love. From all of you.''

There was a furious pounding on their door, and the muffled voice of Kitty, telling them it was time for the ceremony to begin.

Yale turned to Cara. ''Ready?''

She nodded and looped her arm through his as they stepped out of the cabin into the front yard, where family and friends waited to witness their vows.

As he stood before the preacher with Seth in his arms, and Cody holding his hand, Yale turned to his bride, seeing the girl she'd been, and the lovely woman she'd become. She'd been engraved on his heart for a lifetime. Thoughts of her had filled his days; dreams of her his nights. And now, finally, his thoughts, his dreams, were about to become reality.

Color flooded her cheeks and he felt his heart overflowing with love for Cara. His Cara. Their love had stood the test of time. He had no doubt that it would last. For a lifetime and beyond.

* * * * *

Be sure to look for
Kitty Conover's story in
BADLANDS HEART,
available in December 2002
from Harlequin Historicals.

On the lookout for captivating courtships
set on the American frontier?
Then behold these rollicking romances
from Harlequin Historicals.

On sale January 2003

THE FORBIDDEN BRIDE
by Cheryl Reavis
*Will a well-to-do young woman defy
her father and give her heart to
a wild and daring gold miner?*

HALLIE'S HERO
by Nicole Foster
*A beautiful rancher joins forces
with a gun-toting gambler to save her spread!*

On sale February 2003

THE MIDWIFE'S SECRET
by Kate Bridges
*Can a wary midwife finally find love and acceptance
in the arms of a ruggedly handsome sawmill owner?*

THE LAW AND KATE MALONE
by Charlene Sands
*A stubborn sheriff and a spirited saloon owner
share a stormy reunion!*

HHL **Harlequin Historicals®**
Historical Romantic Adventure!

**Embark on the adventure of
a lifetime with these timeless
tales from Harlequin Historicals**

On Sale January 2003

**LADY LYTE'S LITTLE SECRET
by Deborah Hale**
(Regency England)
*Will a wealthy widow rediscover true love
with the father of her unborn child?*

**DRAGON'S DAUGHTER
by Catherine Archer**
(England & Scotland, 1200)
**Book #3 of *The Brotherhood
of the Dragon* series**
*Passion blazes when a brave warrior goes
in search of his mentor's secret daughter!*

On Sale February 2003

THE SCOT by Lyn Stone
(Edinburgh & London, 1870)
*Watch the sparks fly between a feisty lass and
a proud Scottish baron when they enter into
a marriage of convenience!*

**BRIDE OF THE TOWER
by Sharon Schulze**
(England, 1217)
*Will a fallen knight become bewitched with
the mysterious noblewoman who nurses him
back to health?*

Harlequin Historicals®
Historical Romantic Adventure!

HHMED28

Two families...
Four generations...
And the one debt that binds them together!

BECKETT'S
BIRTHRIGHT

The dramatic prequel in the **Beckett's Fortune** series from
Harlequin Historicals and Silhouette Desire!

Just as Eli Chandler is about to get hitched to a pretty con artist,
his intended bride is kidnapped! Determined to see justice done,
the honor-bound ranch manager sets out on a bold adventure that
brings him face-to-face with his new boss's tempestuous daughter,
Delilah Jackson. When all is said and done, will Eli be free to say
"I do" to the one woman who's truly captivated his heart?

Don't miss any of the books in this riveting series!

AUGUST 2002
BECKETT'S CINDERELLA by Dixie Browning
SILHOUETTE DESIRE

NOVEMBER 2002
BECKETT'S BIRTHRIGHT by Bronwyn Williams
HARLEQUIN HISTORICALS

JANUARY 2003
BECKETT'S CONVENIENT BRIDE by Dixie Browning
SILHOUETTE DESIRE

BECKETT'S
FORTUNE

Where the price of family and honor is love...

Harlequin Historicals®
Historical Romantic Adventure!